The Wolf Vet

Strawberry Moon

Cleo Mercer

Don't miss out!

Want to be the first to hear about new releases and special offers?

Follow Cleo on Instagram:

https://www.instagram.com/cleo_mercer_writes/

Want free books?

Go to https://linktr.ee/cleomercer to sign up for Cleo's newsletter.

Please visit Cleo's website to find books, behind-the-scenes details, and swag.

Author's Note

Dear Reader,

A quick heads up, this book is not intended for young readers. It contains extra steamy scenes.

The Wolf Vet was originally published in episodic format on the app Radish. I loved releasing episodes one at a time because I got feedback from readers in real-time. Those readers had a real impact on the direction the story took.

This book can be read as a stand-alone, but belongs to a larger series—St. Louis Blue Bloods. Find out what the rest of the pack is up to by reading the next books in the series.

Thanks for reading *The Wolf Vet: Strawberry Moon.* Enjoy,

Cleo

The Wolf Vet

Strawberry Moon
By Cleo Mercer

1.

The moving van disappears around the bend, and I am truly alone. I said I wanted a change. Well, here it is.

Strawberry Moon Veterinary Clinic.

The sign, hand-painted with white blooms, hangs at an odd angle. The property sat empty for ages, leaving the barn full of racoons and the house full of cobwebs.

At least the view is good. The south side of the property opens up to a little ravine and you can see for miles. Wide open sky. Pine covered mountains.

Behind me, though, is a different story. The trees crowd up to my property, dark and silent. Jury's still out if they're with or against me.

A soft breeze whispers through the branches, swinging the off-kilter sign with a forlorn creak.

Despite the summer heat, a shiver works its way down my spine.

"Oh, hell no." I squint at the sign. "You just made your way to the top of the list."

I'm not a natural-born country girl. My last clinic was on the edge of St. Louis. We treated everything from parakeets to Great Danes, some farm animals too, but I was just an employee there. Don owned all the buildings. Knew how to fix things when they broke down.

The idea of being responsible for a big property like this is daunting, but the last vet was on her own, too. If a seventy-eight year old woman could handle this place alone, so can I. There's a barn full of abandoned tools that came in the auction and at least one of them ought to be able to fix a broken sign.

I slip into the barn's storage room, passing through dusty bars of light. My sneakers kick up little clouds of dust as I go.

Convincing myself that I do not think the silent barn is creepy, I find the ladder in a dark storage room towards the back. Cobwebs pull away from it as I lift it from its place on the wall. Dust coats my skin, tickles my nose. But five minutes later, I'm perched at the top of the ladder, hammering the sign back in place.

"See if you can creep me out again." As if on cue, a distant wolf calls to his brethren and a chorus of wolves howl in response. It's a reminder that I've moved to a part of the country where I am no longer at the top of the food chain. Back home, the biggest threat we have comes in the form of a mosquito.

But this is my home now. The Black Hills. And I've got to remember to keep an eye out for mountain lions and rattlesnakes.

And, apparently, wolves.

I'm a rational person. I know the wolves aren't coming for me, and yet, it makes me pretty glad to be at the top of the ladder. I'd be even happier if I was behind a locked door.

Pausing, I listen for more wolves, but hear wheels on gravel instead.

A patrol car appears through the break in trees and parks next to my little SUV.

I hurry back down the ladder, listening to the car door open and close before my sneakers touch the ground.

A man in a sheriff's uniform hesitates by his car door.

Good Lord, he's handsome. Strong jaw, covered by a dark five o'clock shadow. Thick dark hair to match. "You must be the new vet."

Pasting on what I hope is a friendly smile, and not a I-want-to-eat-you-up smile, I close the distance. "I must be."

Light brown eyes take in the stack of boxes still waiting to be moved into the barn. He glances back at his patrol car with a slight frown. "I thought you'd be settled in by now."

I follow his gaze and spot a square head with floppy ears resting on the back seat. "Who do you have there?"

He opens the door and stands aside. "Found him on the side of the road. His paw is in bad shape."

I peer in at him and the little guy looks back with a lackluster thump of his tail. It's an American Bulldog with a big spot on his back and the saddest eyes I have ever seen in my life.

Straightening, I'm hyper aware of my proximity to the sheriff.

He's ridiculously tall. Or, maybe, I'm ridiculously short. I have to crane my head to meet his gaze. "Can you lift him for me?"

He nods and I lead both man and dog back to the house. "I don't have anything unpacked, but I'll see what I can do. Did you try the other vets in the area?"

"You're it, ma'am."

I glance over my shoulder as I open the front door. Who's he calling ma'am? If anything, I'm a few years younger. "It's Zoey. And you are?"

"Hitch Florean."

"Nice to meet you, Hitch." I flick lights on as we go, noting the musty smell. There must have been a leak at some point. I'm sure this place will be full of surprises. Probably not as pleasant as Officer Dreamy back there.

The left wing of the old house was converted into a vet's clinic. We pass through the lobby. Cracked vinyl seats line each wall. I point at the first exam room. "You can bring him in there. I'll go get my kit."

Hurrying out to a stack of boxes, I shuffle through paperwork and winter sweaters, before finding the box I want. Hefting it in my arms, I make my way back to the exam room.

Hitch is waiting, his big hands brushing soothing strokes across the dog's back.

He looks back at me and gives me a shy smile. I realize, with no small amount of surprise, that Sheriff Florean is nervous around me.

Little, regular-ass me.

Wonders never cease.

2.

"Hold him still for me."

Hitch complies, pressing a gentle hand across the dog's flank. I examine his paw, searching for breaks. "Lucky for this little guy, I think it's just a sprain. You said I'm the only vet around?"

Hitch nods. "Next closest one is forty minutes away in Rapid City."

"You're kidding." I look up, finding myself snared in those eyes. They're not light brown after all, they're hazel.

He shakes his head. "I wish I was."

"What have the people in Hill City been doing up to now?"

He gives me a grim smile. "Driving forty minutes."

I whistle and the dog perks its ear up. "No collar on this one."

Hitch nods. "I think he was dumped."

"I guess he'll just have to stay here for the time being. I'll be his foster mama until we can find his forever home." I move back to my box and rifle through the medications. "Should we give him a name?"

Hitch runs his hands along the dog's back. "Sure. What do you think?"

I return to the table with a syringe. This dog is no dummy. He takes one look at the syringe and decides now

5

would be a good time to make a break for it. Hitch manages to hold him safely in place. I run my hand along the dog's smooth head, murmuring soothing sounds. I'm well aware that this puts me in very, very close proximity with the good sheriff yet again. I can smell his aftershave. My fingers brush his forearm and we're both acting like there's not a massive amount of tension in the room. His gaze meets mine, lingering just long enough to see something more than neighborliness lurking below the surface.

His Adam's apple bobs, and I could swear his eyes get darker. It's fascinating, but then my patient is scrabbling against the table. I'm a vet first and foremost. I can admire the homo sapiens later. "Just a big, sweet baby." I murmur, soothing the dog long enough to stick him with the syringe. When the needle doesn't hurt the way he expected, the dog relaxes. "How about Baby?"

Hitch looks up at me with a crooked smile. "You want to name this big dog Baby?"

He should talk. If that dog is big, then Hitch is gigantic. Broad-shoulders. Height. He makes a Baby look like a lap dog. "It fits, don't you think?"

Baby looks up at Hitch and licks him square on the lips. I'm secretly jealous.

Hitch pulls back, too little too late, but he's smiling broadly now and that is not something I was prepared to see. I thought he was cute before, but when he's smiling like that, he makes me nervous all over again. I dig out a sharps container to get rid of the syringe.

Hitch watches me out of the corner of his eye. "How are you settling in?"

"It's going to take some time to get used to the landscape. I thought I heard a wolf earlier."

Hitch has his arm around Baby, guarding him while he sits happily on the table. Hitch's expression hardens. "Yeah, we've got a sizable pack around here."

I pause. "Seriously? That's kind of cool."

A tendon in his jaw tenses.

My stomach swoops. "Unless it's not cool? Are they dangerous?"

One eyebrow arches. "Wolves?"

"They generally leave people alone, right?"

He lets his hand run across Baby's back. "Generally." His tone is neutral. I would have preferred a lighthearted response. One that might ease the growing concern in my chest. He looks at me. "I'd just stick to the park trails. And if you spot one, give it wide berth."

"You are not instilling me with a bunch of confidence, Hitch."

He winces, helping me set Baby on the ground. "I wish I could tell you they weren't a problem, but over the last year, we've had more issues."

"I suppose that's what happens when we humans take over their natural habitat."

He tilts his head, looking unconvinced. "Yeah. I suppose so."

When we start to leave, Baby whines, limping after us. I stoop to pick him up, but Hitch gets there first. "Let me." Hitch lifts him with ease. "Where do you want him?"

Hitch looks pretty damn cute holding Baby in his arms.

I press my lips together to keep from beaming at the two of them. "Would you carry him to the porch for me? I need to move the rest of those boxes, but I don't want to leave the poor little guy alone."

"Little." Hitch shakes his head, smiling.

I set up a temporary bed on the porch, an old blanket and a cushion. Hesitating between his squad car and the porch, he turns back. "I'm still on duty, but if you need help with those boxes… or just settling in, I can stop by another time."

Cleo Mercer

Maybe this is some of that small-town niceness people are always talking about. A tiny part of me, or maybe a big part of me, hopes this handsome stranger is offering so that we can spend more time together.

You'd think I'd be over men. I definitely declared it so more than a time or two.

But Hitch isn't just a man, he's a work of art.

Handsome.

Kind.

And just a wee bit shy.

Which is really, really cute. I just want to take a bite of him.

I'll have to settle for moving boxes together.

3.

Baby and I survive the first night. *Barely.*

Baby was a very apt name. For such a big dog, he's a massive a scaredy cat. And in an old house like Strawberry Moon, there's plenty to be freaked out by. Creaking pipes, settling boards. Pretty sure we've got squirrels in the attic.

I'm hoping that was a squirrel, anyway. Otherwise, we've got ghosts. And I've already got wolves in the neighborhood. I'm good on monsters

I spend the first full day cleaning up the house. It's slow work, but satisfying.

And I locate the source of the musty smell. A leaky sink in the bathroom. The entire vanity will have to be gutted. But it can be fixed.

On the second day, I get to work on the clinic. In time, I'd like to paint the paneling in the lobby a cheery white. I'll replace the paisley drapes and the orange chairs. For now, I settle for removing the top layer of dust.

I'm working on the exam room when Baby looks up, ears perked forward. He scrabbles to his feet, taking a few limping steps, listening. He lets out a low *woof*. Glancing back at me, he gives me a nervous look. I pat his head and work my way through the clinic, stepping through the clinic's entrance just as two black motorcycles pull into my drive.

Cleo Mercer

I get a glimpse of two big men climbing off their bikes. Even at a distance, there's something distinctly menacing about them.

I am not a tall woman. I'll admit to that. Shortness is an inherited affliction. My mother gave me her auburn hair, her fiery Irish temper, and her complete lack of height. What we lack in height, we Coopers make up with stubbornness.

This is my land, my clinic, and I refuse to be intimidated by the two very large bikers lumbering my way. They both wear black t-shirts, dark jeans, and have tattoos covering their bodies.

The bigger of the two has long, sandy hair and a thick beard. He's got a chest like a barrel and a body builder's arms.

His friend is just as tall, but slimmer. More athletic. He's clean shaven and blue-eyed. His hair is short on the side and carefully brushed back—a styling miracle, considering he just had a helmet jammed on that hairdo. From the chiseled jaw up, he could be an investment banker. An attorney. But from the neck down, he's nothing but ink. Skulls and roses and moons.

They stop a few feet away and Baby's ears pull back. He lowers his head and growls at them. The clean-cut guy looks at baby. "Quiet." It's a low command. Not a shout. Not overly aggressive. But dominant, which is a bold move, considering Baby is not his dog.

Baby whines quietly in his throat, but obeys, laying on his belly.

"You the new vet?" The bigger guy asks.

I cross my arms. If Baby doesn't like them, then I don't either. "Who's asking?"

The big guy glances at his friend and they trade amused grins.

"I'm Andy Haugen. And this is Pretty Boy."

I laugh, covering my lips when I see that they're completely serious about the second name. "Oh. Okay. Andy and… Pretty Boy. What can I do for you?"

Andy shoves his big hands in his pockets. "Nothing at all, darlin'. We just came to welcome you to the neighborhood. I'm the head of a little motorcycle club down the road." Andy nods over his shoulder and Pretty Boy immediately returns to the bike to dig through the side saddle. "We missed having a vet around here. Did you know Maria?"

"The last vet?" I shake my head. "No. I'm afraid not. I bought the place on auction."

Andy seems visibly disappointed by that. Pretty Boy has made his way back, they exchange glances again and I'm starting to get a little fed up with the silent conversation these two are having.

Pretty Boy comes closer, offering me a fancy bottle of Bourbon.

"I don't drink."

That's a lie. And that bottle in his hands is a good one. But I'm leery of accepting gifts from these guys. Some instinct is telling me there's more to these bikers than meets the eye. And what meets the eye is scary enough as it is. Motorcycle club? That's a polite way to say biker gang.

Pretty Boy holds the bottle out. "Keep it. Maybe you can share it with your guests."

Left with no other option besides throwing a fit, I accept the bottle, ignoring the little jolt of energy that passes through our fingers when they touch. He tilts his head, studying my face. I can feel my cheeks heating up, no doubt highlighting the smattering of freckles across my cheekbones and nose. I tip my chin up and stare right back, meeting that gray-eyed stare eye for eye. He huffs an amused laugh, gaze eventually dropping to my mouth.

Cleo Mercer

I try to act unimpressed by Pretty Boy, which is difficult, considering he looms over me. And is viciously good looking. Are all the men around these parts built like this?

I kind of hope so.

But I'd prefer ones who aren't literally covered in bad boy vibes. I've had enough of that kind of man. I'm ready for someone *nice* for a change.

Andy comes closer, reaching down to pet Baby. He scratches him behind the ear and Baby's back paw starts thumping on the porch. His tail wags happily. Turncoat.

He glances up at me. "We really are glad to have you here. That means Pretty Boy can retire his stethoscope."

"You're a vet?"

Pretty Boy's lips tug into a smirk. "No."

What's with the attitude? "If you're not a vet, what are you doing treating people's pets?"

He gives me a serene smile. "They weren't pets."

I put my hands on my hips. "What were they then?"

He meets my gaze. "Wolves."

4.

I don't love the idea of a biker gang being headquartered just down the road.

It shouldn't come as a surprise. Strawberry Moon is twenty miles from Sturgis—home of the biggest biker rally in the world.

But it's one thing to think about motorcycles as a hobby and another thing entirely to think of bikers as an organized group. They didn't say they were part of a gang, but they didn't need to. There was an almost professional way those two moved together, like they were military-trained. My ex had enough friends who were part of an underground network that I can spot them when I see them.

And those two, Andy and Pretty Boy, were definitely not just a pair of regular guys.

I'm hoping that biker club is like a hornet's nest, if I don't kick it, maybe they'll leave me alone.

But even after they left, they stayed in my thoughts. Like a dog worrying a bone, I kept thinking about them. Especially Pretty Boy.

A dumb nickname. Why would he let them call him that?

Granted, he is quite pretty. Actually, pretty doesn't really do it justice.

Cleo Mercer

And he is a boy. Well, man, really. Maybe the name is meant to be ironic. An intentional understatement. Because handsome beast doesn't quite roll off the tongue.

That beast dominates my thoughts well into the night.

I lay in bed and try to clear my mind. But when I close my eyes, I see those clear, blue eyes.

I try to counteract him by remembering Hitch—so sweet and shy. But Pretty Boy dominates my thoughts. That assured smirk. The way he seemed to be laughing at everything I said.

He's a bully.

But damn it, he is pretty, too. And if he won't leave my head, I might as well put him to work.

I fantasize about making him get undressed. Preferably on his knees. He'd be covered in ink, across muscular shoulders, down his abs. Maybe I would make him crawl to me. Kiss my feet, my ankles. Work his way up to see if those lips are as good at making a woman come as they are at smirking.

He follows me into my dreams where we wrestle for dominance. In the end, he wins, making me come even in my sleep. I wake up at an ungodly early hour, cranky and horny.

Even after coffee and an hour spent in the office, paging through the last vet's files, I'm still feeling cagey and restless.

Throwing on a tank top and running shoes, I hit the trail that leads towards the ravine. The sun is just peaking over the ridge, casting everything in soft, orange light. It's beautiful. Savage.

Pine trees spring from impossible angles, climbing up from lichen-covered granite. The path zigzags down the ravine. It's wide enough to take at an easy jog but has drops steep enough to slow my pace. I wouldn't want to fall over the side of that, you'd definitely break some bones on the way down.

There's a brook at the ravine's base. Clear and cool, it burbles over the boulders and fallen trees. It's beautiful.

This is a rare place that is untouched by man. It's looked exactly like this for centuries. Maybe longer. You can't look at the jagged edges of granite and not think about shifting tectonic plates, primordial destruction. It makes me feel small. Insignificant.

And there is something about that clear water that calls to mind the movement of time, the enormity of the mountains I've moved to. Reaching down, I dip my fingers in the clear, cold water and draw an infinity symbol across my wrist. It's an odd tick, something I picked up from my grandmother and my mom. Kind of like crossing my fingers or throwing salt over my shoulder, it always felt like good luck to touch a place to my wrist. Like the water from a place holds magic.

A branch breaks behind me and I whip around finding myself face to face with a gray wolf. My heart lodges in my throat and I try to gauge the distance between us. Maybe twenty feet. We both stare at each other, frozen.

You wouldn't have to be a vet to recognize that this wolf is not thriving. It's thin and its fur is ragged. Those eyes are yellow, nearly orange. Some part of me is still trying to compare this animal to a husky, but when its lips peel back, I'm quickly dragged back to reality.

Foam drips from it teeth.

Rabies.

Not good. Not good at all.

Thanks to my line of work, I'm up to date on my rabies shots, but a rabid animal is an unpredictable animal. Just meeting a wolf would be dangerous enough, but I'm basically face to face with the berserk version, and that's not a great place to be.

I feel stupid for forgetting the warning about wolves.

Cleo Mercer

I wish I had Baby with me. Then again, I'm glad Baby is safe at home.

If it wanted to, it could leap onto me and take me down with ease.

I reach deep into my memories, trying to remember what to do when you're attacked by a wild animal. If it's a bear, you're supposed to play dead.

I think.

But I have enough experiences with dogs to know that turning your back or lowering yourself is not a smart move.

I watch with growing horror, as the wolf gathers itself, back end coiling up, ready to jump.

5.

Adrenaline surges through my veins. A primal scream works its way out of my throat. More of a roar, really.

The sound startles a few crows from the line of pines at the top of the ridge. They burst into flight, sailing overhead.

The wolf startles, backing up a few steps. Maintaining eye contact, I hold my shaking arms out and yell again. My paltry surge of energy has worn thin, and this scream comes out hoarse and broken. It feels like I'm in a nightmare. One where my body isn't doing what I want it to do. I'm paralyzed. I want to curl into a ball and hide my face, but I force myself to hold its gaze. I scream one more time, digging deep.

The wolf stares at me for a few agonizing heartbeats. Then without warning, it turns tail and sprints away.

Backing up slowly, I make sure the wolf really has left, before I turn and run the rest of the way home.

☽

I tell myself that wolf didn't follow me—that it was just a rare wildlife encounter, one that I won't have to repeat. I might be able to fool my rational side, but I can't fool Baby. He follows me around all morning, from room to room, standing guard while I unpack dishes. Push furniture around. I'm struggling with the armoire when I hear the

17

front doorbell buzz. Hoping it's my first customer, I hurry downstairs, Baby limping behind me.

I swing the door open and pull up short. The screen door separates us, but for the briefest moment, I feel like I'm staring down my second wolf.

Pretty Boy stands tall and smug on the other side of the screen. Damn. I was hoping my memory was editorializing, but Pretty Boy is every bit as *pretty* as I remembered. High cheekbones. Straight nose. Sweet, blue eyes that could fool a Sunday School teacher, but not me.

I don't bother opening the door for him. "What can I help you with?"

"Andy sent me."

"Okay." I drawl. He probably doesn't deserve the hostility he's evoking in me. But he reminds me too much of my ex. Smug. Inked up. I've had enough bad boys for one lifetime. I know better than anyone how these types of relationships play out.

Not that Pretty Boy is interested in me.

Except, he is staring pretty hard.

He's looking more closely than is strictly necessary, and the way his gaze is scanning my body isn't exactly neighborly. After my run, I changed into a pair of jean shorts and a tank top, but now I'm wishing I had on a bath robe. Or a winter parka. But those blue eyes could probably cut through anything.

He tilts his head, a smile tugging at his lips. "You going to open the door?"

I shake my head. "Haven't decided."

He huffs a laugh. "Okay. Well, they sent me over here to bring you back for lunch."

"Who's they?"

"Cherry and Andy," he says.

"Cherry." I repeat the word, one eyebrow shoots up.

"Kali. Andy's woman."

Do these people know about regular names? "Why do they call her Cherry?"

He gives me one of his mysterious smiles. "Short for Cherry Bomb."

That doesn't really clear things up, but I'm not going to give him the satisfaction of taking his bait to ask more questions about Cherry. I leave the topic in favor of a new one. "Why do they call you Pretty Boy?"

"To fuck with me. Why do they call you Zoey?"

I cross my arms. "Because it is a name. The one I was given at birth, as it happens. What's your real name?"

"Peter." He glances over his shoulder. "Now that we've been formally introduced, are you coming or what?"

"What," I reply, voice flat.

He laughs, eyebrows climbing. "You're turning poor Cherry down?"

Anxiety coils in my stomach. I'm between a rock and a hard place. If I say no, I risk upsetting a gang leader's 'woman'. If I say yes, I get to have lunch with a biker gang. No thanks and also, no thanks.

"I'm still trying to get moved in. It's a lot of work for one person and I really don't have time to take a break right now."

He peers past my shoulder. "Well, that's simple enough. You come with me, and the club will help you get settled in."

Oh Lord, that was not at all what I was trying to accomplish. "Not necessary. Really. I can handle it."

He grins. "I'm sure you can. But if I come back without you, Andy's going to have some very pointed questions for me."

"Sounds like a personal problem to me."

He studies me for a few heartbeats. "You don't trust me."

19

Butterflies expand in my stomach. "What makes you think that?"

"You still haven't opened the door."

I swing the door open and he catches it. It was just a flimsy sheet of mesh separating us, but with that protection gone, I suddenly feel very exposed. "Happy?"

"Ecstatic." His gaze flits across my face. "You're nervous."

"I'm not."

"You are." He glances over my shoulder, then back at the yard. "You were nervous before I even got here. I can smell it on you."

It's like he's crawled inside my head.

I wrap my arms tighter around my body. I was doing a pretty good job being brave until this asshole showed up. Standing here, with the door hanging wide open, I'm suddenly afraid a wolf could show up on my front door.

Peter's expression grows dark. There's a savage coldness in those blue eyes that both scares and delights me.

His gaze captures mine and his voice seems to drop an octave. "What happened?"

6.

His voice is almost a growl. I can feel it in my chest. It rumbles down my spine, like striking a match, it warms my core. His nostrils flare slightly and his gaze only darkens. "What happened, Zoey?"

I'm feeling a little light-headed. Giddy or antsy, it's hard to say which. "I saw a wolf on the trail."

His eyebrows knit together. "What color were its eyes?"

"Its eyes?"

His tone is hard. "Gold or silver?"

"Gold."

He seems to ease a bit at that.

"But I think it might have been rabid."

His spine seems to snap upright. In a heartbeat, he seems to loom a few inches taller. "You're coming with me."

I laugh anxiously. "I think not."

He lets out an exasperated breath. "You can come willingly, or I'll toss you over my shoulders. Up to you."

I take a small step back. "And then what? Are you going to ride that motorcycle with me across your lap?"

The image of me laying across his strong lap, maybe with his hand on my ass, hits me hard filling me a sudden flush of pure lust. His eyes dilate and I get the impression he's having a similar visual. He takes a long, deep breath.

21

Cleo Mercer

"Look, Andy's been really concerned with the… rabid wolf issue around here. He's going to want to know what you saw. You can either come with me and tell him yourself or wait for him to roll up to your front door. Keep in mind, with option two, you get to explain why you turned down the lunch Cherry lovingly made you in her own kitchen."

"In her own kitchen?"

Peter nods.

"So, not at the club?" I peer past him, as though I can see Andy and Cherry's house.

"No. Not at the club."

"Why didn't you say so? I'll grab my keys."

He opens the door wider for me. "You don't need your keys. You're riding with me."

"On your bike? No."

He sighs. "Is everything going to be an argument with you, woman?"

"I'll drive myself."

He tilts his head. "You know the way?"

I glare at him, refusing to answer the question.

He gives me a smug smile. "You're coming with me."

After a brief stare down, I give in. Better to get it over with than to keep arguing with him all morning.

Nerves buzz in my stomach. I make sure Baby is safe and comfortable in a kennel before reluctantly following Peter out to his bike. Walking behind him, I'm reminded yet again that I am a rather short individual and Peter is rather tall.

I should be intimidated by a man like that. But I'm not.

He was wrong when he guessed that I don't trust him.

It's not that I don't *trust* him. It's that I don't *like* him.

Two entirely different concepts.

His bike is black with the emblem *Royal Enfield* pressed into the side. It's a classic bike, powerful and predatory looking.

I put my hands on my hips. "Oh darn. Only one helmet. Guess I'll have to take my car."

He rolls his eyes, handing me his helmet, before climbing on. "Let's go, smart ass."

Taking one last look at the house, I throw caution to the wind and shove the helmet over my head. Careful not to touch him, I climb on behind him.

My nose is filled with his scent. It's woodsy and undeniably manly. He smells good.

Which is kind of annoying.

I hesitate, balancing on the seat. I'd really rather not get any closer. But when he kicks the bike into gear, I lurch forward wrapping my arms around his middle. I can feel him laughing, it rumbles through his chest. And then we're flying down my short, curved drive.

His bike hits the highway and my lips curve into a wide smile. Wind whips over my bare legs, my shoulders and the bike rumbles underneath me. Peter can't see my face, so there's no need to hide the pure pleasure that's fizzing through my veins.

My thighs wrap around his hips, and I lean into him, letting my chest press against his strong back. I wonder if he can feel the way my heart is racing.

While the trees are blurring by and we're nothing but metal and thunder racing down the highway, I can admit to myself that I'm drawn to this big, inked idiot. As long as he keeps his mouth shut and I don't have to see that arrogant smirk on his face.

Fifteen minutes. That's how long I can suspend disbelief. But then he's pulling up a steep drive, stopping in front of a truly magnificent cabin. A confection of glass and raw timber.

This is not the home of a regular blue-collar joe. This is the home of the wealthy elite.

Or a crime lord.

7.

Peter kills the engine on his bike and slips off first. He turns back, and I feel a little silly to be straddling his bike on my own.

Stepping closer so that his hips press against my thigh, he eases the helmet off my head. My hair falls around my shoulders and into my eyes. He gently pushes it behind my ears, letting his fingers trail down my hair. Coiling a lock around his long finger, he studies the auburn color before letting it fall again. These gentle, intimate touches are stoking a fire in my core, but at the same time, I feel uneasy. I barely know him, and yet, I let him touch my hair. I don't put up a fight when he puts his hands around my hips, easing me off the back of the bike.

Hard to act tough and feisty when he's got my thoughts on a merry-go-round.

His gaze finds my eyes, traveling down to my lips, and dragging lower to my cleavage. My tank top was pulled down a bit during the ride and I'm sorely tempted to yank it back up to a more modest level. But that feels like losing the battle, so I tip my chin up instead. He takes a short, quick breath through his nose, almost like he's scenting the air. Whatever he smells either makes him angry or hungry. I can't really say for sure which, but the look he's giving me is intense enough to make me squirm.

The front door opens and Andy steps out, a friendly smile on his face. Now that I've gotten over the shock of his gigantic size, he's not so intimidating. Not like Pretty Boy who follows a bit too close as I make my way up to the front door. When I climb the three steps to the deck, Peter lightly puts his fingertips on my lower back.

Andy grins at me, gaze flicking back to Peter. "Took you long enough. I was about to send the posse out."

Peter stands at my side, his arm brushing mine. "She didn't come willingly."

My cheeks heat and I'm tempting to smack him for telling on me. "He forgot to say please."

Andy laughs, a warm booming sound, before turning back to the door. "Well, come on in. Cherry is dying to meet you."

I can't hide my awe when we walk into Andy's place. It's expansive. There's a stone fireplace in the middle of the room with a fire roaring away, despite the fact that it's June. The entire eastern wall is solid glass offering a view of the Black Hills that spans as far as the eye can see. The kitchen to our left is massive and open with big granite counters. Cherry stands at a chef-grade stove.

She is not even close to what I pictured.

I would peg Andy to be in his forties. Cherry, on the other hand, can't be much past her early twenties. She's got long, black hair and tight little curves that make me feel plain and shapeless. I'm not wearing any makeup, but Cherry's is flawless. Smokey cat eyes. Plump, red lips. She wears short black shorts and a thin-strapped tank top showing off her tattoos. If this is the sort of pin up woman these guys are used to, I'm afraid I won't be up to their standards. I look like a summer camp counselor in comparison.

Cherry is in a class all by herself. But when she looks at me, and her eyes light up, I find myself hoping we can be friends.

She snaps the towel that was on her shoulder at Andy. "You didn't tell me how beautiful she is."

Andy grins sheepishly. "That seems like a problematic thing to tell one's girlfriend."

Cherry wrinkles her nose, glaring at him. "Yes, but now that you've left it out, that's awfully suspicious." She turns back to me, closing the distance to wrap me in a hug. "I'm just kidding, baby. Not about the gorgeous part. Because you are stunning. Pretty Boy, did you see these eyes?"

He's leaning, his hip against the counter. "I did."

Cherry takes both of my hands in hers. "I'm Kali Bata. They all call me Cherry." She grins at me. "And you are Zoey Cooper."

I nod. "You got it."

"How rude were they?"

I shrug. "Andy was a pure gentleman."

Andy barks a laugh, grinning at Peter.

Cherry's eyebrows raise. "Pretty Boy was the one who misbehaved?" She looks over my shoulder at the man in question. "He's usually the only civil one amongst them."

Andy's chuckling as he makes his way over to the stove. "The star pupil is finally getting in trouble."

Peter tilts his head. "Am I in trouble?"

Kali looks at me. "That depends. How rude was he?"

I narrow my eyes at him. "Very."

Peter scoffs. "I was the picture of patience with this one."

Kali turns to study Peter's face. "Interesting." She turns back to me, taking my hand. "I'm so glad you moved up here. We ladies are seriously outnumbered out here. You have no idea what I put up with."

Andy hooks an arm around Peter's neck. "Come on, brother. Ain't no winning when you're in the wrong."

Peter resists. "In the wrong?" He closes his eyes for a beat, shaking it off. "Zoey saw a wolf on the trail."

That comment seems to suck the air from the room. All three people turn to stare at me.

Andy's voice is gentle, but his expression is dead serious. "What kind of wolf?"

I shrug, feeling uneasy under all the pointed attention. "A *wolf* wolf."

Peter meets my gaze. "She says it was rabid."

Kali makes an almost inaudible sound of distress in her throat. "What color were the eyes, baby?"

8.

I swallow, my palms starting to sweat. "I didn't get that good of a look. Maybe orange? Yellow?"

Kali lets out a soft breath. The three of them exchange looks. I get the distinct feeling they're going to wait until I'm gone to talk about this wolf.

Kali goes to the wine fridge at the far end of the island. "This calls for a drink." She looks up at me. "You like white or red, babes?"

"Red."

"Excellent." Kali pulls a bottle out along with two wine glasses. "I was a bartender in a previous life. That was before I moved up here."

Andy and Peter move around the kitchen behind me, plating the steaks Kali made. They set the table and I find myself sitting down to a hearty meal of steak and potatoes. Mostly steak. The guys each have a cut of meat bigger than their heads. I don't have much of an appetite.

For one thing, I never eat a heavy lunch.

But for another thing, Peter has pushed his chair close to mine. He stretches his legs out, casually invading my space. I tell myself that they're just legs. So what if they're damn near tangled up together? And if I'm feeling a little buzzed by the connection, that's just the wine speaking.

Andy sits in the chair opposite mine. He's got his chair pushed up next to Kali's. "Where did you see the wolf, Zoey?"

I struggle to keep my voice even. "There's a ravine on the south side of my property."

Andy nods. "We know it. Silver Creek runs through there."

My knee accidentally brushes up against Petere's thigh. "It was down by that creek."

Kali pushes her empty plate back. "What color was the wolf?"

I think of the wolf, the way its lips curled back. The fear I felt in that moment. A shiver passes through my body. "Gray."

Peter shifts in his seat, casually moving his elbow onto my arm rest. I'm distracted by the tattoos on his arm. Black roses twine up his forearm. Words in Latin. It's oddly soothing to look at. Like one of those Magic Eye puzzles from when I was a kid.

Their conversation resumes around me. It sounds like shop talk. They discuss where everyone was today. I don't know who they're talking about, so I tune them out, letting my mind wander. I'm trying to adjust my dream for Strawberry Moon. At one point, I imagined I'd have a little farm. I thought I'd have chickens. Goats, possibly. But if this territory is full of wolves, some of which are rabid, that seems like throwing chum to sharks.

Peter unexpectedly, climbs to his feet, cupping my elbow. "Come on."

I look around, realizing that Andy and Kali have moved back into the kitchen. They're talking quietly, heads bent together, while they wash dishes.

I let Peter lead me through the sprawling living room, past multiple couches and chairs, until we're passing through a glass door. We step onto a patio. A soft breeze swirls around my legs, tosses my hair.

I stop, letting the view expand around me.

Cleo Mercer

It's so different from back home. St. Louis is a river town. If you make it outside the city limits, you're immediately swallowed up by a different kind of forest. Oak. Sweetgum. Dogwood. It's humid and green and verdant.

It's like a Christmas tree farm went haywire out here. The air is dryer, too. I like the way the breeze brushes across my shoulders. I lean up against the deck's railing and let my gaze wander.

"We'll find that wolf." Peter leans beside me, his arm pressing up against mine.

I look up at him. "*You're* going to?"

"Yeah." He shrugs. "We'll find it. You don't need to worry."

"Who said I'm worried?"

He studies my face. "You wear your worries like perfume."

Clearly, I'm not coming across as the carefree, independent woman I'm trying to become. My shoulders slump slightly. "I've got a lot on my mind."

"Such as?"

I meet his gaze and look away. "Just... starting over in a new place. It's hard. And, yeah, I guess maybe the whole rabid wolf thing has me a little freaked out."

He pushes upright and slides an arm around my waist. Back home, everyone was a hugger. Friends. Co-workers. I tell myself that this is just like that.

Just a friendly hug.

Except for the part where Peter and I are not friends.

I hesitate because I think I'm supposed to. Because I don't know him very well. He's clearly not a boy scout.

But that logic is a flimsy shield to hold up between someone who radiates power and heat.

His arm feels good against my back, his fingers scorch my skin through my shirt. He's pulls at me, at something deep inside me.

I turn into him, and he wraps both arms around my body, tugging me closer. Reluctantly, I allow my weight to ease into him. This is what I needed. Human connection. Even if this particular human is an arrogant tease.

It's lonely trying to make it on my own.

But that was the goal.

It's the sole reason I moved to the middle of nowhere. I wanted to prove to myself that I could do it on my own. That I'm as strong as I think I am.

But that was before the whole rabid wolf thing. Blood-thirsty predators are a bit much, even for an independent woman.

I let out a slow, shuddering breath and lean into him. My cheek rests against his chest. He smells so damn good.

He braces one hand on the small of my back, fingers spreading wide. His touch lights my skin up with a sparkling feeling. That slow burn that's been stoking in my belly since he showed up sparks to life. There's a little flutter in my core, wetness begins to gather between my legs.

Breathing in through his nose, his right hand trails up my spine.

9.

The glass door opens again and Andy steps out. I disentangle myself from Peter's arms as casually as I can. Kali trails behind Andy. She looks positively pint-sized next to the giant of a man. I move back to the railing and Peter leans up next to me. He has this ability to lounge wherever he is. Strength and laziness all rolled into one. It makes him seem deceptively cuddly. It also makes the times when he is alert seem all the more intimidating.

At the moment, he's relaxed, leaning on his elbow. His forearm manages to fit into the small of my waist. This is how you stand next to a girlfriend. Or a lover.

Not a woman you just met.

I don't want to send mixed signals. I should move.

In a minute. I'll definitely move away. Just a few more minutes.

I glance up at Andy. "Peter said you'd try to track down that wolf."

Andy nods, squinting out over the hills. "We'll find it."

There's a note of confidence in his voice that surprises me. "And then what?"

Andy turns his gaze back to me. "What do you mean?"

"What will you do once you find it?"

Andy glances at Peter, before turning his gaze back to mine. "You're a vet. You know what the chances of survival are for a rabid animal."

"Are you sure it has rabies?"

Andy glances at Peter again.

Peter cranes his head to look at me. "We're going off what you said. What made you think it was rabid?"

I toss my head, feeling my temper creep up on me. "I thought I saw some foam around the mouth." I pause, not liking the grim look on Andy's face. "But that could have been slobber. You shouldn't euthanize a healthy animal without confirming that it's sick."

In the back of my mind, I know this wasn't a healthy animal. But I'm a vet. I didn't go to school so that people could put animals down at the first sign of illness. "Could it be rabies? Sure. But it could have just been dehydrated. It was coming to the creek. Please don't kill an innocent animal based on my account alone. I really couldn't stand that."

Peter's watching me, studying me with open curiosity. "An innocent animal? A wolf?"

"Those wolves were here long before you or I ever set foot in these hills."

Andy huffs a laugh at that comment.

I glare at him. "I'm serious. This is their home, not ours. We need to learn to live with those wolves and not treat them like invading monsters."

Andy and Peter are trading mysterious looks again and that has my temper stoking into a full-on inferno.

"Please tell me you don't hunt those wolves for sport."

Andy gets a pained look on his face. Kali puts a hand on his forearm. Her voice is soothing. "We're just caught off guard, babes. We don't run into a lot of animal lovers out this way."

I feel a little deflated. "I'm a vet. What did you expect?"

Andy laughs, breaking the tension. "God, it's good to have a vet back in the area."

Peter slips his arm around my waist again and tugs me flush against his side. Maybe, if you squint your eyes just right, you could convince yourself that it's just a friendly gesture. But it feels like more than that.

It feels a little like he's staking his claim.

Part of me rebels at this idea. I did not just escape one controlling relationship to leap right into the arms of the next man I found.

But on the other hand... being independent doesn't have to mean celibate, right? There's only one thing more distracting than Peter's pretty blue eyes. And that's the darn wolf. I can't be responsible for an innocent creature being killed.

I make eye contact with Andy. "Promise me you won't euthanize that wolf if you find it. Not without bringing it to me first."

Andy's expression holds the faintest note of challenge in it. "You sure you want that?"

I tip my chin up. "I've handled bigger animals than that little wolf. Bring it to me if you find it."

Peter waits quietly, watching Andy for his reaction.

Andy's smiles gamely. "Whatever you want, Doc."

Peter's thumb glides along my hip. "I promised Zoey that we'd help her finish moving into Maria's old place."

Andy nods sharply. "You bet. Round up the boys."

I hold up my hands. "You don't need to do that. I can handle it. I'm almost unpacked."

Peter shakes his head, ratting me out. "She's not."

Andy nods. "Call Rabbit and Dante."

Peter nods his head at me. "Let's go, Baby."

Babes.

Baby.

It doesn't take long for these people to welcome me into their ranks. Too bad those ranks happen to be part of a biker gang. But if I have to be with or against, I'll be with all day long.

Peter takes my hand and tows me through the house again. Outside, he puts the helmet on my head, eyes searching mine briefly before he flips the visor down.

It's safe behind this visor. He can't see my flushed cheeks. Can't hear my racing heart. I climb on behind him, this time bracing myself on his strong shoulders as I sling my leg around his hips. He hooks both hands under my knees and snugs me up against his body. And then he kicks his bike into gear. I'm already craving the feel of the bike rumbling beneath me. Of flying over the road so that the world becomes a watercolor blur.

It feels me with a joy that tears down my inhibitions, makes me feel free.

10.

The Black Hills Motorcycle Club refers to themselves as The Pack. As more and more pack members show up at Strawberry Moon, I start to notice a common thread.

One, all of these men are huge.

And two, there is an abundance of wolf tattoos. Maybe I was off-base to worry that these guys would want to harm an innocent wolf.

Not only do they help me unload the rest of the boxes, they clean the barn top to bottom and fix the leaky sink in the bathroom.

Kali and another woman, Angela, help me get the clinic into working order. Peter always seems to find an excuse to stay nearby. When I'm in the barn, he's out there boarding up the broken window. When I move into the house, he takes it upon himself to move the furniture where I want it. I suspect he's a bit territorial. If another club member spends too much time talking to me, or lingers for too long, Peter's there to move them along. Between Baby and Peter, I've got two males guard-dogging me all day long.

A few hours and a dozen pizzas later, I'm completely, one hundred percent moved into my new home.

I stand on the wrap around porch watching the pack members ride off into the night one by one. Peter stands by my side as we watch Kali climb onto Andy's bike with him. She waves over her shoulder, before jamming the helmet over her long black hair. Her back arches prettily and that round ass sticks out and I feel a jab of envy wishing I knew how to look that sexy.

I turn back to the house, Baby and Peter trailing behind me.

Baby lays by the oven on the rug he's claimed. He lets out a long sigh before flopping onto his side.

Peter comes up behind me. "I left my tools up in your bedroom."

"Okay." I lead him up the stairs, ultra-conscious of the fact that he's getting an eyeful of my ass as I climb the steps. With each step, the butterflies in my stomach get more agitated until it's a full-out butterfly cyclone in my tummy. My heart is beating too fast and I'm just glad he can't read my thoughts. Because Pretty Boy and I are alone.

Alone alone.

Walking to my bedroom, I'm doing my damndest not to think about what the two of us could do in there. It's a one-job mission. Retrieve Peter's tools. Thank him for his help. Not on my knees, even though that's what my horny little heart is thinking about.

We silently walk down the long hall and I step into my room. My heart feels full when I look at my bed. Kali or Angela must have made my bed at some point. Where there was a bare mattress and a bunch of boxes, my furniture is arranged and my big, gray duvet is pulled neatly over my bed. It looks like I actually live here now.

I turn back to Peter, noticing the heat in his eyes.

My voice comes out sounding shaky. "I don't see your tools."

"Huh." He steps closer.

I take a step backwards and he follows.

If I wanted to get away from him, I wouldn't have led him up to my room. The jury is still out on this guy's personality, but my southern half made the decision on his body hours ago.

I let him back me up against the wall. He reaches out, putting his big hand on my hip. After a beat, my own hand feathers over his. As soon as my fingertips glide over the back of his hand, he snags my wrist and pins my hand over my head. He's so much taller than me, he has to stoop to be at my eye level. His nose runs along my cheekbone and he breathes me in. "I've been watching you all day."

My head automatically leans towards his, following his teasing touch. "I noticed."

His voice is low, raspy. "Could you tell what I was thinking?"

"Maybe the same thing I was thinking?"

I duck out from under his arm, slipping my wrist from his grip. Moving to perch on the edge of the bed, I watch him prowl closer, a playful look in his eye.

I cross my legs and lean back. "Let me see the rest of your ink."

Reaching behind with one hand, he pulls his shirt over his head. He has roses on his arms. His neck. But his torso tells a darker story. I uncross my legs, leaning forward, elbow planted on my knees. It's not a ladylike stance, per say, but I'm drawn in. Skulls. A reaper's blade. A weeping saint, or maybe she's a goddess. He's moved closer.

Close enough I could lean forward and kiss the inky lines on his abs. Instead, my gaze drags up his torso, over his chest. He's got a strange look in his eyes. Like there's a door to his soul and he's got it cracked just an inch. He takes my hands and puts them around his waist.

"I can smell you." He murmurs.

My cheeks color as I try to guess what he means by that. He weaves his fingers through my hair and pulls. He forces my head back, leaning down to breathe in along my neck. His fingers find the edge of my shirt. Slowly, giving me a chance to protest, he pulls it up and over my head. I'm wearing a dark red bra. Nothing special. But when he passes those tattooed hands over my chest, it's like my perspective takes a one-eighty and I feel powerful and sexy. His warm palms sooth my frayed nerves and I lean into his hands, willing him to go harder. To inflict a little pain. His palm slides to the middle of my chest, resting over my heart. It beats wildly against his hand and his gaze meets mine.

And then he pushes me onto my back. He works deftly at the button on my shorts, the zipper, dragging my shorts down my legs in a swift movement.

11.

He's on his knees at the foot of my bed. Those big shoulders force my thighs wide. He kisses the inside of my knee, kissing and licking his way up my thigh until he reaches the hem of my panties.

He presses his face to my panties and breathes deep. His breath is warm and teasing. I reach down and finally allow myself to touch his hair. The sides of his scalp are shorn close, prickly one direction, smooth when I sweep my hand down. Then my fingers find the longer length on top of his head. I expected it to be hardened with gel. The way it stays combed back from his face made me assume he cemented it in place. I was wrong about that one. There's no gel, no pomade. Just soft, smooth hair. Thick and obedient. It follows my fingers, looking charmingly mussed when my fingers pass through it.

Then he's tugging at the edges of my panties, slipping them over my hips. "Take off your bra, Baby."

I obey the command even though this leaves me completely naked and him still in his jeans. He watches my every movement with eyes that remind me of a predator. I am not a sex pot. Not like Kali. No one would ever call me Cherry Bomb.

I'm very much in the cute category. The girl next door.

But the way he looks at me makes me feel like maybe I can be more than just the sweet and innocent one. Maybe I can be who I want to be. Who I really am.

It makes me feel fierce.

I push up on my elbows and take a handful of his hair. Holding tight, I tug his head to the side mimicking the same thing he did to me earlier. It's a little like a kitten fucking with a tiger, but his eyes spark with lust. He likes a little pain, too, it seems. "I want you to do everything I say."

He closes his eyes, leaning into my hand. "Okay."

An immense wave of power surges through me. Such a big man and he's putty in my hands. I guide his head between my thighs. "Kiss me."

He obeys, soft lips kissing the inside of my pelvis. Working his way down, he stokes the fire in my belly with his feathery kisses. When he gets to my apex, he forms his lips around my clit and sucks gently. A surprised whimper is caught in my throat. His shoulders stiffen up at the sound and he slips his arms under my thighs, forcing them wider. He finds my center, keeping his tongue soft and flat, he drags it back up to my clit and down again.

On the rare occasion that my ex did attempt oral, he was sloppy and blind at best. I didn't really expect this to be any good. I didn't expect him to be better than anything I could do for myself. My fingers run through his hair, scratching lightly at his scalp, murmuring soft words of encouragement. When he sucks my clit again, a moan escapes my lips and this time I don't try to mute it. I prop myself up on my elbows, watching, intoxicated, as his head moves between my legs. His tattooed neck brushes us against my smooth thigh. If I look to the side, I can see his reflection in the mirror leaning up against the wall. He's on his knees, inked back strong and bent towards me. I like

41

seeing him kneeling at my feet like this. It makes me feel less overpowered and more in charge. "Touch yourself."

He turns his head to the side, nipping at my thighs, but keeps those baby blues trained on my face. Without a word, he drags the zipper down on his jeans and tugs himself out. I've never watched a man jerk off. Not in person, anyway. I can't quite see the whole picture, and part of me wants to be the one kneeling so I can see his cock up close. But he's got his tongue inside me and it's a struggle to keep my eyes open.

He fists his cock, quick on the downstroke, going slow as he pulls back. It's a visceral demonstration of what it would be like if he was inside me. I'd ask for a demonstration here and now, but I'm too close to the edge and I can't find the words to put the breaks on. With his left hand, he puts two fingers at my entrance and pushes them inside. I sigh with pleasure. It's not his cock, but it's a close second. My head tips back, but I can still feel his eyes on me, watching my every reaction as he plays my body like a fiddle.

Sweet, aching tension builds in both my clit and where his fingers delve deep and sure. He winds me tighter and tighter until my hips are twitching and bucking under him and then the coil springs loose and pleasure rushes through my body. It's like a twin orgasm, one from inside and one from where his lips work over my clit. I cry out, nonsense spilling from my lips. And he kisses me gently, wringing out fluttering aftershocks. With my body still twitching and dazed, I weave my fingers through his hair and pull. "Now you." I pause. "Come."

12.

It's the same command I'd give a dog. In control. Leaving no doubt as to who is the alpha.

He presses his forehead into my belly and lets out a soft grunt. "Fuck."

I prop my limp body up on my elbows and watch him drag his own pleasure out with his fist. He's rough on himself. I picture myself being the one wrapped around that shaft, feeling those brutal pumps and a shiver of anticipation ripples through me. Turning his head to the side, he meets my gaze. Something about those cool blue eyes has the ability to cut right through me. Then his eyes are squeezing shut, he clamps his teeth around my hip and bites. It's sharp, but not sharp enough to break skin. And besides, I'm too fascinated by the sight of Peter coming to be worried about a little pain. His back gleams with a fine sheen of sweat, highlighting ink and muscle alike. The sharp, defined muscles in his arm, his forearm, tense and shift as he jerks himself off.

It's a pleasure to watch. I let my fingers slip down his neck and over his hard shoulders. I can feel what I can't see—his muscles are warm and tense. My fingertip comes away slick with his sweat.

I've always had a superstitious affinity with water. Without much thought, I draw a symbol across the inside of my wrist.

Cleo Mercer

I'm not sure what instinct drives me to do it, it's just something I occasionally do.

Spring water from the foothills of Sedona. Holy water from the back of the church on Easter. It goes on my pulse point, right on my wrist.

My mother always joked we came from a long line of hedge witches. That could be it. Some ancient instinct guiding me towards sources of power—like I can borrow some of that magic.

I scrawl the letter P, feeling my pulse flutter under my touch.

The letter P for Peter.

And Power, because that's what he is. Raw and untamed despite his diplomatic reputation. I see past that, to what he is.

I like getting the uncut version of him, seeing him unravel. It's euphoric.

And the epicenter of that pleasure seems to be the place where his teeth mark my skin. Pleasure radiates out from those marks, golden and buzzy, until my entire body is a satisfied puddle of goo.

When he's done, he stays on his knees, forehead resting on my tummy. I let my fingers trail through that soft, thick hair twining it around my fingers, nails scratching lightly at his scalp.

His sucks in a long breath, pushing himself upright. He stares at the teeth marks on my hips for a long time. His hand finds my hip and his thumb brushes over the mark, as though he can scrub those two half-moons away. Then those clear blue eyes lift to meet my own gaze. A strange expression flickers across his face. Is that regret? Concern? His thumb is still covering the marks on my skin.

I put my hand over his. "Don't worry about that."

His gaze falls to my hand.

I let my fingers smooth over the back of his hand. "It's not like it's permanent."

His gaze raises up to my face with something very close to panic flitting through his eyes. Then he's pushing upright, climbing to his feet with brisk movements. He snags the tissues from my nightstand and cleans up without a word.

Nerves tighten my stomach and I push into a seated position, watching him pull his shirt back over his shoulders. "You're leaving?"

He gives me a strange look and I'm suddenly very conscious of the fact that he is fully dressed, boots and everything, and I am completely naked.

His eyes scrape over my face, flitting down to my hip, before looking away. That smug look is back on his face. "Should I have brought my toothbrush?"

He might as well have slapped me. Scrambling for my tank top and panties, I shrug into them in record time. It's not like I expected him to write me love poems and braid my hair. But I was hoping for something more than just oral, even if it was mind-blowing. I wanted to see what else he could do.

But apparently, it's just in and out with this guy.

Hurt starts to unspool in my chest, but I rebuke it, shoving it back in its box. I did not want a relationship with this guy.

He is a biker.

In a gang.

And he is staring at me.

I spread my arm wide, gesturing for him to lead the way. "I'll walk you out."

He seems a bit surprised, like he expected me to beg him to stay. Not fucking likely. If he wants to go, he can go. Last time I checked, he was the one on his knees, not me. My ego might be slightly bruised, but I won't beg.

I follow him down the stairs, feeling more sure of myself with each step. A sense of achievement is growing in me. Turns out, I am capable of a one-night stand. All I had to do was smother the hopeless romantic in me.

Baby hears us coming and scrabbles upright, meeting us at the door. I push the door open and stand aside. He brushes by me, hesitating on the porch. He turns back. "I guess I'll see you around?"

A smirk tugs at my lips. "I guess you will."

He glances back at the dark night, before fixing me with those blue eyes. "No more off-trail runs, okay?"

I cross my arms, stretching to my full height. I am fully aware that I am standing in my doorway in nothing but my panties and a tank top.

"Zoey." He growls my name.

I sigh. "Fine. But y'all need to keep your promise."

"What promise was that?"

I tip my chin up. "You find that wolf, you bring it to me."

His gaze flicks down to my hip and he shrugs. "Your wish is my command."

I watch him move across the yard to his bike, so graceful despite his size. He climbs on his bike, and it roars to life. It's like that rumble is calling to me, stoking the fire in my tummy. That tongue of his was pretty damn good, but it left me feeling incomplete. I wanted more, but maybe there will be other chances.

I turn back into the house, scowling. But when I spot Baby asleep on his rug, I can't help but smile. I'm feeling pretty good as I climb the stairs, more positive with each step.

I've made new friends, friends who were willing to help me move my crap, which is high praise in my mind. And I've found a potential fuck buddy. I've never had one of those before, but I can definitely see the benefits.

I'll just have to get used to sleeping alone.

13.

It's really for the best that Pretty Boy didn't linger. Sent a clear message. This is just for fun.

There's a small part of me that's offended by that notion. Am I so easy to walk away from? If I had my way, I would have kept him around for a little longer.

A part of me that wanted to cuddle up with him tonight, fall asleep in his arms. But the larger part of me is relieved that I didn't accidentally land myself a biker boyfriend.

He's kind of like a human bonfire. Beautiful. Powerful. But if you stand too close, you're bound to get burned.

I pause by the bed, glancing at the mirror. It's possible I'll never be able to look in it's reflection without thinking of Peter on his knees, his cock in his fist. He certainly knows his way around a woman's body. An odd flare of jealousy flickers in my belly at the thought of other women having his attention but I quash it.

He's not mine. I don't want him to be mine.

This move, this new start, is all part of my bid to be my own person. To prove to myself that I can do it.

I take a quick shower before bed. And then I lay in my bed, letting the past few days wash over me. I was frightened by that wolf, but now I feel more grounded. I've got the people around me who seem to be willing to help if I just ask. I drift off to sleep with a bone-deep satisfaction, something I should thank Pretty Boy for later. Even though he's not here, he's given me the best night's sleep I've had in years.

◗

The next morning, I start my day in the office. The last vet, Maria, left her filing cabinets full of patients' files. Odds are, some of these pet owners may return. It's a gift to find them. I organize her paperwork, keeping the useful stuff and tossing the rest into the recycle box.

Baby is a wonderful assistant. He grins at all of my amusing observations and keeps an eye on the lobby for me. My one complaint is that tail. When it's wagging, it's a straight-up weapon. I'm sitting on the floor, sorting through papers and Baby is doing his best to help. His paws scatter a cat's file, making it clear where he stands on the feline issue. He licks my cheek, ass wagging like crazy when I kiss the top of his head. That tail is out of control, knocking my coffee over as he jumps back.

"Oh shit!" I scramble to grab the mug, but its contents are already cascading across the floor. I rush to the kitchen, returning with a rag. Baby's head is lowered in shame, he looks up at me with an apology in those brown eyes. I laugh, ruffling his ears. "It's not your fault, Babes. I shouldn't have had my coffee on the ground."

I kneel to clean up the mess, but it's already seeping through the floorboards. I pause, distracted by the tapping sound of coffee dripping below my knees. Pulling back, I study the floorboard, noticing a tiny chink in one of the planks. There's something oddly intentional about it that has me curious. Finding a letter opener, I prize it into the plank and three planks on a hidden hinge easily lift up. I sit back, momentarily stunned. I glance over at Baby who seems just as shocked as I am.

"What do you think old Maria was hiding down here?" I ask Baby. "A pistol and pearls?"

I shine my cell phone's flashlight into the opening first, revealing a small cavity. There's a leather doctor's bag and several folders. Lifting everything onto the floor beside me, I open the doctor's bag first.

The first thing I pull out is a muzzle. It looks like its designed to fit a person's head but has the snout opening for a dog. Old Maria must have been into some kinky shit. Gingerly setting it aside, I remove an antique wooden case. I carefully open it and sit back, stunned.

"What the fuck?"

It's lined with red velvet. There's an old fashioned pistol. I glance at Baby, attempting a weak smile. "I was only kidding about the pistol."

I empty a box of bullets into my palm, they look slightly misshapen. Homemade. My fingers gingerly pass over a line of vials, each sealed with wax containing what looks like mercury. Or quicksilver. I lift a jar out and read the crabbed handwriting. *Wolfsbane*.

There's a velvet pouch and I upend it on the floor. Five wicked looking claws tumble onto the ground.

Whatever Miss Maria was into, this is not a casual collection. Why would she hide it under the floorboards?

I carefully place everything back in the bag before lifting the folders. Flipping the first one open, I find a mismatched collection of pages torn from books.

The first page has the title *The Wolf Hunter's Guide*.

A whisper of fear slips over the back of my neck. I want to dismiss Maria as a lonely kook with a strange hobby. But some deep instinct is warning me that there are darker forces at work here. Crazy or not, something compelled an old woman to gather this collection. To hide it from prying, powerful eyes.

Something, or someone, was scaring that old woman. And I think I have a pretty good guess as to who it was.

14.

The doctor's kit goes back under the floor. But I move the folder, with its scraps of paper and journal entries to my desk. It's all nonsense, from what I can gather. Victorian-era photographs and sketches. There's a drawing of a human skeleton with a canine skull.

Maria has some odd observations here and there about wolf poison and the moon's course through the night sky. Suddenly, the clinic's name, Strawberry Moon, takes on a new perspective. It has shit to do with fruit and everything to do with the moon's cycle.

I sit back feeling uneasy. This woman clearly had some very deep, troubling preoccupations. The guys never mentioned that she was unstable. I wonder if she was able to keep her delusions under wraps—hidden from them. She seemed particularly obsessed with something called a Vargulf. A rabid wolf, from what I can gather. She had working theories about how to cure the disease, but I feel like I'm reading Macbeth. Eye of newt, toe of frog. That kind of nonsense.

The bell over the clinic's door chimes and I jump, startled. Scooping the journal entries back into the folder, I go out into the lobby and meet my first, real customer in Hill City.

He's a tall man, stooping and thin, with a thick beard and a bald patch on his head. He reminds me of a skinny friar. He's got a box and as I come closer, I see a beautiful long-haired Siamese wrapped up in a towel. "The wife accidentally ran her over."

I nod sharply, turning back to the exam room. "Bring her in here. I'm Zoey Cooper."

"I heard you was moving into Maria's old place. Good to have a vet nearby again." He sets the box on the exam table. "I'm Bernard Stevens."

I ease the injured cat out of the box, giving it an injection for the pain. "What's this little sweetie's name?"

He tilts his head. "It was Prissy."

Prissy? Heck of a name, but… okay. I exam Prissy's back leg. "It's broken."

He nods. "Best if you just put her down."

I look up, shocked. "Oh, I think you misunderstood. It's just broken. She'll recover from this."

Bernard tips his head. "No. I think it's best if we just let Prissy go. The new wife don't like her, to be honest. She belonged to the ex. Was an anniversary present. She's been nothing but trouble. I think it'd just be best if we put Prissy out of her misery."

Disgust and anger swirl in my stomach making me feel almost nauseous. "I'm not going to euthanize a perfectly healthy animal, Bernard."

He and I both stare down at Prissy. She's looking worse for the wear, but despite the dire appearance, her injuries aren't life-threatening.

Bernard shrugs. "I would've put her down myself if I had a gun."

I find myself putting a protect arm over Prissy. Bernard takes note of my new stance. He pulls out his wallet. "How's this? I'll pay for her to be put down and you can do whatever you want with her. Sound fair?"

I pull myself upright, trying to appear taller than my five foot two inches. "You can keep your money, Bernard. I won't take it."

Cleo Mercer

He gives me a long look, shaking his head with a quiet huff. "Suit yourself. She's all yours." He takes a few steps back, stopping at the exam room door. "Welcome to Hill City, Miss Cooper. We sure are glad to have you here."

There's something creepy about the way he said that. I try to focus on the beautiful cat and what she needs, but Bernard and his wives stay just at the periphery of my thoughts. I can't seem to shake the cold sense of disgust that I feel. I didn't get into animal sciences to euthanize living creatures, but it seems that's everyone's first go-to. Well, they've met their match in me.

After Prissy's cast is finished and she's resting, I go outside for some fresh air. Baby follows me out, taking up a spot at my side. I let my fingers trail over his head, trying to shake the feeling of despondency that's settled on my shoulders.

When I hear car wheels on the gravel, I'm almost afraid Bernard has come back for the darn cat. But it's a sheriff's car.

The door opens and Hitch unfolds, standing tall and strong. His gaze flits from my face to Baby's. A smile tugs at his lips and he closes the distance. "Came to check on our patient. How's little Baby doing?"

"See for yourself." I pat Baby's head.

Something in my tone must have given me away, because Hitch studies my face. "You doing okay?"

I intend to tell him everything's great. I have my clinic and my fresh start. But what comes out of my mouth sounds more like a tortured croak. "No."

Without a word, Hitch sits down at my side.

After a beat, he puts his arm around my shoulders and I lean into him, helpless to stop the tears from pouring down my cheeks.

15.

Hitch has a calming presence. Must be part of the job. Soothing hysterical citizens. But his arms are strong and his silence is reassuring. He doesn't mock me or make me feel like I'm on edge all the time. My last boyfriend was an MMA fighter. He sort of existed on the fringes of right and wrong. And there's Pretty Boy, who can't decide if he wants to tease me or fuck me.

Hitch's solid goodness is a refreshing change. Eventually, I gather myself up enough to tell him about my morning and my run-in with Bernard the would-be cat killer.

"Can I see it?" Hitch's deep voice resonates through his chest.

I push myself upright, disentangling myself from his arms. "The cat? Sure."

He follows me back inside and we find Prissy sleeping peacefully in her crate. I open the door so that Hitch can run the back of his knuckles gently over Prissy's flank. Even in her sleep, she starts to purr.

"What will you do with her?" He murmurs, keeping his voice low so as not to wake her.

If she was in perfect condition, a pure-breed cat like that would be an easy animal to place. But she may never get full mobility in that back leg.

I shake my head. "I'm not sure. There might be a cat rescue in Rapid City. I'll have to look into it."

He glances at me, hazel eyes finding mine. "Can I have her?"

My heart seems to expand in my chest. "You want her as a pet?"

He gives Prissy one more careful pet before stepping back. "Used to have a cat like that as a kid. I wouldn't mind having a little friend around the house."

Tears start to burn in the corners of my eyes and Hitch gives me a look of pure concern. "Are you okay?"

I nod, giving him a watery smile. "You can have her on one condition."

"What's that?"

"Give her a better name for God's sake."

He chuckles. "That can be arranged."

We creep back into the lobby, and I start giving him paperwork to fill out. "I'll keep her overnight for observation. You can get her in the morning. And Hitch?"

He looks right at me. Damn, he's handsome.

I swallow the lump in throat. "Thanks."

The front door chimes, yet again, and we both turn to watch Pretty Boy darken my doorstep. His gaze flits across my face, before traveling over to Hitch where his expression hardens. "Florean."

Hitch's shoulders straighten and the lightness in his eyes fades. "Mackavoy."

I've learned two things. Pretty Boy's last name. And the fact that they clearly do not like each other.

Peter saunters in with Baby on his heels. "On county business, sheriff? Or are you here as a patient?"

Hitch hooks a thumb over his belt. "Zoey is looking after my cat."

Peter smirks. "Not surprising."

Hitch tips his head slightly. "What's that?"

"You're a cat guy."

"I guess I am." Hitch turns back to me. "Are you okay here?"

He's asking, in so few words, if I want Pretty Boy to leave.

Peter seems to bristle at that, but I smile reassuringly at Hitch. "Nothing I can't handle."

Hitch studies my face for a few moments before reluctantly turning to leave. Pretty Boy stands in his path, not bothering to move and Hitch lets his shoulder clip Peter's on his way by.

I wait until the door is closed before turning my attention on Peter. "Can I ask what you're doing here?"

He shrugs, coming forward to lean on my counter. "Came by to check on you."

"Why?"

"Just to make sure the big bad wolf didn't get you."

I smirk at that. "Pretty sure I'm staring the big bad wolf down right now."

His eyebrows knit together briefly before he manages to smooth his features. "I've been thinking about you."

I've been thinking about him, too. Dreaming about him, actually. Those skilled lips. The way his tattoos stretch and move across his skin. His hand on his shaft.

The memory warms me through, and I try to ignore the fluttering feeling in my core. "I hope you're not looking for trouble. Last time you left me high and dry."

His lips curve up. "I seem to recall taking pretty damn good care of you."

"Good care of me? You left a mark."

His gaze drops to my wrist and before I can move, he snags my arm. He raises my wrist and breathes deep, blue eyes lighting on my face. His thumb presses into my wrist, in the exact place where I drew his initial.

Cleo Mercer

I've taken a shower since then. Washed my hands a dozen times. Scrubbed up for work. And yet, with the way he's zeroed in on my wrist, it feels like I branded myself.

My cheeks catch fire.

He can't guess what I did, can he?

16.

I take my wrist back, but his gaze stays trained on my face. It's like he's seeing me in a new light. He doesn't look disgusted or anything, just incredibly serious.

Too fucking serious.

I need to change the topic before he starts asking questions. "That's not where you left a mark." I tug down the side of my scrubs to reveal the upper curve of my hips. "Here."

His teeth left a strange bruise on my skin. A faded red. I expected the mark to disappear right away, but when I woke up in the morning, it was exactly the same.

I expect some sort of saucy response from Pretty Boy. A smug grin. But he winces instead.

Not the response I was going for. I laugh in surprise. "Relax, Pretty Boy. I'm just teasing you. It's just a little bruise. It will fade."

"No, it won't." His cell starts ringing in his back pocket, but he doesn't break eye contact with me.

I give him a bemused smile. "You going to get that?"

He reluctantly pulls his phone out and presses it to his ear.

"Yeah." He pauses, listening. "Where?" Another pause. "Okay, I'm on my way."

I lean on the counter, resting my chin in my palm. "I take it you have to go?"

He shoves his phone in his back pocket. "They found the wolf."

I straighten immediately. "If you find it…"

He gives me a tight smile. "We'll bring it to you."

☽

It's not until Pretty Boy is long gone that I realize he doesn't have my cell number. None of them do. And since the land line is defunct, there's no way to get a hold of me. As the hours wile on, and no one shows up with a wolf, I start to feel the fool.

What made me think a hardened biker gang would listen to my demands? I have no influence with them. No leverage. If they wanted to kill every last wolf in the Black Hills, what could I do to stop them? Maybe Hitch and I could band together and bring them down.

Nursing wild west fantasies, I move around the clinic. Prissy is a model patient, but she's only one cat and doesn't take much of my time.

I said I wanted time to myself, but it's turning out to be a lot lonelier than I expected. Good thing I have Baby to keep me company. He follows me up to my room later that night, watching me brush my teeth before bed. I change into a soft blue tank top and matching shorts. We both pause, listening, as the faint call of a wolf slips in through the window. I wonder if it's just my imagination, but then it's followed by another call, slightly closer.

Baby's head is tilted, he looks over his shoulder at me.

"It's all good, Baby." I ruffle his ears. "Just Mother Nature making her presence known."

But I'm too unsettled to lay down and decide to make my way back down to the kitchen. I put on the kettle hoping some chamomile tea will soothe my overactive thoughts.

I tune out the initial sounds of engines roaring by, but as they grow louder, I realize they're pulling into my drive.

I peer into the dark summer night, temporarily blinded by several sets of headlights.

Two bikes pull up to the house. A pickup truck follows close behind, whipping around to back right up to the clinic door. Something about the speed at which the truck approached, the gravel spitting from the tires, fills me with dread.

A man with short black hair and grim expression climbs out from behind the wheel and drops the gate on the back of the truck. I'm outside, barefoot and in my pajamas, before I have a second thought. There's a limp form in the back, covered in blood and grime.

It's a wolf.

As I get closer, I quickly realize that this is not the rabid wolf I saw earlier. This wolf is darker. Bigger. Peter materializes from the shadow, sweeping forward, a grim look on his face. He's followed by one of the bikers who helped assemble a bookshelf for me the other day. Dusty, I think his name was.

I step to the side. "Bring it into the exam room."

Peter and Dusty carefully lift the wolf and carry it inside. The dark-haired man gives me a brief, strong handshake introducing himself as Dante before following on their heels.

Peter watches me enter the exam room, his gaze flits across my bare legs, the thin material stretched across my chest.

I realize I'm wearing light pajamas in front of his biker friends, but there isn't really time to worry about my clothes. Not with that wolf bleeding out in front of me.

"What happened?" I come closer and Peter gets in my way. He snags a box of blue, latex gloves from the counter and makes me put a pair on.

Dusty puts both hands through his curly brown hair, clearly agitated. "He was attacked by the rogue wolf."

59

Peter still holds me back, forcing my arms into my lab coat. He meets my surly gaze. "Just in case he's sick, Zoey. Protect yourself first."

I'm curious why they're so sure the wolf is a male when its legs are drawn up close to its body. I come closer, finally getting a chance to examine the tears across its flank and chest. "The wounds I can repair." I pause, looking up. "But he's lost a lot of blood."

They exchange looks.

When Dusty finally speaks, his voice cracks with emotion. "Where's Andy?"

17.

The front door opens, and Dusty's head pops up. "That's him."

Dante follows Dusty out to the lobby, but Peter stays nearby. Hovering.

I put him to work, asking him to bring me the light, hand me surgical equipment. We can hear Andy's voice rumbling in the main area. More and more people are showing up, the growing din in the lobby is hard to ignore. They're checking to see where everyone is. Reporting locations and alibies.

It fills me with a growing sense of unease.

Peter looks up, nodding at someone over my shoulder. I have to keep my focus on the wolf's wounds, but I don't have to turn to recognize Andy's voice.

His voice is low and solemn. "We'll need to test for sickness."

I shake my head. "The only way to do that is to examine its brain. Meaning, it'd have to be dead." I pause, glancing over my shoulder. "As you can see, this wolf is still alive."

Andy's dark eyes meet mine, that expression is hard. "There's a lab in St. Louis that can test overnight."

That brings me up short. "With what?"

"A blood sample."

I tilt my head, confused. "Is that legit?"

Andy crosses his arms. "We've used it dozens of times in the past." He turns to Peter. "Get a blood sample and Dante can run it to the Mail-X in Rapid City."

Peter nods, searching my cupboards for a vial and a syringe. I pause, helpless, with a clamp in one hand and a needle in the other. Peter meets my gaze. "Trust."

"Trust?" I scoff, keeping my voice low. "I barely know you, Peter."

Peter gives me a tight smile and because my hands are occupied, he moves in and takes the blood sample himself.

I put the last suture in place and step back. My shoulders ache and my head is starting to throb, but the wolf is still holding on. That's got to be a good sign. Peter watches me toss my gloves. "Triple wash your hands."

Andy appears in the doorway again. "Is she done?"

Peter nods, his expression grim.

"Let's get him back to the house."

I stand in between Andy and the wolf. "You aren't moving him."

Andy's face softens. "Move aside, Doc. This wolf belongs at the house."

I laugh at that. "Do you even hear how crazy that sounds?"

Andy draws up even taller, looming over me. "He's coming with us."

My chin tips up. "Like hell he is." I lick my lips, nervous. "I'll call the sheriff."

Andy nods at Peter. "Take care of your woman."

"I'm not anybody's woman." I plant my fists on my hips, but Andy ignores me, walking over to the exam table. I try to stop him, grabbing his arm, but then Peter slips his hands around my hips. Twisting, I turn away from him, but his forearm locks around my middle. My hands grasp at his arms, trying to pry him off me, but he only holds me closer. When Dante slips around us to help Andy pick up the injured wolf, I lose it.

"Let go of me!" I'm kicking, pulling to either side, but Peter just lifts me up like I weigh nothing.

"Shit." Dante hisses, stepping back. Peter turns to look, keeping me pinned against his chest. Something is terribly wrong with the wolf. Its fur is falling away.

That's not quite right. It's melting. Disappearing from sight. Something's wrong with my eyes, maybe it's the stress, but the wolf seems to waver in front of me. The longer it wavers, the less canine it looks until the bones seem to rearrange themselves.

In the back of my mind, I'm thinking of Maria's journals. My memory is supplying me with a clear answer to what I'm seeing.

But seeing and believing are two entirely different things.

I blink and in that brief moment of time, the wolf fully disappears, leaving a slender man on my exam table. He's covered in blood and grime, tattoos and wiry muscle. I take a look at his gentle face, screwed up with pain, and his moppish haircut. He can't be much more than a kid.

Peter's grip loosens around my middle, and I take the opportunity to twist free. I launch myself between the men and this kid. Covering him with my body, I turn to glare at them. "Get the fuck away from him, you animals!"

I lift up enough to check his chest for wounds. Sure enough, he has oozing wounds in the same place as the wolf. My brain is having a hard time processing the change I just witnessed, but one fact remains clear to me—this kid needs help, and these assholes aren't going to transfer him anywhere.

"Pretty Boy." Andy growls, low and harsh.

Peter comes forward, his firm hands clasp my sides. I'm ready for him this time. Turning back, I elbow him hard in the face. He grunts in surprise but isn't deterred. He locks both arms around my middle and starts to lift me again. I hook my ankle around the back of his calf and pull hard, causing him to lose his balance. But, in the meantime, Dante and Andy have moved forward and are lifting the kid from the table.

"No." My cry is ragged, and tears of anger are tracking down my cheeks. "Stop! Please!"

Andy and Dante both harden their expressions, carrying the boy between them.

18.

"I won't help you." My voice is ragged, and my heart is racing.

Andy pauses, his back turned to me. I can't see his face, but I can see Dante. He's watching his boss very carefully.

There's a sliver of a chance. "How many of you are werewolves?" There's a wobble to my voice, but I keep my chin up. I test Peter's grip, but he's still holding me tight.

When Andy doesn't deny that any of them are werewolves, I press on. "That's why you wanted a vet, right? Maria was your personal doctor, wasn't she? I found her old notes." I swallow. "I won't help any of you if you don't let me treat that kid. I swear to God."

Andy's shoulders tense. A moment, that probably only lasts a few heartbeats, stretches between us. He finally tips his head. "Bring her."

Then Dante and Andy carry the boy away.

"What's happening?" I struggle against Peter, trying to look up at him. "What's that mean? Where are they taking him?"

Peter's expression is grim. "He's going to let you treat Rabbit back at the house."

"Rabbit? That's his name?"

Pretty Boy takes a shuddering breath. "Yes."

"Why not leave him here? I can't treat him there."

He lets a slow breath slip between his lips. "We have a better set up than you do."

I stop struggling, trying to process everything that's happening. Peter's still holding me, but he isn't restraining me anymore. I'm not sure if he's holding me up or if I'm holding him up. "Is Rabbit a friend of yours?"

Peter pauses. "More like a brother."

"If he has rabies, he needs to go to the hospital, Peter. Now. If the virus passes the brain barrier, there's nothing anyone can do for him."

Peter shakes his head, hands tightening around my waist. "They don't treat our kind."

"Our kind." I repeat his words. "You're a wolf, too?"

He's quiet for a moment. "We can't go to the hospital."

I put my hand over Peter's. "He might die without treatment."

Peter releases his hold on my body. "That's the reality we live with. If they knew what he was, they'd lock him up in a government facility. It's what they'd do to any of us." I turn, meeting his cold blue eyes. He studies my face. "That's why we need you."

Those words sink in. The enormity of what he's saying. Energy coils up through my body. I nod, hurrying into my office. He follows close behind, watching me sift through Maria's notes. I find the journal entries I'm looking for. Maria's recipe for treating werewolf rabies. I glance up at Peter. "Vargulfism? Is that what you call it?"

He nods, coming closer.

"The cupboards. Help me find everything she has on this list."

He takes the list from me, watching me pilfer through Maria's leftover stocks. "What is it?"

"Maybe nothing." I admit, snagging a few bottles of herbs from the shelves. "But if he is sick and we don't try, what happens?"

Peter has to clear his throat. "He'll die."

"So, we have to try, right?"

Peter doesn't respond. Instead, he checks the list and starts searching the cupboards for the herbs we need. We shove everything in a backpack.

Angela, one of the pack members, agrees to stay behind to watch over Prissy and Baby, at least until Hitch comes by in the morning to pick his cat up.

And then Peter and I are stepping into the warm night. Peter stops by the bike, pulling out a second helmet. He came prepared this time. I let him put it over my head, waiting patiently while he latches it under my chin even though my heart is going a million miles a minute. And then I'm climbing on the bike behind him. The bike roars to life underneath us and the wind whips through my thin pajamas. It probably would have been wise to change, but it's too late now. I lock my arms around his middle and lean into him feeling his broad muscles stretching beneath me, absorbing as much of his warmth as I can. I flatten one palm against his chest. I can feel his heart pounding, even over the rumble of the bike. He's scared, too. He's just doing a better job of hiding it.

As long as we're on the road, flying through the dark night, we stay suspended in time. There's no phone calls or texts to alert us to Rabbit's condition. I know, the second our feet touch the gravel, it will all come rushing up at warp speed. An impossible set of realities that defy reality. But for a short time, riding Peter's bike, the world stops turning.

When we get to Andy's cabin, I'm surprised by the number of bikes I see there. I count at least a dozen before Peter pulls me from the back of the bike. He leads me up to the cabin and when he swings the door open, the low murmur of the pack washes over me.

Cleo Mercer

It occurs to me then, that they called themselves a pack right in front of me. I just had no way of connecting the dots until now.

I can feel almost everyone's eyes on my body. They're no doubt curious about the new doc in town. Peter tugs me protectively under his arm, leading me down a set of stairs to the basement. My feet slow as I reach the bottom step.

19.

Everything down here is state of the art. And while they do have a small exam area, complete with a stainless-steel table, the majority of the basement is dedicated to observation rooms. I come closer. There's something sinister about those rooms. They have windows in each door and it's through those portholes that I can see each chamber is essentially a padded room with a cement floor. And at the center of each room, a drain. Presumably for clean-up.

I find Rabbit in the last room. Andy bars my path. Kali leans up against the wall next to him. It's clear she's been crying. She gives me a weak smile and I do my best to shore her up with confidence I don't feel. I try to move past Andy, but he blocks my path. "He's resting now, doc."

I look up at Andy's grim expression. "What did you give him?"

"Klonopin."

I do a double take, shocked. "How... why do you have that?"

He tips his head. "We have our ways." He turns with me, and we both look through the window. "Only thing we can do is wait."

"Wait? Like hell we will." I look over my shoulder at Peter. "You got my bag?"

Peter hefts it. "Where do you want it?"

Cleo Mercer

They're all staring at me, and I feel the pressure mounting. "I'm not sure. I need a second."

Kali pushes away from the wall. She puts her small hand on Andy's forearm. "We need to give her space to work, baby."

Andy frowns, curious, but glances over at Peter. "No one goes in or out unless I say."

Peter gives him a sharp nod.

"I've got to speak to the pack." Andy pats Peter on the shoulder and makes his way up the steps, hand in hand with Kali.

I spread Maria's notes out on the exam table and Peter moves closer, leaning a hip on the counter at my side. "You sure you know what you're doing?"

I look up at him. "The truth?"

He nods.

I sigh. "I'm going to do my best."

Peter moves to stand by Rabbit's door. He leans on his side, his gaze never straying from his friend. I try to turn my attention to Maria's notes. I read her recipe five times over. She used it to treat raccoons and even a bat or two. Never with much success. According to her notes, the treatment bought her patients an extra week or two, but eventually, they all succumbed. Considering rabies usually kills its victims within a week, she was making progress.

But as I'm reading her instructions, I get the nagging feeling that something doesn't seem right.

My grandma was a big herbalist. She hated prescription medications, saying there wasn't anything in the body that couldn't be healed by Mother Nature. She knew how to strip bark to make tea that would soothe everything from arthritis to a sore throat. She kept an acorn in her pocket for wisdom and a bay leaf under her pillow for dreaming. She was kooky like that. Superstitious. We'd laugh about it, but Lord help us if someone spilled the salt.

I spent enough time with her to learn a thing or two, and even I know that a weak tea means you'll lose a friend. And essentially, that's what Maria was making. A tincture. Or a tea. My gut tells me it wasn't strong enough.

I read through her process a few times, trying to think like a vet, but my grandmother's voice keeps overriding all of my schooling. Checking that I have everything I need, I gather it up into the backpack and come to stand next to Peter. We both watch Rabbit sleep. The Klonopin will knock him out for quite a while. That's not a drug they should have access to, but with hospitalization taken off the table, I'm sure they've had to circumvent the rules a time or two over the years.

I study Peter's face, noting the concern etched into his features. I want to reach out and wrap my arms around him, but he's giving very strong *don't touch* vibes. Instead, I gather up my notes and turn to him. "I need to use the stove."

He nods, leading me back up the stairs. It's quieter in the main room, but the tension is thicker than before. People lay sprawled out on couches or curled up on the floor. Andy sits in an armchair, holding Kali against his chest.

They're all waiting to see if Rabbit pulls through, which puts a gargantuan amount of pressure on my shoulders. What will a pack of werewolves do with a little human if she accidentally poisons one of their packmates? Possibly the same thing they would do to that little doctor if she lets a wolf die on her watch. Either way, I have to try.

20.

I stand at the stove, willing my grandma to look down on me and guide my hands. Peter comes up behind me, holding out a flannel shirt. I let him slip it over my shoulders, relishing the way the soft fabric feels on my skin. I didn't realize how cold I was. He might have noticed, or he might have just been feeling territorial. I'm showing miles of skin. In my defense, I wasn't expecting guests. Or an emergency evacuation from Strawberry Moon.

I glance up at him, giving him a ghost of a smile. "Thanks." Keeping my voice low so as not to wake the slumbering wolves, I turn back to the stove. "Standing around in my pajamas. What must everyone think of me?"

He leans up against the counter, standing close. "The general consensus is that you're pretty bad ass to make a home visit in the middle of the night." He tips his head down. "And just fair warning, they all have pretty spectacular hearing. So, keep that in mind."

My cheeks color and I glance over my shoulder. Nobody stirs, but I decide to keep my thoughts to myself, anyway.

There's no one to tell me that the tea is finished. I just know. Some instinct tells me that the color is right, the smell is right. I glance over at Peter who's been sitting on the counter staring off into space. Pouring the tea into a mason jar, I turn to look at him. "It's ready."

He slides off the counter and looks over at Andy, who is already on his feet. An uneasy shiver works down my spine as I realize they were watching me closely the whole time. Kali trails behind Andy and the four of us make our way down to the basement.

It's bright down here. The ceilings are high, and the furnishings are comfortable. And yet, there's an entire hall lined with padded cells. It gives me the heebie jeebies. I lead the way, stopping in front of Rabbit's cell. I try the door, but it's locked.

Andy pushes past me, holding out his hand. "I'll take it."

Kali makes a tiny sound of distress. She clearly doesn't like the idea of her man exposing himself to rabies, but just one look at his face makes it clear that the decision is made. I reluctantly hand the tincture over. It sloshes in the mason jar, amber-colored and still warm.

Andy closes himself in the room and the three of us watch as he carefully approaches Rabbit.

Andy settles onto the floor, pulling the unconscious kid into his lap. His touch is tender as he pushes Rabbit's light brown hair out of his eyes. They call Peter Pretty Boy, but Rabbit is downright beautiful. Angelic, even. And clearly, this guy has a place in everyone's hearts. They obviously love him, so I can't understand why they'd even consider killing him. Andy tilts Rabbit's head back, metering out small sips of the tincture, waiting and watching for him to swallow, before trickling more into his mouth.

When the tea is gone, he carefully lays Rabbit down and comes out to join us. He looks down at me. "Now what?"

All three of them are looking to me for answers, and I don't have a thing to say. I've gone completely off script. "Now we wait."

Andy nods, looking at Peter. "You two should get some rest. Take her to the west room."

Peter puts his hand around my forearm, but I easily twist out of his grip. "I'll stay with my patient."

I can see that they care about Rabbit, but I still don't trust their judgement. I didn't want to euthanize a cat, I sure as shit don't want anyone harming this kid. Not while he still has a fighting chance.

Peter pins me with his gaze. "You need rest."

My jaw clenches. "I'm fine."

He frowns. "You've been swaying on your feet for the last three hours."

Kali brushes her hand across my shoulder. "It's four in the morning, Babes. You need to rest."

I meet her gaze. "If you guys want to go to sleep, go to sleep. I'm staying here."

Peter squeezes his eyes shut briefly, before glowering at me. Those eyes are shockingly blue against his bloodshot eyes. He looks tired and out of patience. "Suit yourself."

Shaking his head, he turns on heel. Andy watches him go, glancing back at us with an exhausted expression. "I'll grab Dusty. He can take first watch."

Kali waits until Andy is gone before turning back to me. "This is really hard for them."

I wrap my arms around my middle. "I can see that."

Her expression is gentle, but firm. "If you can see that, then you can see that Rabbit isn't the only one who's suffering. Rabbit is like a little brother to Pretty Boy." She pauses. "Look, I know Pretty Boy comes across as this quiet sweetheart, but he's not made of stone."

A sweetheart? Are we talking about the same guy?

Kali briskly rubs my arm, up and down. "Go check on him. He's having a hard time."

I want to point out that I barely know the guy. If he's struggling, I'm betting he'd rather talk to a trusted friend, not a random lady from St. Louis. But Kali is a very persuasive person. I get the feeling she knows how to get her way.

My gaze travels past her shoulder at Rabbit's sleeping form. "You'll come get me if anything changes?"

She nods.

"I mean it, Kali. Please. Don't let them do anything to him without me."

She nods again. "I promise."

With that weak promise in place, I reluctantly head up the stairs. I have to slip between Dusty and Andy on my way.

Andy pauses mid-sentence. "Down the hall and to the left."

It's a bit strange how they all assume Pretty Boy and I are a package deal. I'll have to untangle that misunderstanding on another day.

Tiptoeing past a sleeping pack of werewolves, I make my way down the long hallway and slip into the last bedroom on the left.

Peter sits on the edge of the bed, elbows on his knees, face in his hands.

My heart lurches in my chest.

He's this big, powerful guy.

But right now, he looks pretty broken.

21.

Closing the door behind me, I pad across the room, stopping right in front of him. It never ceases to amaze me how big Peter is. Even sitting down, he's at eye level. He straightens, looking at me for a few heartbeats before tugging me between his legs. His hands slip around my waist, and I let my fingers weave through his hair. "You're worried about Rabbit?"

He pauses. "Yes."

"What do you need?"

He leans into my touch. "Distract me."

My fingers slip down the tendons in his neck, smoothing over warm skin. His muscles are tense, hard as granite. He runs his hands over my tank top. "These pajamas." An exhausted smile tugs at the corner of his mouth. "I think you got everyone's attention."

I blush. "You said they didn't care."

"No." His fingers slip under the thin fabric, skirting my ribcage. "I said they thought you were bad ass. But every last male and female in that room was interested."

"Interested?"

His thumb grazes the underside of my breast. "Interested."

Male *and* female? I try to remember who was around. Dusty and Dante. Andy. Kali. There's no way. He's clearly mistaken.

I roll my eyes. "I think not."

He grins, that infuriating mysterious smile of his. "I have a pretty good sense of smell, Babe. The nose doesn't lie. I can smell them, and I can smell you. I know without a doubt they liked the way you look, just the same way I know you like to see me suffering."

My head pops up. "Do not."

He laughs. "Oh, yes, you do. As soon as you walked in here, that little heart of yours started racing and your pussy warmed up."

My cheeks catch fire. He may have a point. The idea of a big, strong alpha made vulnerable is pretty fucking enticing. But I am not a fan of him being so aware of my body.

His fingers glide up my back. "You liked smacking me, too."

He's right about that, too. After the way he'd been restraining me, popping him on the jaw was incredibly satisfying. My gaze trails along his jaw. I touch it gingerly. "Sorry about that."

He chuckles. "No, you're not." His hands slip over my ass. "Where'd you learn to throw a jab like that?"

His touch is light. Teasing.

"You won't like the answer."

His gaze darkens, his grip tightens. "Try me."

"My ex."

His expression hardens. "He hit you?"

"No, no, no. Nothing like that. He's an MMA fighter. He taught me self-defense."

He frowns. "You're right. I don't like that answer."

Dax and Peter have more in common than I'd like to admit. Apparently, the bad boy thing is a fatal attraction of mine. And while Peter doesn't seem to be as selfish as Dax was, he's a million times more dangerous. If I had any sense, I'd be looking for the nearest exit. But I'm drawn to him. I can't help myself.

Cleo Mercer

My hands smooth over his tense shoulders. "Take your shirt off."

His lips curve into a grin.

I squeeze his shoulders and jostle them a bit. "I'm going to give you a massage."

He clicks his tongue, but helps me pull off his shirt. My fingertip traces the scrollwork along his biceps, palm sliding over the rose on his shoulder. His chest and shoulders rise subtly under my touch with each increasingly ragged breath he takes. Circling my fingers around as much of his thick arms as I can, I tug until he slowly unfolds, climbing to his feet. Hooking my fingers around the waist of his jeans, I try to pull him towards me, but it's a little like tugging on a brick wall. His eyes stay fixated on me while I unbutton his jeans and drag the zipper down. Watching him shrug out of his jeans, I place my palm flat on his chest. I think I can almost feel his heart racing under my hand as I push him towards the bed.

"Lay on your stomach." I murmur.

Surprisingly, he turns and drops onto the mattress. I crawl on behind him, sitting on his firm ass.

My fingers explore the tattoos on his back, following the roots and trunk of a braided tree. "What's with the tree?"

He turns so his cheek rests on the bed. "That's Yggdrasil. The Norse tree of life. It supports the universe."

My fingers brush the raven's wings on either shoulder blade, trace the Norse ruins on his spine. Unlike his packmates, I don't see any wolf tattoos on his skin. I let my hands follow the curve of his back, working knots out of his tense muscle. But in the silence, my mind starts to wander towards the basement. If I'm worried about Rabbit, Peter must be close to coming unglued. I promised him a distraction and silence isn't going to do it. "So, you're a werewolf?"

He's quiet for a few moments. "You going to freak out on me?"

I grin at that. "Later. I'm still in shock. I'm sure when I get home, I'll lose my shit."

My thumbs follow the tight muscles in his neck and a thought occurs to me. "Is that why you don't kiss?"

"What?" He moves his arms, lifting his head and shoulders.

My hands pause on his shoulders. "Would I get infected? If you kissed me?"

He rolls over and I find myself sitting on his stomach. He puts his hands on my hips. "You can't get it that way."

Something in my chest seems to shift. "Then how do you get it?"

He breathes out through his nose. "You have to be bitten."

My hand moves to cover the bite mark on my hip.

He puts his hand over mine. "Not like that."

My heart is starting to race. "Why hasn't that mark gone away?"

"That's not..." He closes his eyes briefly before fixing those bright blue eyes on mine. "That's just a mark. You can't get infected that way. You'd have to be bitten by someone in their wolf form. That's why we were all so scared to have you that close to Rabbit."

I consider that for a few heartbeats, distracted by the way his thumb is running up and down my hips. "So, why don't you kiss?"

"Well, damn, woman. Give a guy a chance to work up to it."

22.

I grin at him. "You're taking too long."

His fingers slide up my side, dragging my tank top up. "I'm enjoying the moment."

I bite my lip when his thumb caresses the side of my breast. "And you talk too much."

He laughs. "No one has ever said that about me before."

"I'm saying it..." But whatever else I was going to say is cut off when he sits up. I slide back onto his hips, only kept upright by the arm he's braced against my back. His lips press against my open mouth, catching teeth and lip and tongue. I cling to his neck, bowled over by a kiss that makes it hard to think straight. He doesn't just kiss me, he savors me, devouring me whole. I find myself tightening my hold on him, rolling my hips against his lap and the growing bulge there. I moan into his mouth, and he shudders underneath me.

He lifts me up, gently laying me down on my back before settling over me. His thigh slips between my legs, snugging forcefully up against my center. I hold onto his neck, grinding against his leg. My panties grow damp and just the contact alone has me very close to the edge. His fingers find the edge of my tank top and he drags it up and over my head, making my hair spill across the pillow. He pauses, gaze roving over my naked chest. I don't have particularly large boobs, and his hands easily cover me. My nipples, taut and aching, are hard points against his palm.

He kisses my jaw, my neck, trailing down to my breast. His tongue flicks my nipple before he takes me into his mouth, sucking and nipping at my sensitive skin. Fingers hooking around my waistband, he drags my pajamas and panties over my hips, leaving me completely naked beneath him.

My fingers scrabble at his boxers, tugging them over his ass. He kicks them the rest of the way off, reaching over to the nightstand. After digging around for a few heartbeats, he finds a condom and slips it on. I half-guide, half-drag his body between my thighs. He kisses my neck, coming back to my mouth to suck on my lip. His cock finds my center and just the tip nudges inside. I couldn't really see how big he was when he was kneeling by my bed, but I'm beginning to realize he's a big guy in more ways than one. I'm ready for him though, I've been ready for him since the moment I laid eyes on him. His hips press forward, burying part of his length inside. A groan tumbles off my lips and his shaky breath feathers my neck.

My fingers caress the back of his neck. "Deeper, baby. You aren't going to hurt me."

I can feel the shell of his ear as he nods, sliding his arms under my body to hold me closer. His hips pull back and then he's thrusting again, delving deeper. He tucks my head against his chest and thrusts again. The bed dips under our bodies and he drives deep inside. He pauses there and I adjust to his length. Wrapping my legs around his waist, I drag him closer, taking him fully inside.

He groans quietly, hands wrapping around my shoulders.

I roll my hips, squeezing his shaft, and he growls, holding me tighter. "You take my cock so well."

My hands move across his back. "Fuck me. Please."

He pulls back, thrusting in sharply. His tip nudges my cervix in a way that makes me feel every last inch of him. I raise my hips with the next thrust, taking him harder, deeper. He picks up his pace, hips grinding against my clit, shaft pressing against my inner wall. And each thrust is punctuated by his tip kissing up against my limits.

I feel fully dominated by him, caught up in his powerful tide. Nonsense tumbles off my lips. His name. Praise for his cock.

I haven't forgotten where I am. That I'm in the middle of a wolves' den. That they have, in his words, very good hearing. I cover my mouth, but he takes my wrist and pins it over my head. "I love the sounds you make when I'm fucking you." His voice is a low murmur in my ear. "Don't stop, baby. I want to hear you scream when I make you come."

Something like a whimper or a moan swirls across my tongue and I nod. His hands move across my breasts, pinching my nipples before slipping between our bodies. He draws fast circles across my clit, making me spasm around him. But he's impaling me with his cock and caging me with his arms. I can't move. I can only submit. The lack of control makes my heart race, heightens every touch.

I try to put my hand over his, to slow him down. "Peter... I'm going to come."

He chuckles, thrusting deeper. "That's the idea."

"No... I'm going to..." It's hard to form words, hard to think straight. "Slow down, baby. You're going to make me *come*."

He pulls back long enough to look into my eyes. He understands what I'm trying to tell him, but instead of relenting, those eyes seem to darken. "Just let go. I want you to come all over my cock like the good girl I know you are."

23.

He's fucking me harder, faster. Each thrust collides with my body, maxing me out. I'm balancing on a razor's edge between torture and euphoria. I spiral higher, higher until, without warning, I tip over the edge. I'm seeing stars, literal stars. I always thought that was urban legend, but I don't just see them, they shower through me, sparkling, radiating pleasure.

He's still moving inside me. He grunts when my pussy clamps around him and his fingers find my clit again. My hips twitch and spasm under his ministrations. I'm helpless, completely at his mercy. And then I'm coming again, this time soaking his shaft.

"Fuck yes, baby." He rasps, pressing his forehead into my shoulder. He goes still for a heartbeat and then he's thrusting deep into me, cock flexing as he comes. My clit has just stopped twitching and then, like he's going for extra credit, he presses on my clit again. A softer, sweeter orgasm flickers through my core, completely exhausting me.

After a while, he pushes up on his elbows and looks down at me. His cock is still fully inside me. I'm hoping he's not planning on moving any time soon because it feels good to just lay together.

There's a twinkle in his eye as he gently pushes my hair behind my ears. "That was... incredible."

I bite my lip, trying not to laugh. "Do you think they heard me?"

"Baby, I think they heard you in Denver."

I throw an arm over my eyes, half-groaning, half-laughing. "So much for first impressions."

He forces my arm over my head, making me look into his smiling blue eyes. I'm momentarily distracted by his dimple. I didn't know he had one of those.

"I think you'll find this is a very sex-positive group. No shame for something so natural." His thumb rubs gentle circles on my wrist. "And anyway, they already know you're mine."

I tilt my head. "What? Did you stake your claim before I got here?"

He huffs a laugh. "I tried, but you were far more effective."

I'm distracted by the feel of his cock inside me, his thumb on my wrist. It's hard to focus on his words. "I was?"

"With your hex or whatever it is you did."

That grabs my attention. "Come again?"

He wiggles my wrist. "The mark you made. With *my* scent."

My cheeks catch fire. "How did you...What are you talking about?"

He shows me my own wrist. "This."

He says it like we can both see the invisible mark on my skin. I could deny it. Play dumb. But there is a loaded look in his eye that makes me absolutely certain he already knows what I did. Which seems impossible, but I thought werewolves were an impossibility a week ago.

My gaze slides away. "But I washed it off."

He moves to the side, pulling out. "We're werewolves, babe. We can smell magic a mile away. And that brand on your wrist is not subtle."

I grimace. "It smells like your sweat?"

"No. Yes. A little. It smells like me." He tilts his head. "You tell me, little witch. You're the one who did it. Why am I explaining your magic to you?"

He climbs out of bed, going to the bathroom to clean up. I'm left staring at the ceiling, wondering what all of this could possibly mean. He comes back with his boxers back on and a towel in hand. He insists on cleaning me up himself, taking the time to explore every inch of my thighs, my tummy. My thoughts are like stripped gears, they slide against each other, failing to connect.

He pauses, studying my face with a hint of a smile. "Should I be concerned?"

"About what?" I ask.

"That spell you cast."

I laugh, exasperated. "I didn't cast a spell. I'm not a witch. I'm a vet, for God's sake."

He settles onto the bed beside me, ticking a list off on his long fingers. "Brews potions. Casts spells. Has a penchant for magical creatures."

"I can see I'm not going to get anywhere with you." I turn to search for my tank top, but he's already holding it. This jerk moves like greased lightning.

"I'll keep this safe for you right over here." He puts it on the nightstand out of reach.

"Why do you get to wear your underwear?" I pretend to pout, but he's surprisingly cuddly and I'm still kind of enjoying the moment.

He tugs me closer. "Because I like you naked."

I rest my cheek on his chest, thinking about spells and staking claims. The truth is, I'm not sure why I did that. I've never done something like that before. I'm not usually a big fan of sweat. But I had this sense that I might borrow some of his power, his strength, if I touched it to my wrist chakra. It was a whim, not a spell. Twisted, maybe. But witchy? No. Because witches don't exist. Not really. And even if they did, I wouldn't know the first thing about claiming someone with a simple rune.

A realization creeps up on me.

I push back to look at him, still caught in his arms. "You marked me."

He grins, that dimple showing up again. "I was wondering when you'd circle back to that."

I sit up, examining the teeth marks on my hip. "Is that what this is?"

"Yes."

I look up at him, eyebrows climbing. "Tell me this will come off."

He rests, unconcerned, on his side, head propped up on his elbow. His thumb follows the curve of the toothmark. "I should have put it somewhere more obvious. Cherry's is right below her ear. Sends a very clear signal."

I pause, picturing Kali. "I thought that was a tattoo!"

"In a sense."

"Peter." My voice carries a note of warning. "It comes off, right?"

"That depends." He raises his eyes to meet mine.

"On what?"

"On how mad you'll be if I say no."

24.

I'm upright and searching for my panties. I have them up and over my hips before he can coax me back to his side. "Calm down, baby."

I poke him in the chest. "Never tell a woman to calm down."

"Okay."

"It's patronizing." I allow him to pull me back to the bed.

"Okay." He pulls the blanket over both of us. "*Don't* calm down."

"Better." I pull the blanket over my chest and cross my arms. "Explain. Now."

"Before you get too mad, I just want you to remember that you also branded me, so you're not exactly innocent in all this."

"Peter."

"I'm just saying." He puts an arm around me and when I don't fight him, settles me closer. "It's part of our mating physiology. It's how we tell the rest of the pack that a mate is taken."

"So, I could bite you right now and leave a mark?"

"I bet it'd leave a mark. Probably take some blood, too, judging by the way you're looking at me right now. But it's more than just the bite itself. It's the intention behind it."

"What was your intention when you bit me?"

A guarded look crosses his face. "What was your intention when you marked your wrist?"

"I was trying to steal your power."

A surprised laugh tumbles off his lips. "Aha! So, you admit it."

"I admit to nothing. I didn't know what I was doing. You did. Big difference."

He gets quiet. "It's not like I planned it or anything."

"Why'd you do it then?"

He looks down at me. "Instinct."

I blow out a long, slow breath.

His fingers trail up and down my arm. When the silence draws out too long, he puts his hand along my jaw. "What are you thinking?"

"I'm thinking I bet you wolves use that instinct card whenever you're in trouble."

His thumb traces my ear. "Am I in trouble?"

"Yes."

"Is this a bad time to tell you that the mark heightens my awareness of you?"

I pull back. "What?!"

"Just your heartrate. I could hear it pretty well before, but now I can sense where you are." He pauses, thinking. "And I'm hyper aware of your hormones, now."

"My hormones." My tone is flat as I repeat the word.

"If you're horny or on your period. Like right now, you're ovulating."

"Stop, stop. I don't want to know anymore."

He kisses the top of my head, weaving his fingers through mine.

I settle in closer. "There aren't really witches are there?"

"I'm sorry we're dumping so much on you all at once." His voice is low and soft.

"There are, then?"

"Yes. There's a big coven in Chicago." He hooks his leg over mine. "Our region's second in command is mated to a woman who's both. Werewolf and witch."

"Andy?" I snuggle in closer.

"No, the region alpha. They're based out of St. Louis."

I glance up at him. "That's where I just moved from." I pause. "What are their names?"

"Henry Rudolfo is the grand alpha to us all."

I sit up. "The Rudolfos are mother fucking werewolves?"

"You know of them?"

"St. Louis is a big city, but it isn't that big. Of course, I know of them. I didn't know they were wolves." I sit back, rubbing my temples. "I think I'm getting a headache."

"Just rest, baby. You're going to need your strength tomorrow."

And just like that, we're both snapped back to the real problem at hand. A young man, Peter's friend, is fighting for his life.

But he's not alone. Not really. Because I'm going to fight for that kid. Even if he does have the sickness, I'm going to make it my mission to bring him back from the brink.

Peter turns off the lamp and lies back. I sidle closer, tracing light circles over his chest. His arm fits around me, holding me tight.

It seems like I barely close my eyes and there's a sharp knock on the door. Squinting in the morning light, I realize at least a few hours must have passed. Peter stirs behind me. His body fits around mine, arms locked underneath my breasts. He's got a very enticing morning wood pressing up against my ass.

I'm still half asleep, grumpily wondering who's banging on the door.

It swings open and Andy stomps in. If he's surprised to find Peter and me mostly naked in bed, he doesn't show it. His gaze skips right past me, landing on Peter. "You better get up. St. Louis sent the results."

Peter pushes upright. "Good or bad?"

Andy's face hardens. "Just... get up."

25.

In the light of day, with everyone fully dressed, I am seriously regretting coming to the cabin in my pajamas. I button the flannel shirt up and it hits me about mid-thigh, screaming walk of shame. Then again, according to Peter, everyone could hear us last night anyway, so my clothing won't exactly add to the scandal.

But clothing is armor and I feel defenseless.

Most of the pack is gone. Everyone else stands around in the kitchen, untouched coffee steaming in front of them. I recognize Dante and Dusty. Kali and Angela. Angela is as tall as Kali is short. She has long, red hair and cat-like eyes. Her expression is wary when she sees me, but she still attempts a smile. She's back from the clinic, which means Hitch must have come by for his cat.

Andy stops in the kitchen, arms folded over his chest. He looks around, meeting everyone's gaze. "We got the results back on Rabbit's test. He tested positive for Vargulfism."

Angela moans, allowing Dusty to pull her against his side.

I glance at Kali, noticing that she's got dried tear tracks on both cheeks.

"What happens now?" My voice cracks the moment like a stone thrown into a frozen pond. They all look at me and I get a very firm reminder that while this group is very tight knit, I am not part of the pack.

I'm an interloper.

Andy gives me a hard look. "There's no coming back from rabies. You know that, Doc."

"So, what? You put him down?"

Andy looks away, squeezing his eyes shut.

They're fucking kidding.

They have to be joking. I look around, waiting for someone to say what the real plan is. But no one speaks.

I look at Peter, meeting his cold, blue gaze. "Peter?"

His eyebrows knit together, and he looks away.

"Rabbit." I swallow hard. "Where is he now?"

Kali meets my gaze. "I checked on him about fifteen minutes ago. He's still sleeping."

The Klonopin should have worn off hours ago. So his condition has either taken a nosedive, or… he's improving.

My ex, Dax, taught me a lot of things about life. Why you don't share a bank account with an asshole. What it really means if his clothes come home smelling like perfume.

But he also taught me how to fight. He taught me to move without advertising my intentions. This little tidbit gives me just enough time to slip away from them. The barest of head starts.

They don't expect me to go against a pack decision. I can see the power Andy has over this group. And, if I'm feeling very generous, I can understand where he's coming from. I can empathize, but that doesn't mean I agree. And unfortunately for Andy, he's not the boss of me.

My feet are light and nothing in my expression gives me away.

I'm circling around them, flying down the stairs so fast my feet barely touch each step. I'm lucky I don't take a tumble. As it is, I'm going too fast when I get to the bottom and hit the opposite side of the hallway. I glance up and spot Andy and Peter hurtling down the stairs after me. My heart seems to be pounding in my throat. Pushing off the wall, I tear down the hallway.

It's empty.

Everyone was upstairs.

There's no one left to stand guard.

No one to stop me from twisting the key in the lock with shaking hands. I fling open the door and slam it shut behind me. I have no plan, other than to put myself between Rabbit and his kill squad. My heart pounds against my chest and I find myself cocooned in the bleach white padded cell. Sound is muffled.

It's just me and Rabbit.

I can hear a scuffle outside. Peter's trying to get to me, but Andy won't let him pass. He won't risk another pack member. More voices join Peter and Andy.

From the sound of it, Peter is putting up a pretty good fight. I know enough about wolves to know you don't disobey your alpha. A distant part of me worries Peter is getting himself into hot water over my decisions. But I can't think about that right now.

Rabbit stirs and I hesitantly come closer, lowering down to a squat. "How are you feeling?"

He lays in the fetal position. Naked and shivering. I've been thinking of Rabbit as a kid. But up close, I'm realizing how wrong that was. His pointed chin is covered in scruff. He's got tattoos all over his chest, and inked wings on his back. There's a silver ring in his nose and two in his ears. His face is delicate, but not young. I'd put him in his early twenties if I had to guess.

But more importantly, Rabbit is not a small guy. Even laying down, I can see that he's got at least a foot on me. If he goes berserk on me, I won't stand a chance. Fear starts to uncoil in my belly.

Cleo Mercer

He coughs, chest spasming, before pushing up onto his elbows.

His gaze stays trained on the floor, like he can't get his eyes to focus.

Doubt slices through me.

All this because I found some old notes on how to make a tea.

I glance up at the window and find myself looking right at a very grim Andy. He doesn't move. Doesn't open the door. He just watches me. Grim and unforgiving.

Guess help isn't on the way.

26.

Rabbit sways, shuddering again.

What's done is done. If I'm going to die, it might as well be defending an innocent kid.

Man.

Wolf man.

I reach forward, helping him upright. I get him settled against the wall where he can lean back.

Unbuttoning my flannel shirt, I tug it off and hang it over his shoulders. He pulls it closer, looking at me with a hint of a smile. "Is this where they stick the naked people?"

I grin, plopping down next to him, wrapping my arms around my thin tank top. "I'm only half naked."

He looks around the cell. "I never wanted to be back in this fucking room."

"They put you in here before?"

He huffs a laugh. "After I was first changed. Some people make the transition gracefully. I was not one of them."

He sighs, giving me a sidelong glance. "Did you get bit, too?"

I shake my head. "I'm just the doctor."

He grins. "Man, if I'd known doctors were like you, I would have been getting my regular physicals."

My gaze scans his body with clinical urgency. "How are you feeling?"

Cleo Mercer

"Like hot garbage."

I give him a gentle smile. "Can you be more specific?"

He passes a hand over his chest. "Everything aches. I'm cold." He shrugs, glancing up at the window. He and Andy trade a long look. Rabbit's shoulders droop. "I've got it, don't I? Vargulfism."

I keep my voice light. "Seems like it."

He frowns, looking at me. "What are you doing in here, then? Why didn't they just put a bullet in my head like we always do?"

Dread, like icy fingers, slips up my spine. It's a harsh reminder that these people are not just another run-of-the-mill biker gang.

They're killers.

Werewolves.

I clear my throat. "We're trying to treat it first."

"Treat it... there's a cure for Vargulfism?"

I study Rabbit's face, comparing his current state to what I know about rabies victims. By now, he should be showing signs of aggression. Light sensitivity. And yes, foaming at the mouth. But at worst, he just looks like he's a bit run down.

His voice is soft. Calm. "I'm not going to get better, am I?"

I can't answer that question. I don't have the answer. "Did you know the last vet?"

"Maria? Barely. She died not long after I got here."

I nod. "She was working on a cure for Vargulfism."

He tilts his head. "No shit?"

"We gave you one of her treatments last night. I don't know what's going to happen, Rabbit. But I know this, I'm going to fight for you. And I need you to fight, too. Will you do that?"

He gives me a lopsided grin, letting his head rest against the wall. "I'm really more of a lover than a fighter. But I'll try."

I reach out and take his hand. His fingers curl around mine.

His other hand smooths over the flannel of Peter's shirt. "Pretty Boy, huh?"

I'm sure a blush is creeping up my neck. "You sound surprised."

"I'm not surprised." He pauses. "I'm shocked."

"That he would let me borrow his clothes?"

A lopsided smile tugs at his lips. "That the high and mighty Pretty Boy finally found someone worthy of his talents."

I huff a laugh. "And which talents are those?"

Rabbit shrugs, grinning. He turns our linked hands over so that my wrist is pointing up. "What kind of voodoo magic is this?"

I groan, letting my head fall back. "I don't want to talk about that."

He squints at my wrist. "How did you get his scent tattooed on your skin like that?" He looks up at me, studying my face. "Are you a witch?"

"Better. I'm a vet." I climb to my feet. "I'm going to work on a second treatment. Is there anything I can get you?"

He grins. "Some underwear might be nice."

"You got it." I walk to the door, chin held high, and glare at Andy through the glass.

My confidence is a frail thing, but I know I've made my point. Rabbit isn't frothing at the mouth. I hold Andy's gaze, challenging him. The size difference, even through a steel door, is stark. I can't keep the derision from my expression. I'm not even trying. If a little old human like me isn't afraid of Rabbit, what's a big bad wolf got to say for himself?

After a few heartbeats, he grunts, opening the door. I slip past him. He and Rabbit exchange silent looks. I know this isn't easy for Andy. He clearly has a big heart. But when it comes to thinking outside the box, he's not exactly light on his feet. He shuts the door behind him, turning to face me. I'm stepping into his space, poking a finger into his chest. "I am the trained medical professional here. Not you. And I say this young man's treatment is working. I'm going to go upstairs to work on his tincture, and you are not going to harm a hair on that angel's head."

Andy's gaze slips over my shoulders and I turn to see Kali standing behind me. Her eyebrows shoot up.

I twist back to look at Andy. "Well?"

Andy lets out a long breath. He pulls his gaze back to me. "Anything else, doc?"

"Yeah. Get that poor kid some underwear. It's cold in there."

Kali follows me upstairs. The kitchen is ominously empty. I watch Kali walk to the front door, swinging it open. "You can let him go now."

27.

Dante and Dusty both have their arms around Peter, and they clearly have had their work cut out for them trying to hold him back. He shrugs roughly out of their arms, striding across the yard. Hopping up onto the deck, he slides past Kali. His gaze is trained on me the entire time, searching my body for signs of harm. Looming over me, he tugs me roughly into his arms, murmuring in my ear. "That was a very stupid thing you did." He presses his nose into my hair and breathes deep. "Don't you ever throw yourself into harm's way like that again."

There's a strain in his voice and his shoulders are so tense he's almost trembling. I doubt he's ever been forced to choose between his pack and his mate. He clearly didn't enjoy the way the process played out.

I'll let him hold me, because damn it, I need a hug right now. But he can't tell me what to do. "No promises."

He growls quietly, turning to look at Kali. "Cherry, don't you have anything she can change into?"

Kali's watching us with keen interest, but she straightens. "She's a little skinnier than me, but I bet I can find something."

I glance at the stove. "I really should get started on Rabbit's treatment."

Kali pauses. "Do you have everything you need?"

Cleo Mercer

I squint, doing quick math in my head. "For one more treatment. I'll have to go back to the house after this one, though."

She nods. "Let's get you changed first."

Peter is reluctant to let me out of his sight, but settles for waiting at the base of the stairs.

I let Kali lead the way. "Why do they call you Cherry?"

She laughs, grinning over her shoulder as we step into her bedroom. "It's short for Cherry Bomb. My first change was pretty messy." She mimics an explosion. "Blood everywhere."

"Oh." I'm not sure what the polite response to that statement is. Add it to the list of small nightmares I'll probably be unpacking later tonight when I'm finally home.

The entire second floor is a dedicated suite for Kali and Andy. They have lofted ceilings and sweeping, panoramic views of the pine-covered hills.

She steps into a huge walk-in closet and emerges with an armload of clothes. "You don't strike me as the cheetah print sort of gal, which knocks out like... half of my wardrobe. You're welcome to whatever you can find."

I grab a black t-shirt dress off the top. It's not until it's settled over my hips that I realize it has the words "Hellraiser" emblazoned on the chest. Beggars can't be choosers.

I follow Kali back down the stairs where Peter is waiting, shoulders tense. His gaze scans my chest and his lips tug into a smile.

I roll my eyes, scooting past him to get to the kitchen. He follows on my heels, my new bodyguard. I can't say I mind it. Because of all the werewolves present this morning, Peter was the only one willing to fight for my safety.

Granted, I was the one who endangered myself in the first place, but the rest of the pack was content to see how the cards fell.

I still don't feel safe here. The thin strands of composure holding me together are snapping one by one. I stand at a werewolf's stove, brewing up a spell. A life hangs in the balance and I have never felt imposter syndrome like this before.

Maybe my thoughts are scrawled across my face. Or, maybe Peter is still conflicted about being kept away from me by his own brothers. He stays within arm's reach, alternating between leaning on the counter and standing behind me with his arms around my waist. I pull strength and warmth from him. Lord knows I need it.

When the tea is finished, I carry it down to the basement with my own hands, but Andy insists on taking it from there. I stand on the other side of the doorway, watching as he sits down next to Rabbit. Andy is big and rugged where Rabbit is slender and graceful, but with their sun-kissed hair, they could almost be brothers.

They hold a quiet conversation, much too low for me to hear. I look at Peter, wondering if he can hear what they're saying. His face is inscrutable, but he reaches out and slides an arm around my waist.

I lean into him, turning my gaze back to Rabbit's cell. My biggest concern is that Rabbit finishes the tea, but the fact that Andy is willing to give it to Rabbit himself gives me hope. It means Andy has faith in me and my cure.

I just hope that faith isn't misguided.

Peter straightens, glancing over his shoulder. He tilts his head, listening, in a move so doggy-like it pulls a grudging smile out of me. Moments later, Kali comes down the steps. "Zoey? You've got a visitor."

I frown, meeting Peter's gaze, before following her back up the steps.

Angela is standing by the door. Dante and Dusty are both on the deck, barring the way. I peek past their bulky shoulders and spot the sheriff's cruiser first. Then I see

Hitch's grim face. He's got his arms crossed, but he straightens when he spots me. "Zoey?"

"Hitch?" The tension in the air fills my stomach with anxiety. "What brings you all the way out here?"

His gaze flits from the wall of muscle in front of me to focus over my shoulder. I can sense Peter standing just behind me. No doubt he's glowering like a fool. I push past Dante and Dusty.

Hitch's gaze slips over my t-shirt dress and his eyebrows knit together briefly. Yeah. I know. Not my style.

"I came by to pick up the cat, but nobody was home. Just Baby raising a racket."

I look over my shoulder at Angela, not bothering to keep the anger from my expression. If looks could kill.

She winces. "I made sure the animals had food and water. They're crated."

Irritation and concern stoke in my belly. We've left an injured cat and an abandoned dog alone. I didn't really have a choice, not with the circumstances Rabbit was in, but my back-up plan failed.

Hitch watches my expressions darken. "You need a ride, Zoey?"

I nod. "I better get back."

Peter grabs my arm. "We can send someone to check on the pets."

I glare at him, temper flaring.

Dusty and Dante fade into the background, clearly sensing a dispute.

28.

My voice is tight with anger. "Like I'm going to trust any of you with that now."

Peter steps closer, keeping his voice low. "Angela is incredibly close to Rabbit. I'm sure she just wanted to get back to headquarters."

I tip my chin up so that I can look at him. He looms over me, but I won't let my size be my excuse for cowering. "Then someone else could have helped at the clinic. You can't leave injured animals alone like that. It's inhumane."

"So is letting a *rabbit* suffer." His gaze flicks over at Hitch, before landing on my face again. "Get your priorities straight."

"That's exactly what I'm trying to do." I take a step back. "Those animals are my responsibility, too. It was a mistake to trust anyone else with them."

I'm disappointed by Angela, but I'm pissed at myself. I'm the only vet present. The health of those little guys is my responsibility and mine alone. I could never regret coming to Rabbit's aid, but I should have done it with a level head.

Taking a deep breath, I press my eyes closed and try to think things through this time. I have to get back to the clinic to check on the animals, but something else is motivating me, too. I want to get Hitch away from this place. For his own safety. For the pack's safety. No good

103

will come from Hitch realizing they've got a deathly-ill kid in their basement. I understand why we can't take him to the hospital, but I'm not sure Hitch would.

I feel strangely defensive of the pack.

It's like I'm standing in front of a thin veil separating reality from something else, something deeper and darker. I'm the person standing between Hitch and those secrets and all I can think to do is to take him away. We'll go back where we both belong, leaving this strange and mysterious world undisturbed.

Peter squeezes his eyes shut, opening them with a sigh. "If you want to go home, I'll take you."

"Hitch has to go back to the clinic anyway to pick up his cat. I'll just ride with him." I try to telegraph my thoughts to Peter. *Let me take Hitch away from here.*

Peter's expression hardens. "You'll ride with me."

I sigh. Exasperated. "I'm going with Hitch, but I'll check on Rabbit later, okay?"

Peter lowers his voice, his usual cool composure frayed thin. "You can go back, but you're not going with him."

I've been down this road before with a pushy boyfriend who always gets his way.

Panicky anger fills my belly. "What, do you think you own me now?"

"Yes."

My nostrils flare and my fingers itch to slap that smug face. "You'll regret saying that."

I spot Kali standing in the doorway. "I'll work on those meds back at the clinic. You can send someone for them later. Preferably not this asshole."

I turn, not bothering to look back at Peter. Part of me is afraid he might try to prevent me from leaving.

Part of me wants to drag him with.

I don't want to be alone—not after everything that's happened. I had hoped Peter and I could lean on each other, but we're shearing apart instead.

Hitch watches me, holding his arm out as I approach. He doesn't touch me, but guides me back to the car, keeping a wary eye on the people behind us. He knows they're dangerous, and he doesn't even know the full story.

Opening the passenger door for me, he waits until I'm buckled in before closing the door and circling around to the driver's side.

It's not until we're back on the highway that he finally clears his throat. "What were you doing there?"

The night's events start to crowd around me, threatening to overwhelm and pull me down. I feel split in half, two sides waging an internal war. I should tell Hitch about Rabbit, just in case they decide to enact their own judgement on that kid's life. But then again, there's no way to tell Hitch what happened without revealing their secret. And that's Rabbit's secret, too. I don't want him being turned into a freak show or a national headline. It's too much responsibility and I'm not sure which way to turn. I'm starting to feel like I need to throw up. "They needed a house call."

He glances over at me, looking pointedly at my dress. It's clearly something Kali would wear.

I stare right back. It's not a crime to take house calls. I didn't let Peter intimidate me and I won't let this guy either just because he's got a star pinned to his chest. "It was an emergency."

His hazel eyes narrow. "What kind of emergency?"

"An animal emergency. What's with the third degree? Am being interrogated here?"

He sighs, sending a hand through his dark hair. "No. I'm not trying to meddle." He glances at me. "I'm just concerned."

"About what?"

"We don't have a lot of trouble around these parts. But when we do, you can about guess that group will be

105

involved. One way or another. It ain't gossip, because they'd tell you themselves. More than one of those gang members have done time."

"For what?"

"Drugs. Racketeering." Hitch turns down my drive. "I just want you to know who you're getting involved with."

"Thanks for your concern."

He looks ahead as Strawberry Moon comes into view. "I don't want to see you get hurt."

"You're sweet, Hitch."

He puts the car into park by the clinic and turns to look at me. "I'm not trying to be sweet."

I'm momentarily caught off guard by the heat in his eyes.

Trying to paste on a light and breezy smile, I push the car door open. "In any event, your concerns are misplaced. I am definitely not trying to get involved with anyone over there. Animals are the only kind of people I tolerate right now."

Hitch follows me up to the house.

My step slows when I see a set of prints in the mud. Paw prints. It might have been from when I took Baby up to the cabin.

But a small voice points out that Baby's paw print isn't that big. Or narrow. I scan the yard, trying to peer into the imposing line of pines. Nothing. Not a crow. Or a sparrow.

Absolutely nothing.

Shivering in the stiff breeze, I lead Hitch up to the front porch.

I unlock the clinic door and listen for sounds of distress. It's completely quiet. I find Baby curled up in his crate, snoozing away without a care in the world. When he hears my footsteps, he pushes upright, tail wagging like crazy. Hitch takes him outside to do his business while I check on Prissy.

She's also sleeping in her crate. I open the door and carefully lift her out. My hand sweeps over her long, luxurious fur and I find myself astounded that anyone would want to put a beauty like this down. There's a ragged sense of victory in saving her from that fate.

A small voice reminds me that I saved Rabbit, too.

But that doesn't make me feel good. It makes me feel sick. I shouldn't have had to step in like that. It shouldn't have come down to one person who would take a step forward and say *no*.

Hitch finds me tearing up as I pet a very awake Prissy. She turns her baby blues on him and starts purring.

He tilts his head with concern. "If you want to keep her, I wouldn't stand in your way."

I sniff. "No. I'm just tired. I'm glad she's going home with you."

He takes her from my arms, being extra careful with her injured leg.

I watch his strong fingers gently brush through her fur. "What are you going to name her?"

He looks up at me, a shy expression on his face. "Luna. The Strawberry Moon cat."

A low rumble sounds in the distance, growing as a bike turns down my drive.

I look up, glaring at the door. "I swear to God, if that's Peter…"

Hitch meets my gaze. "You want me to get rid of him?"

29.

We both step outside to find an abandoned bike right by my clinic door. It's a Harley with an orange fender. Not Peter's bike, then.

Hitch glances at me, moving into the drive. The gravel crunches under his boots as he steps in front of me.

Dante emerges from the place where my driveway bends past the trees. He's carrying a beat-up cardboard box. When the box wiggles, I push past Hitch and rush over. Dante stops just short of my porch and I peek inside. A furry, white head pops up. A coo slips off my lips, because spoiler alert, I love dogs. I'm not sure what this pretty girl is. Judging by her body, she's got some dachshund in the mix. But her fur is long and silky and she has floppy ears like a spaniel. And then, there's that fascinating nose. It's probably a mild case of Vitiligo, but the nose itself is mostly white with black patches.

"Come here, sweet girl." I lift her out of the box, feeling her body shiver against my chest.

Dante gives me a grim look. "Someone left the box by the end of your drive."

My head rears back slightly. "How'd we miss that?"

Dante shrugs. "It had slid down into the ditch."

Hitch gazes down the lane. "Bound to start happening. I hate to say it, Zoey. But people might start dropping unwanted animals at your doorstep."

I press my cheek into the top of the dog's head. "Let them come."

I carry my new friend into the clinic. Baby is waiting, his tail wagging like a wrecking ball. When I'm certain both dogs are comfortable with each other, I lower to the ground, letting Baby sniff our new visitor. "What should we call her?"

Dante takes a seat in one of the orange vinyl chairs. "Dolores."

I look up at him, surprised that he would offer a suggestion. He shifts awkwardly. "My Great Aunt Dolores had hair like that."

I look down at the little dog, ruffling her soft fur. "Dolores. What do you think, ma'am? Does it suit you?"

Dolores sits on her haunches, her head coming up primly. It seems she approves.

I don't need to ask Dante why he's come. And even though I told them to keep Peter away, some small part of me thought he would come, anyway. I'm surprised by the tiny flicker of disappointment I feel, but I quickly sweep it away. The pack is respecting my wishes in at least this. I have to take the small wins.

Rabbit is still my patient, and I don't want anything jeopardizing the shaky bridge I have between my world and theirs. Not until I'm sure he's going to be okay.

Hitch seems more than a little reluctant to leave me alone with Dante. But short of moving in, he eventually has to leave. I send him home with care instructions for Luna. It's not until his squad car has disappeared down the drive that I turn back to Dante.

He has Dolores on his lap and Baby at his feet. Apparently, they recognize an alpha when they see one. I don't follow pack law, but I do follow the laws of biology. And he's another hulking man taking up space in my little clinic. Not for the first time, I bemoan my mother's genetics, the pint-sized height the Cooper women inherited.

"What's your last name, Dante?" I lean against the lobby's counter, crossing my arms.

Dante is a handsome man in his own right. A slight hook to his nose. And dark eyes so intense they could cut diamonds. "Torres." He meets my gaze. "And you're Doc Cooper."

I nod. "If you're out here, you must have drawn the short straw."

His lips pull into a hint of a smile. "You barred the only civil guy we have from the clinic, so they had no choice but to send me."

I laugh. "Pretty Boy is your most civil pack member?"

He nods, completely serious.

"Terrifying." I nod towards the exam room. "Are you here for the medicine or did they put you on babysitting duty?"

He pauses. "Yes."

He's here for both reasons, then. A hum of warning sounds in the back of my head. Why are they already keeping tabs on me? It's not like I'm going to turn them into the authorities. I start gathering up ingredients from Maria's stores, stealing a glance at Dante. Baby and Dolores are following him around like he's the head boss. They trust him, but do I?

Hefting the box of supplies, I shove it into Dante's arms. Might as well put the big boy to work if he's going to be lurking around. Taking another box of bottles and flasks, I lead him into my kitchen. Baby and Dolores settle on the rug, and I line up the ingredients. "I'm going to run out of wolfsbane before long."

Dante sits on the stool by the counter. "Make a list and we'll track down whatever you need."

I pause, turning to look at him. "How's Rabbit?"

Dante meets my gaze. There's something there that resembles respect. "He was sleeping when I left. He seems comfortable."

"That's good." I nod, making the decision to go back later in the afternoon, even if it does put me right back in the wolf's den. I want to check on him myself. "And how's everyone else?"

I get the feeling that Dante is not a very expressive person. But there's a hint of a smirk in his eyes. "If you're asking about Pretty Boy, he's a mess."

30.

Am I that transparent? With a pot of water heating on the stove, I turn to the coffeemaker. "What's wrong with Pretty Boy?"

Dante's eyebrows flick up and he grins, tipping his head. "You tell me."

I ignore the comment, turning back to my ingredients to crush herbs. "Why don't you have a goofy nickname?"

He barks a laugh. "Everybody's probably too afraid to try."

"Who came up with Pretty Boy?"

Dante moves to the cupboards, searching for coffee mugs. "I think that was Dusty. Those two didn't get along at first. Dusty's a farm kid and Peter graduated from the School of Mines."

"In Golden?" That means Peter is an engineer by trade.

"That's the one. Pretty Boy was such a preppy kid when he came to us. Uptight. No tattoos, yet."

It's easy to picture that version of Peter. I can see him working in an office with a crisp oxford and slacks. Those tattoos start to take on a new meaning. It almost seems like they mark the point of no return. One life ends, the other takes over.

The smell of crushed leaves fills my nose. "You all broke him down?"

Dante shrugs. "We had an influence on him."

"So, is he an engineer, then?"

Dante tips his head again. "In a matter of speaking."

I'm tired of riddles. And if Hitch is to be believed, it's best if I don't dig.

"Not everyone can settle into pack life." Dante pours me a mug of coffee. "We ain't exactly fancy."

"What happens if they don't mesh with the pack?"

Dante's expression is grim. "They're free to go off on their own. Assuming they're stable. But the life of a lone wolf isn't an easy one."

I pause, pestle raised above mortar. "What's it like? Being…"

"A wolf?" Dante sits on the stool. "There are some who think being a werewolf is a holy calling. Especially if you're born that way. But out this way? We view it as what it is… a curse."

"You can be born that way?"

"Some shifters are." Dante nods. "They're called Lycans. Pure bloods. Our region is run by a pack of them. They call themselves the Rat Pack."

"Why the Rat Pack?"

"Because all them wolves in St. Louis are Italian and they love them some Sinatra."

St. Louis again. No matter how far I move, that city seems to keep its hold on me. "What are their names? Your pack leaders?"

Dante holds up his hand. "The big dog is Henry Rudolfo. His next in line is Harris Barone. And then, there's Lennon Accetti—"

"Lennon Accetti is a werewolf?" I lean against the counter. I might need to sit down.

"You know of him?"

"You could say that." Dax was one of Lennon's biggest fanboys. Lennon Accetti is a powerful name back home. He owns half the clubs in the city. And Lennon was always at Dax's fight nights, seeing as how he owned one of the arenas. When Dax was fighting, Lennon always made sure I sat in the VIP area with him. Thinking back, it doesn't really surprise me that he isn't strictly human. There was something wolfish about that man. He radiated power and confidence beyond your typical bad boy.

But then, I'm thinking about Peter again. Why did he have to go and ruin a good thing? There's a thin line between being a sexy alpha and being a scary alpha, and he crossed right over that line when he said he owned me.

Fuck that guy.

I need to stay clear the hell away from him. Socrates reduced philosophy to one line, know thyself.

I have many faults, but being unaware is not one of them. I know where my weaknesses are. I know which temptations can push down the best of intentions. And I know a man like Peter Mackavoy is my kryptonite.

I didn't drop my life back in St. Louis and move out to the sticks to make all the same mistakes.

But my calling is still the same. I'm here on this earth to help creatures, big and small. And there is one patient out at the cabin who is still not out of the woods. The trick will be in treating Rabbit without running into Peter.

The events of the last forty-eight hours are catching up with me. Three hours of sleep just aren't cutting it, but there's more to be done. Letting the tea simmer on the stove, I dash upstairs to shower and change into a pair of fresh scrubs.

These scrubs, a soft blue color, make me feel more like myself. Feeling refreshed, I head back downstairs.

When the tincture is complete, I carefully meter it out into half a dozen mason jars. The amber liquid sloshes against the glass and I silently pray that it will work.

Dante offers to give me a ride to the cabin, but I refuse. It's best if I stay off those bikes for the foreseeable future.

When he sees me fretting over the dogs, he tells me to bring them along. I weigh the costs and benefits of throwing these dogs into a new environment versus crating them again. As a vet, I'd tell my dog families to give new dogs a chance to adjust before bringing them into yet another new environment. But I can also see the way Baby and Dolores are following Dante around with little cartoon hearts in their eyes. When he promises to look after them, the decision is made. He helps me load them up into the back of my car and then we all hit the road.

I've traveled the road enough times in the past few days, I know the way. The highway curves around the mountains, pines stretching up and over the road to obscure the sun. They call this area the Black Hills, but it's a misnomer. They are mountains cut from lichen covered granite. Cold and mysterious.

If there is such a thing as magic, these mountains vibrate with it.

I pull up to the cabin, parking at the end of a row of bikes. Climbing out of my car, I let Dolores and Baby out before hefting the box of jars. Dante quickly scoops Dolores up, and I follow him towards the cabin. We pass by Peter's bike and I do my best to ignore the way it makes my heart stutter.

In a row of chunky Harleys and lowriders, his bike stands out. Sleek. European. Pretty.

My heart starts to beat even faster, and it's like I can sense him.

Wherever he is, I hope he stays out of sight. I'm here for one purpose only. And that purpose has nothing to do with him.

31.

If I was worried about how the dogs would react to the pack, my concerns were misplaced. As soon as we arrive, it's like a pair of celebrities have rolled up. Dante quickly shushes everyone, refusing to give Dolores up. Dusty immediately takes a shine to Baby, leading him over to the rug by the fireplace.

Andy finds me in the kitchen putting the tinctures in the fridge. "Can I have a word?"

I straighten, trying to tamp down my immediate dislike. "Sure."

Following behind him is like trailing behind a flannel-wearing yet. He slides a glass door open and we both step onto the deck. Leaning on the railing, I let my gaze wander. A lone hawk rides air currents over the trees, seeking dinner.

Andy clears his throat, leaning on his elbows at the railing. "Rabbit seems to be holding steady."

"Thank God for that."

He turns his head, studying me. "Thank *you* for that."

I shrug, turning to lean against the railing.

His gaze follows the hawk. "Back when Sam was still in charge, we had to do clean up duty for a pack out by Big Sky." He casts me a sidelong glance, before looking at his hands. "One of their pack mothers had contracted Vargulfism, and they didn't have the heart to end it for her." He clears his throat, voice going raspy. "That shit spreads, as you well know, with rabies. Tore through the entire pack. By the time we got there, they had nothing left. It was a blood bath."

My heart lurches in my chest. "That's terrible."

He straightens. "I know you must think the worst of me that I would even think about killing Rabbit. If it isn't obvious, the idea… it wrecks me. But it's a reality we all live with. If you catch Vargulfism, you're as good as dead. None of us wants to follow the fate of the vargulf. We'd all want to be put out of our misery."

"A mercy kill."

He nods, giving me a strange look. "How did you know you could save Rabbit?"

"I didn't. I just needed to try." I pause. "Maria had her notes, and it seemed like she was onto something. I thought there was a chance."

He shakes his head. "Witches and wolves don't typically mix. Our worlds are very separate. Hidden from each other and everyone around us. It's all smoke and mirrors to stay out of the public eye. But if witches had the ability to cure Vargulfism, it just makes me wonder what else we're missing being so siloed."

"I'm not a witch. I'm just a vet."

He smiles at that. "Whatever you are, I'm damn grateful you moved to Hill City." He pauses. "I know there's plenty of them out there that aren't a big fan of our little pack. We're just trying to get by, like anybody else."

"Except for the whole werewolf thing."

He laughs. "Except for that. The system isn't set up for our kind, so we have to operate outside of it. Some would say that puts us on the wrong side of right. I guess I'll leave it up to you to decide if we're the bad guys or the good guys. But I'll say this much, we owe you, Doc. You saved one of ours and we're in your debt. Whatever you need, you just name it."

"Right now, I need to see my patient."

He nods. "In the basement."

I leave Andy on the deck, passing through the living room. Baby and Dusty are taking a nap by the fireplace, and Dante is reading a book with Dolores on his lap. Grabbing a jar from the fridge, I make my way downstairs. I expect to find someone standing guard outside of Rabbit's cell, but the hall is empty. The key is left in the doorknob, but it's still locked. The pack no longer feels like Rabbit needs a guard, but he's still locked up. They're hedging their bets.

I peek into the holding cell and spot Rabbit and Peter sprawled out on the floor. They've dragged in some sleeping bags and pillows, camping out until Rabbit is better. I'm not surprised to see Peter there. But it doesn't stop my heart rate from picking up. As though my heart is pounding too loudly, he stirs and pushes upright. After a few beats, he looks right at me. I've been caught.

Skewered, actually, by bright blue eyes that aren't smiling. Not in the least.

He wears an expression that says he has a lot to say, but won't be uttering a word of it.

He's mad.

We'll fuck him, if he is.

I'm not here to see Peter. I'm here for my patient. Unlocking the door, I make my way inside, pointedly ignoring Peter.

Rabbit yawns, stretching as he sits upright. He wears an old band tee and gray sweats.

I settle down next to him, replacing the empty jar of tea with a fresh one. "What's your real name, Rabbit?"

He swirls the tea, glancing up at me. "Vince."

"What's your real name, Doc?" He throws the question back at me, his tone tongue-in-cheek.

I give him a wan smile. "It's Zoey."

"Okay, Zoey. What's this tension I'm sensing?" His gaze bops over to Peter before settling on my face.

I shrug. "What tension?"

He laughs. "You are acting like Pretty Boy is invisible and Pretty Boy is staring holes into the back of your head."

I hear Peter scoff behind me.

32.

"Keep drinking that tea, Vince." I say. "You're hallucinating."

He laughs, shaking his head. "I'm definitely not. Seeing as how I'm grounded to my room and there's no escape, let's hash this out so you two crazy kids can have a happily ever after."

I shrug. "I have nothing to say."

Vince raises his gaze to Peter. "How about you, Pretty Boy?"

In the corner of my vision, I see Peter settle against the wall. "I'm not discussing it with you, Rabbit."

Vince's gaze flicks between the two of us, before landing on me. "What'd you do?"

My mouth drops open. "Me?"

"I mean, Pretty Boy couldn't misbehave if he tried." Vince tilts his head. "That leaves only you, Doc. What'd you do to piss our resident saint off?"

I glance back at Peter, who looks rather pleased with himself. Glaring at Rabbit, I cross my arms. "I'm sensing favoritism."

Rabbit looks at Peter, waiting.

Peter sighs. "It was between me and Hitch, and she picked Hitch."

My shoulders sag. I turn, glaring at him. "It was just a ride, Peter. Calm down."

Peter meets my gaze. "I thought you said we aren't allowed to tell each other to calm down."

"No, I said never tell a *woman* to calm down."

Rabbit tilts his head, eyebrows pinching together. "You took a ride from Hitch over my boy?"

I shrug. "He was already going back to the clinic."

Rabbit grimaces. "Yeah, but... Hitch? That nerd?"

Feeling ganged up on, I hook a thumb at Peter. "He said he owns me."

Peter clicks his tongue. "You're taking that out of context."

Rabbit wrinkles his nose. "I don't know a lot about women, but that seems like a bad move, bro. Regardless of context."

Sensing victory is near, I go for the final blow. "And he bit me."

Rabbit's jaw drops. He looks at Peter, a slow grin tugging at his features. "You did not."

Peter throws his hands, exasperated.

Rabbit's grinning ear to ear. "Ho-ly shit. Does everyone else know?"

Peter sighs. "Not yet."

Rabbit laughs. "Damn. That's out of the blue, but congrats, dude."

"Okay." I climb to my feet. "Clearly, you're exhausted and not thinking straight. I think the patient needs his rest."

Shooting Andy a text, I stand by the door waiting for him to let me out. When he finally comes, Peter follows me out.

Andy stays behind to keep Rabbit company and the two of us make our way upstairs. At the landing, Peter tugs lightly on the back of my scrubs and I reluctantly follow him outside. He has his head turned, looking into the forest. He glances back at me. "You want to go for a quick hike?"

I hesitate. "With that rabid wolf in the area?"

His expression grows somber. "I'll be at your side. You have nothing to worry about."

"Hmm."

He tips his head towards the path. "There's something I want you to see."

Curiosity wages war with caution. I might be pissed at Peter, but I do believe he is capable of keeping me safe. "Fine. But if I get bit by the rabid wolf, I'm coming after you first."

He laughs. "Deal."

He leads me up the gravel lane, sheering off on a path that curves up the mountain. The trees rise on either side of us and beneath a thick layer of pine needles, slabs of granite form the foundation. Peter always stays within arm's reach. He helps me up a ridge that a shorty like me can't quite master. We skirt along the ridge, weaving through spindly pine trees. The sunlight filters down in a bright patchwork and it's hard to believe that somewhere in those dappled shadows, a monster lurks.

Peter looks back over his shoulder. "That wolf only attacked Rabbit because we had it cornered."

"Okay."

He squints at me. "You don't need to be afraid."

"I'm not."

He shakes his head. "Liar. I can feel your heartbeat."

"Okay, maybe I was thinking about that wolf." I pause. "How'd it get away?"

He helps me over another boulder. "When Rabbit was injured, our priorities changed. We had to let it go."

We stop on a ridge, and I turn to look at the horizon. A valley opens up below us, rich with wildflowers. I breathe deep, and even though my nose is just a regular old human nose, I can still smell the rich loam below, the hint of pine.

He dusts off his hands, staring at the valley. "I've been out of human society for twelve years now."

I look over at him, surprised. "When did you..."

I trail off, not sure if it's a werewolf faux pas to ask about the moment when a wolf bite turned everything upside down.

His eyes are ice blue and steady. "I was twenty-two."

I do the math, doing a double take. "You're thirty-four?"

He nods.

"How? I thought for sure you were younger than me."

He frowns, a twinkle in his eye. "Is that a compliment or an insult?"

I laugh. "You look young."

His smile fades. "That's the virus at work. It slows the aging process."

That brings me up short. "How old is Andy?"

"Forty-seven."

My eyebrows fly up. "Wait a minute, how old is Vince?"

"Rabbit's twenty-three."

I sigh with relief. "Well, I guessed one out of three."

"Anyway, the point is, Zoey, that sometimes we forget the rules of human society."

I squint at him. "Is this you apologizing for what you said earlier? About owning me?"

He drags a hand over his face. "Yes."

33.

I put my hands on my hips. "For future reference, saying you own a woman is not a very progressive way of thinking."

He nods. "I realized that right after I said it. But in my defense, I was pissed."

"I'm not sure that's a great defense."

"I guess not." He tilts his head. "So, why'd you go with him? Were you trying to fuck with me?"

"No." I sigh, exasperated. "I was trying to get him out of there. I could see the wheels turning in that head of his. He was suspicious. And you had a dying man in your basement. Not a good combination, Peter."

He pauses. "When you put it like that, it sounds pretty reasonable."

I laugh. "Because it *was* reasonable. Unlike you, Bitey McBitepants, I know how to plan ahead."

Peter is quiet for a while. "I should have talked to you right away about the bite mark, but I thought it might overwhelm you to hit you with everything at once."

I don't like that he controlled the situation like that. But he's right. I would have flipped out. "Fair enough."

He runs a hand through his hair. "I thought you might be pissed, but then the next day, you turned up with your own claiming mark and I just assumed we were on the same page."

"Not a great assumption, considering I had no idea what any of it meant."

He gives me a wan smile. "Yeah. I realize that now." He picks up a pebble and tosses it. "There isn't really a human equivalent for a claiming mark. Maybe aside from a wedding band."

My cheeks heat up. I can't quite keep the shock out of my voice. "We're married in the eyes of your pack?"

"No, no, no." He pauses. "But it means that you're mine and I'm yours, and no one else is supposed to disrupt that."

"How is that any different?" I splutter, pausing. "And you did that after one day of knowing me? Are you nuts?"

His shoulders raise up. "Like I said, we don't do things the human way. When it comes to picking mates, it's more of an instinct thing."

"Well, bully for you. What about me?"

His eyebrow arches. "You're the one who put a spell on your wrist saying I'm your property."

"It's not a spell!"

He laughs. "Whatever you say, Babe. Do you want to see what we came to look at?"

I growl at him, gesturing for him to lead the way.

He carefully eases over the edge of the ridge, landing lightly on the lip of rock below. I've never been a big fan of heights and the sheer cliff below that ledge makes my stomach knot up. Of course, Peter's got that doggy radar, and senses my fear. He holds his arms out. "I won't let you fall. Just trust me."

I frown at him, muttering as I awkwardly sit on the edge of the ridge and let him drag me down to the platform below. Once I'm safely on my feet, I look back up, realizing it wasn't such a death-defying drop after all. If I look below the ledge, there's a clear goat path zigzagging down the hillside. I turn to look at the space we're standing on and find that we're in a shallow cave. He eases down to the back of it, stopping at a crevice between two boulders. He gestures for me to come closer. I crowd in next to him, looking at him expectantly.

"Listen." He takes my hand and puts it over the gap between stones. Part of me is expecting a rattlesnake to lash out at my palm, but instead, I feel the rush of air. The sound of wind is unmistakable.

Peter watches my face. "The Lakota call it *Oniya Oshoka*. Mother Earth is breathing." He stares up at the rock wall, like he can see beyond it. "This is one of the natural openings to Wind Cave. I'll take you there one day, if you want."

"Mother Earth is breathing." I murmur, repeating his words.

"The air comes from deep inside the earth. The air on the surface is denser than the air below, and that's what causes the air movement, but the Lakota believe—"

"It's a source of power."

He meets my gaze. "Yeah. The portal to the spirit world."

I hold my hands over the crevice, feeling soft, dry air whisper over my skin. My palms tingle, almost like I'm holding a buzzing cicada in my hands. I look up at him. "Do you feel it, too?"

He sits down on the cave's sandy floor. "What do you feel?"

I sit down beside him. "Energy."

He nods. "The locals say there are vortexes all over the place."

I drag my gaze away from the invisible wind rushing over my palm. "What the heck is vortex?"

"Places where energy is coming or going."

I glance up at him. "You must feel it too?"

He shrugs. "I come up here to think, sometimes." He nudges me with his shoulder. "It's a good place to meditate. But no, I don't feel anything physical. I thought you might, though."

"Not with the witch nonsense again."

"Yes, with the witch nonsense." He studies my profile. "You really don't have any witches in the family? No old family stories?"

I pointedly ignore his stare.

"Ha! You do have witches in the family. I knew it." He grins.

I glower at him. "You couldn't know it, because I don't even know it. It's not like great grandma owned a cauldron." Except, she did have a big cast-iron pot she was fond of. I'm going to have to call my mom when I get home. I glance over my shoulder. I get the sense that we're sitting somewhere sacred. Almost like a cathedral. I put my finger up to my lips. "Shh. Show some respect."

He shakes his head grinning, but presses his lips together.

If I close my eyes and focus on the sound of the wind rushing out of the cave, it almost sounds like whispering. That air eddies and flows around me, and I'm not a point of interest to that wind, but an object to move around. I open my hands, letting them fall palm up on my lap and that buzzing feeling balances in my hands. I breathe deep, picturing that energy flowing up my arms and into my chest. It rises with each breath, passing through my heart chakra. On the next breath, I picture that glowing ball of energy moving up each vertebrae, until it's glowing in my skull. I can see myself sitting there at the edge of that little cave, glowing with energy, with Mother Earth's breath. It fills my body and swirls inside my skull.

The energy grows, more and more light flows into me, until a simple meditation exercise becomes something overwhelming and frightening. I'm paralyzed by it, unable to move, unable to do anything but receive. I've never given much thought to the power of the cosmos, or the likelihood of there being a supernatural world, but now I'm caught in its awesome power and it's like underestimating the power of a riptide.

Whispers, in a language I can't understand, fill my head. They don't come from outside, but from within. Like something has been unlocked inside of me. Voices from the past crowd in, filling my head with pressure. It hurts, as though someone is pounding a nail between my eyes from the inside.

It grows, pounding and seething. And then all the light narrows down to one narrow corridor. A part of me worries that this is the light at the end of the tunnel. Am I dying?

Peacefulness settles around me. A sense of oneness with the world. It's beautiful, but overwhelming.

Something snaps.

My entire body seems to crumble.

And the lights go out.

34.

My consciousness comes and goes.

There I am, hanging limp as Peter lifts me over the side of the ridge.

The next thing I know, he's holding me in his arms, sprinting down the path. Moving impossibly fast for someone who's holding another person in their arms.

It's hard to keep my eyes open, like pushing a boulder uphill. I can't quite do it.

And then we're back at the cabin. People are crowding around, but then someone, Andy? Is barking at them to give me space. I'm laid on a soft bed and it feels like relief. All I want to do is sink into the blankets and take a long nap.

I wake up later, opening my eyes long enough to know Peter has pulled my upper half onto his lap, cradling my head in the crook of his arm.

My eyes drift shut, and I listen to the conversation around me. I'm too tired to chime in, content to just listen, to feel his low voice vibrate through his chest.

"I've got Briar on a video call." Andy's voice reaches my ear.

I hear a woman's voice, sultry and velvety. It's like I can feel her presence despite being cast from a speakerphone. "Ah. There she is. How long has she been resting?"

Peter's voice rumbles beneath me. "She's been unconscious for three hours."

Three hours? Is that possible? I just closed my eyes.

"She's not unconscious, she's listening to us." Briar says, ratting me out.

I force my eyes open, looking up at Peter's concerned face. His expression is pretty cute, and I smile, despite myself. But it takes a lot of energy when all I really want to do is go back to sleep.

I can hear Briar chuckling. "Don't force yourself, Baby. Go ahead and rest, I'll talk to your boys."

"She's going to be okay?" Peter asks.

"Yes." Briar's voice is soothing. "This happens to witch folk sometimes when we tap into too much magic. It's not unlike a near death experience. Sometimes people faint or, if it's strong enough, they might go into a coma." Briar pauses. "Zoey says she's not a witch? She didn't come from a coven or anything?"

"No." Peter adjusts underneath me, letting his fingers weave through my hair. "She's pretty adamant she's not, but... I shouldn't have taken her out to that vortex. I just thought maybe it would open something up for her. I didn't know it was dangerous."

"It's not." Briar interrupts him. "Don't beat yourself up, Pretty Boy. She was bound to have one of these experiences sooner or later. You can't run from the shadow. It finds us all eventually. She's fortunate you were there to help her. Where'd you guys find this little witch, anyway?"

Andy's voice rumbles from a few feet away. "She just moved here. From St. Louis, actually."

Briar clicks her tongue. "No kidding?"

Peter's hand smooths up and down my arm. "She says she knows Accetti."

"Really?" Briar sounds genuinely surprised. "Hang on."

I want to chime in that I don't know him, I just know *of* him. But then there's the sound of a shuffle on the other end and a voice meets my ear that sends a shiver down my spine. It's low and smooth and mischievous.

And familiar.

Lennon fucking Accetti. "Hey, I recognize that little nugget."

Briar's muffled voice filters in from the background.

I force my eyes open, certain my cheeks are flaming red.

I hate being vulnerable.

Having an entire audience while I get over whatever hangover this is, is nothing short of mortifying. Add to it that one of St. Louis's most powerful men is getting an eyeful of my groggy, saggy self.

He's grinning down at me from Andy's phone, and I wave weakly.

"He-ey." I draw the word out, aiming for lighthearted, but exhaustion coats every syllable.

Accetti's smile is broad and magnetic. "You're that boxer's girl. Zoey."

"Ex." I manage to murmur.

Peter's stomach tenses slightly under my body, like he's bracing himself. I can't check his expression, not in front of everyone, so I keep my gaze trained on the phone.

Lennon's glancing over his shoulder, Briar joins him on the screen. "She's one of ours. A witch."

Lennon grins at her. "*You're* one of ours, Briar. Werewolf, last I heard."

Briar nudges him. "But I am a witch, first and foremost. And that little Irish cutey is Team Witch."

Peter's arms circle around me. "You can tell all that over a video call?"

"Oh, yes, honey." Briar says. "My sight may not be as good as my mother's, but even I can see Zoey's aura. She's a strong one. A healer, would be my guess."

"A vet." Andy inserts.

131

Cleo Mercer

Briar hums. "Listen, Miss Zoey, I'm sure this is all a lot to take in. The headline here is that you are not dying, you are not sick, you just had your first experience with magic and that takes it out of everyone. Just rest up and, girl, come see me sometime. We have a lot to talk about."

35.

As though Briar's words are law, everyone filters out of the room.

I'm exhausted.

Beyond exhausted.

But my mind's going a hundred miles an hour and won't let me be.

I just want my own bed. Funny how after just a few days, Strawberry Moon already feels like home.

"Where's Baby and Dolores?"

Peter's hand, warm and callused, travels up and down my arm. "Hanging out with everyone in the main room. I think you might have a hard time reclaiming Dolores."

"From Dante?"

I can hear the smile in his voice. "They're smitten."

"Far be it for me to get in between soul mates."

His hand hesitates on my shoulder before moving up to my hair. I wonder if he's going to ask about Dax, but he weaves his fingers along my scalp. "How are you feeling?"

"Drained."

He goes still, when he speaks, his voice is low. Almost hoarse. "I'm so sorry I did that to you."

"You had no idea I'd react like that."

He's wooden beneath me. "Exactly. I should be looking out for you, not throwing you into danger."

"Briar said it was bound to happen sometime. I'm glad you were there." I let my fingers spread across his chest, feeling his heart pound beneath my palm. "Peter?"

"Yeah?"

"Will you take me home?"

He sucks in a shallow breath, his voice comes out gentle—a whisper. "Yeah. Of course."

I sit up a little and he shifts out from underneath me. He hovers close by watching me with an eagle's eye as I push up out of the bed. I want to make a crack about him treating me like a little old lady, but truth be told, I feel a little light-headed. His arm slides behind my lower back and I'm grateful for the support.

We find a subdued group in the main room. Andy sits with his arm around Kali. Dante's got Dolores in his lap and Dusty's sitting by the fireplace with Baby.

As soon as we start to approach, Baby is on his feet, tail swinging back and forth. He trots over, putting on the breaks as he gets closer like he senses I'm not my best self.

Dolores, meanwhile, lets her head flop down to rest on Dante's lap. Cradling her in his arms, Dante stands, but holds back. "I can dog sit Dolores if you don't have the energy to look after her tonight."

Peter gives me a secret look. *See? Smitten.*

I lean into him. "Sure, Dante. That'd be a big help."

Kali packs up food for us and fusses over me until Andy wraps a gentle arm around her middle. "We better let the good doc get home, Cherry." He nods at me. It feels a little like getting a seal of approval from Chuck Norris. "Take care, Doc."

Peter ushers me outside and I blink, momentarily bewildered by the darkening sky. "How is it nighttime already?"

"You were out for quite a while." His voice is quiet as we walk to my car. "I was really worried."

I watch him help Baby into the back seat before opening the passenger door. "If you get worried every time I take a nap, you're in for a hard time, my friend."

He gives me a neutral look. I'm deflecting. He knows it. I know it. But I've never been any good at accepting compassion. Before he can push, I ease down into the passenger seat amid a sea of paperwork, a spare pair of tennis shoes, and half a dozen tennis balls. He sits behind the wheel and finally cracks a smile when he finds his knees up by his ears. "Like a clown car." He murmurs, adjusting the seat.

After a beat, I reach out to take his hand. He keeps his gaze trained on the road, fingers curling around mine. I'm squeezing his hand harder than is strictly necessary, but he's the only thing anchoring me down. I look out the window, just barely making out the first evening stars through the looming pine trees. It's peaceful out there, maybe a little foreboding, but quiet. Inside my head, it's like a hurricane. My thoughts spin so fast I can't hold on to a single idea.

Everything I thought I knew about the world, about myself, was only partially true. I only saw the surface and now it feels like I've slipped below.

I'm sinking.

"Are you doing okay?" Peter glances at me before turning his gaze back to the road. "With all of this?"

I give him a shaky laugh. "It was easier to swallow when you were the only monster in the room." I wince at my choice of words. "I didn't mean..."

He gently squeezes my hand. "I know what you meant."

"It's just, I could compartmentalize when it was you and not me. But now that I'm supposedly a part of this world, too? It's a lot to take in."

135

Cleo Mercer

He glances at me before turning down my driveway. I know what he must be wondering. Just what will it take for me to accept the facts?

I get lost in my thoughts again, and then I realize we're parked outside Strawberry Moon. He's already let Baby out and is swinging my car door open. I peer up at him, a silhouette against the twilight. "What now?"

He offers me his hand and I take it. "If you tell me to go, I will. It'd hurt like hell, but I would. But then I'd just send someone else in my place to make sure you're looked after."

Exhaustion has made mincemeat out of my chronic need to play it cool. I'm too tired to put up a front. "I don't want anybody but you."

36.

Judging by the way he hovers at my side, I think Peter would have preferred to carry me inside.

I let him guide me into the living room. He stops by the couch. "Sit."

A ragged laugh bubbles up from my chest. "Yes, sir."

Baby and I watch him pass back through the house, listening to the door open and shut. Baby lies on the rug by the TV with a satisfied sigh. I decide to follow suit, slouching back into the cushions. It's been such a whirlwind since I moved to Hill City, I haven't really had a chance to sit in my own living room. Flicking on the TV, I listen to Peter return. He moves around in the kitchen. There's the clink of silverware. Plates being pulled down.

I glance at the coffee table and spot my phone, abandoned. Shocked that I could go so long without having my phone with me, I snag it and check my notifications. A call from the bank and the electric company. A few messages from friends.

But none of that scoops my chest out the way the text from my mom does. It's an innocuous text, but I stare at it, feeling strangely anxious.

<How are you settling in?>

How am I settling in? Well, let's see. I live down the road from a werewolf pack. There's a rogue wolf in the woods somewhere. And, oh yeah, turns out I'm a witch.

Cleo Mercer

Part of me knows that I need to ask her about our family history, but I'm not sure how to pick at the edges of that question without giving away too much.

I love my mom. I would do anything for her. But I'm not sure she can handle the truth about the paranormal world. This is a woman who is on her church's vacation bible school committee. Something tells me, if the witch thing is genetic, it skipped her generation.

Peter saves me from having to deal with that thorny issue by returning with two plates. "You need to eat."

I exhale, muscles feeling limp as noodles. "I will later."

I fire off a text to my mom. <Doing great.>

He sits next to me. "You'll do it now."

One of my eyebrows flicks up and I toss my phone to the side. "You think so?"

"Yes."

I open my mouth to reply, but pause. When was the last time I ate? Rewinding the clock, I realize I haven't eaten all day. Hard to have much of an appetite when your whole world is being dumped on its head. "Maybe just a bite."

Under his close eye, I force myself to eat some of the dinner Kali sent home. Each bite feels like a stone going down. I have to swallow past the anxiety and nausea locking my throat.

Meeting his gaze, I tilt my head and give him a cheesy grin. *Happy?*

He nods, satisfied. "Good."

I laugh again, feeling exhausted and loopy. "Question."

He sets our plates aside and leans back, throwing an arm around my shoulder. "Shoot."

"Your friends are very adamant that you are the civilized one."

He smiles at that, but holds his tongue.

I crane my head to study his profile. "Supposedly so polite, but when you're around me, you act like a caveman."

A surprised laugh softens his features. He pokes my side. "Mine."

That single word sends a silly, stupid little thrill straight to my core.

I shake my head, as much exasperated with myself as I am with him. I should know better than anyone what the flip-side of the territorial boyfriend is. It shouldn't turn me on as much as it does, but apparently, I have a weakness for possessive men.

"My last boyfriend was domineering, too," I say.

Peter's smile fades, but he holds my gaze. "Was he also a biter?"

I grin. "No. That's your thing."

His fingertips feather over my arm. "Is that why you broke up?"

I think that over, realizing with a modicum of surprise that no, that wasn't why we broke up. He was bad with money. Had questionable judgement. Never knew when too much was too much. But even that wasn't the reason. "He cheated on me."

Peter's fingers curl around my arm, and he tugs me closer. "Then he was a stupid fucker."

"Yeah."

He kisses the top of my head. "Want me to beat him up?"

My lips pull into a crooked smile. "He'd put up a good fight. Being a boxer and all."

"Think he could take a werewolf?"

"I'd pay good money to watch that match."

"No payment required. I'd fight him for free."

I laugh. "See? Caveman."

"Only where you're concerned." He bends down, pressing his lips to the crook of my neck.

37.

I'm very interested to see where this will lead, but I need to tell him what I saw before I forget again. "That wolf was back."

He pulls back, studying my face. "The vargulf?"

"Maybe? I saw a print outside."

He's sitting upright, pulling away from me. "Where?"

I watch him glide to his feet, regretting the loss of his warmth. "In the driveway."

"Stay here."

I watch him sweep out of the room. After a few beats, I push myself up to my feet and follow behind him. Not wanting to be left out, Baby moves to his spot on the kitchen rug.

I stop in the doorway, suddenly intimidated by the darkness beyond. We need to install a light out there. It's too dark. Too foreboding.

Makes me feel like an interloper in my own home.

Peter pauses just beyond the porch, pulling his shirt over his head. He meets my gaze, giving me a stony look.

I lean against the doorframe. He doesn't need to tell me not to follow him into the darkness. I don't have a death wish. But if he thinks I'm going to cower in my house, he's wrong about that, too. I watch him quickly strip down. A soft night breeze passes over us as though to underscore the fact that he's naked under a starry sky. Exposed.

But he doesn't look vulnerable. He looks like he belongs. Wild and free. Like he and the night are one and the same. The shift happens even as I'm watching, but between the shadows and my brain's confusion, I blink and the human version of Peter is gone. A black wolf, as big as a mastiff, looks at me with glowing eyes.

It should be unnerving. I should probably step back inside and bar the door. But instead, I feel a small flutter of wonder. And pride. That big, beautiful creature is mine.

Mine.

Maybe I'm part cavewoman, too.

He fades back, instantly fading into the shadows. I listen carefully to the quiet night sounds. The breeze tugs at the light fabric of my scrubs, beckoning me to join him. When he returns, it's from the opposite direction I'm expecting. He's back in human form and very, very naked. I stoop to pick up his shirt and jeans and he grabs his boxers.

Slipping them over his hips, he follows me back into the house and shuts the door behind us.

We pause in the kitchen, and I watch him, waiting for his verdict. "Well?"

He scrubs a hand over his face, obviously debating what to say. "Why don't you come stay with me for a few days?"

I pause, heart rate speeding up. "Did you find it? The vargulf?"

He hesitates.

"Peter. Is the vargulf back?"

Coming forward, he pulls me against his body. His arms cage me in, pressing me against his bare skin.

I feel my courage wilting. "Why aren't you saying anything?"

He takes a shaky breath. "I don't want to scare you."

I shiver. "I'm already scared. Just tell me."

"It's been back. A few times." His hand cups the back of my neck. "I don't want you out here by yourself."

Maybe I'm drawing strength from his warmth, but running away doesn't seem like a viable option. "I won't be chased off my own land." I can feel his body tensing against mine, bracing for a fight. I smooth my hands over his chest. "But you can stay here... if you want."

He presses his forehead against mine, nodding. "Okay."

I can feel his breath feathering against my lips. It only takes a small lift on my tiptoes and then our lips are pressed together.

His fingers spread wide across my back, trying to gather me up against him. I can feel the warmth of his skin, the wild beating of his heart. When he parts my lips with his tongue, a cascade of euphoria shivers from the point of contact all the way down my spine.

I realize, with a soft moan, that I am gaining strength from him. My exhaustion ebbs back replaced by a flow of energy. Strength. Courage. Hunger. These are just some of the tones of Peter's personality.

I've always been someone who notices people's energy. I can't literally see it, not the way Briar can. But I have called myself an empath—a hopeless energy sponge. For better or worse.

But as Peter's energy renews my tired body, fills me with a hunger that isn't quite my own, I'm realizing I'm more than just an empath.

I'm a witch.

My instinct tells me that Peter has energy to spare. And with that gut feeling, I choose to siphon off some of the power that emanates from his body. Breaking the kiss, I murmur against his lips. "I need you. Now."

38.

His breath feathers my lips in a soft puff. "I'm trying to be careful with you, baby. But you're making it hard."

He touches his forehead to mine, slipping his hands under my scrubs, callused hands gliding up my back.

I sneak my fingers under the waistband of his boxers, letting them ease over his firm glutes. Almost mirroring my movements, he grabs my ass. He lifts me up, dragging my center up and against his groin. I groan at the friction and his hips thrust involuntarily. He hoists me higher and I wrap my thighs around him, letting him carry me where he will.

Opting for the closest option, he takes me back to the living room, gently depositing me on the couch. He's put me eye level with his hips and his not so subtle hard on. "Take your shirt off, Zoey. I want to see all of you."

I watch, mesmerized as he grips his shaft through his boxers. My shirt comes up over my head and I throw it in the corner.

"Pants, too."

I immediately comply, perching on the edge of the couch, waiting for my next instruction.

Those blue eyes stare at me so intently. "So fucking beautiful."

I'm drawn to him, to the warmth of his skin. My fingertip touches the ink to the right of his belly button and his abs twitch. I thought it was just a skull, but there's a scythe, too. A reaper, then. "Why a grim reaper?"

He reaches out, gently teasing my hair back. "That's a long story."

All of my fingertips span out over the tattoo. "You'll tell me one day?"

His chuckle is gritty. "I'll tell you now, if you want. But it's a little hard to think straight with your hands on me."

I lean forward, so close there's less than a millimeter between my lips and his abs. "How about now?"

His fingers scoop behind my head, fingers slipping through my hair. "Even harder."

I press the gentlest of kisses to his abs, feathering my lips against his skin until I reach his bellybutton. Drawing a circle around it with my tongue, I work my way down, noting with pleasure the way his body seems to almost tremble against my touch.

His reactions feed into me. Like sipping on helium, I feel buoyed up by him.

I pull on his boxers, freeing him. Running his tip across the seam of my lips, I slowly take him in, listening to the soft hiss of breath above me. "Fuck." He sighs. "Babe, *I* should be taking care of *you*."

I circle my tongue around him before popping him out of my mouth. "Then let me use you."

His hands cradle my head, thumbs gently sliding along my temples. "What do you need?"

"Lay down."

He kicks off his boxers and just as quickly, I scramble out of my panties.

"Condom." He murmurs, hustling back to the kitchen. I'm unhooking my bra as he comes back, cock jutting out in front of him proud and bobbing. He rolls the condom down his shaft, giving himself a quick stroke.

I swallow hard, forcing my gaze to meet his. The heat there is scorching. I feel momentarily stunned—the hunted facing a predator.

Better yet, facing a wolf.

A smart woman would probably run for it, but I stay rooted to the spot, a grin stretching my lips.

He comes forward, slowly, slowly. Until I have to crane my head back to take him in. Until he's kneeling between my legs, dragging my thighs wide, the cushions sinking beneath his weight.

And then he's gliding down on top of me. I can feel his length pressing against my stomach. Soft skin and hard flesh trapped between our bellies. I arch my back to bring him closer and he groans into the curve of my neck. He hovers there, still conflicted. "Are you sure you're up for this? You were in pretty bad shape back there."

"Yes." I breathe, putting his hand between my legs. "Please. I need you."

His middle finger slips between my folds, and he makes a barely muted sound of torture when he feels how wet I am. I wrap my hand around the back of his neck, dragging his lips to mine. His tongue nudges my lips apart just as his cock eases inside.

His hips twitch, sinking a few inches in one, hard stroke. He stops there, taking a shaky breath, forehead pressed against my neck.

I hook my ankles around his hips and drag him closer, deeper.

"Oh, fuck." He murmurs. "So tight."

I need more of him. I need him to move faster. Rolling my hips, I can feel his hard length stretching me, making room. I tuck my head into the crook of his neck, lips brushing his skin, breathing in his scent. "Give me everything you've got," I murmur. "Lend me your strength."

He braces his forearm by my head, his free hand scoops under my lower back. Anchoring my lower body, angling my hips the way he wants, he starts fucking me faster. Quick, forceful thrusts, mirrored by slow, dragging withdrawal.

I'm so aware of his presence, his power, I can almost feel it tingling against my sensitized skin. He's filling me, body and soul, physically dominating me. But my spirit flies with him, too, euphoric and greedy.

I want to pull him to me and make him part of me. I want to eat him up.

With each forceful thrust, he's winding me tighter and tighter. It's blissful torture. I can't decide if I want him to keep going forever or to just give me the relief I'm breaking into pieces over. Turning my head, I nuzzle my nose against his arm, distantly noticing the veins there, the swirling tattoos. My hands slide up his back and he's deep inside, but it's not enough.

I want him all. I want him to be *mine*.

39.

Scraping my teeth along his forearm, I find the one patch of bare skin. No inked roses or skulls. Just Peter.

That's mine. That's where I want to leave my mark.

Guided by a foggy sense of purpose and an unholy amount of greediness, I fit my teeth over his skin and bite down.

He gasps, hips involuntarily jerking, burying his entire shaft, and then he goes still. A heartbeat later, a tremor goes through his entire body and his back arches. "Fuck." He groans, pressing his forehead into my shoulder. I can feel him jerking inside me, pulsing as pleasure rolls over him.

His hand curves around my head and he pulls me closer. It's fascinating to watch. I feel a little overawed. I had a vague sense of what I was doing, but it still felt like roleplaying to me. Until now. Until I see the effect on him. And I remember that effect from when his teeth closed over my hip. I rest my hands over his back, smoothing gentle circles across his skin. My own frustrated climax is still there, needful between my legs and his still body, but I'm guided by a strange outrushing of tenderness. Possessiveness.

In one quick movement, he pushes his thighs up under mine, bracing his arms around my back. And then I'm being scooped up, perspective changing so quick it almost makes me dizzy. I'm sitting in his lap. He's still inside me, but he's holding me so lovingly. A surprised laugh, a muted sound of joy, falls off my lips. Have we really only known each other for less than a week?

"You bit me." He murmurs into my hair, I can *hear* the smile in his voice. His hips start to rise and fall screwing another gasp from me. "Did you know what you were doing?"

I pause, momentarily distracted by the feeling of his still, blessedly hard shaft, tugging in and out.

"Zoey." His voice rumbles against my neck making me shiver.

"Yes. I knew." I gasp.

He thrusts deeper. "You've claimed me twice over. What does that make me?"

I smile against his chest. "Doomed."

He bounces me on his hips, telling me that maybe we're both in trouble.

With my world dumped on its head, everything I thought I knew fluttering around me in tattered pieces, I'm so grateful to have something, *someone*, to hold on to.

I'm distracted by warm and fuzzies so the climax creeps up on me, a gradual note of bliss that stretches and crescendos. Warmth and pleasure rush outward, flushing over my stomach, my chest, sailing up my throat in a ragged groan. He holds me close, one hand cradling my head, the other holding me up. Supporting me.

When my breathing settles, he carefully lays me down. I lay back on the cushions, eyes closed, trying to bottle up the feeling. I hear his soft step return, and then he's scooping me up. I grab onto his neck with a surprised yelp. "I can walk."

"No."

Feeling a little silly, but also pretty impressed by his casual display of strength, I hold on and rest my cheek against his warm chest.

He carries me up the stairs and down the hall. Laying me down in the center of my bed, he crawls in behind me. Bodily turning me onto my side, he snugs up against me, holding me in a tight bear hug. I run my fingertips over his forearm. Dislodging it from under my chest, I reposition his arm so we can both inspect the marks near the inside of his elbow. Two half-moons. I touch my fingertip to the canine tooth mark, canted to the side. I wasn't blessed with a perfect smile, but laid out on his skin like that, it almost looks like that's how it was always supposed to be. My crooked tooth. That's how we know it was me.

I bring his arm to my lips and kiss him there. A gruff, satisfied grunt vibrates in his chest.

"Still sensitive?"

He slips his arm back under my chest and hums happily. He takes a deep, satisfied breath. His middle rises and falls against me, filling the curve in the small of my back and then receding. "I don't think I've ever been this relaxed." He nuzzles his lips against my hair. "Or exhausted."

"I sucked the life out of you."

He chuckles. "I can't tell if you're joking."

A wide, devious smile pulls at my lips. "I'm not."

"If sucking my life force out makes me feel like this, you can have at it. Whenever you want." He pauses. "Sure you're not a vampire, too?"

I go still. "Vampires don't exist... do they?"

He laughs sleepily.

"Peter?"

He adjusts his hold on me, somehow making me fill all the empty spaces between us.

"Pretty boy!"

But his breathing has calmed, smooth waves breaking against the beach. He's fallen asleep.

Cleo Mercer

"This fucker." I murmur to myself. But his utter contentment is contagious. I find myself feeling wonderfully soothed. Completely and utterly safe.

Which is saying something, seeing as how I'm sleeping with a werewolf.

40.

I stretch under the quilt, squinting against the bright morning sun. Rolling onto my side, I run my hand over the empty half of the bed. Pushing up onto my elbows, I pause. His side is still warm, which sends an alien feeling of relief through me.

Intellectually, I know that we've both exchanged some sort of claiming mark, but it's still hard to catch up with the idea. I'm slowly learning about him. He's an engineer by trade, a bad ass by choice… I guess. His reputation proceeds him, and thank God, it's a positive one. That has to count for something. And yet, I feel a little like I'm standing too close to the edge of something.

I hear a pan being pulled from the cabinets in the kitchen below. Butterflies sprout wings in my tummy. It's too soon to say if those are nerves or happiness. Trying to buy myself time, I take a quick shower and get dressed. The scrubs, yet again, act like a shield. It reminds me of who I am, even if everything else is in flux. I am a healer. An animal lover.

A werewolf lover, too, apparently. The butterflies are back in force. I can't keep hiding in my room forever. I step carefully down the stairs, moving silently. I wanted to sneak up on them, choose my own moment to see and be seen. But when I step into the kitchen, both man and dog are waiting for me. Baby has fresh water and food and seems rather pleased with himself as he stands guard over Peter.

Still wearing nothing but boxers, Peter is a person worth standing guard over. The sunlight hits his skin just right, making it almost glow, and he looks like King Midas, made of gold and black etching. He gives me a curious smile, coming forward to wrap me in his arms. "Regretting saying I can stay?"

I swallow hard. "No."

"I can feel your heartbeat, you know."

I realize with a start, that I can sort of sense him, too. But where my pulse feels fluttery and erratic, his is steady. Calm. He seems so sure of himself. Of us. And that feels like something I can hold on to. I relax against his chest. His hand slips under my scrubs, sailing up and down my spine. "I made breakfast."

"I see that." I let him guide me to a bar stool. "You didn't have to do that."

He shrugs, plating scrambled eggs and toast. We sit in companionable silence while we eat. The only sound is Baby chomping merrily away on his dog food.

I'm thankful that he isn't grilling me. He isn't demanding declarations of love. I bit him, didn't I? Even if it seems a little overwhelming and scary in the morning light, the act is done. And in a turn I would have called ridiculous just a week earlier, I know deep down that I'm tied to him now.

Maybe I'll ask if the bond can be undone. Or, maybe I can ask Kali or Rabbit. It's not that I want to run... except maybe, I do want to run just a tad bit. It's an awful lot to take in for such a short amount of time.

My pulse must give me away again, because Peter reaches out and puts a heavy hand on my thigh. The weight of his touch, the small circles he draws on my inner thigh, imbues me with some of his confidence. I take his hand and kiss the back of his knuckles before placing it back on my leg.

Without so much as a word, we can say so much.

We're so caught up in our own quiet world, our separate trails of thought, that the car wheels on the drive seem to scrape against the temporary calm.

Peter's head turns to peer out the window. An old sedan pulls up to the house, and he glides to his feet. His jeans and t-shirt are still in a pile by the door, and he manages to pull them on before a knock raps our guest's arrival. At a nod from me, he swings the door open.

A cute little old lady in a muslin two-piece suit stares back at him. Her gaze strays to his bare feet. It's an innocent enough state to be in, but a dead give-away. He's no casual guest.

She is completely unphased, but Peter's ears turn an interesting shade of pink.

"Ma'am." He says, nodding to her.

She pretends to frown at him. "How many times do I have to tell you to call me Lorna?"

He grins back at her. "My mother would throw a fit if I did that."

It's the first time he's mentioned another family member. Curiosity sparks in my chest, but that can wait.

Lorna turns her blue eyes on me. "I didn't want to impose on you, dear. But is there any chance you're taking patients?"

"Of course." I step forward.

Lorna nods, turning to look at Peter. "Would you mind getting Ollie from the car?"

Peter hesitates for only a brief moment before nodding. "You bet."

Lorna looks at me with a twinkle in her eye. "Ollie and Peter aren't on the best of terms." She grins. "I don't think he's a cat person. Or more accurately, Ollie is not a Peter person."

She comes forward, offering me her hand. "I'm Lorna. I own the bookstore in Hill City. Ollie's our guard cat, and Peter is one of our best customers."

I take her soft, delicate hand in mine. "I'm Zoey Cooper."

"The new vet." She smiles at me. There's a hint of nostalgia there. Sadness, too. "I was good friends with Maria. The vet who owned the clinic before."

My heart seems to miss a beat. "Oh. I'm sorry for your loss."

She bats my limp offer of sympathy away. "Time passes. The shock has worn off. I still miss her, though." She pauses, smiling again. "She would have been thrilled to see another young lady take over after her. She was about your age when she moved in, you know."

Peter enters the open doorway with a cat carrier emitting very displeased, low cat yowls. "Where would you like him?"

Lorna and I exchange grins. "In the exam room, please."

We follow behind Peter as he passes down the hallway that leads to the clinic. Ollie stares at Lorna through the patchwork opening in his carrier. His expression can only be described as betrayed.

Peter sets Ollie's carrier on the exam table and beats a hasty retreat. Lorna watches him go with barely concealed glee on her face. "He tries so hard to be polite, but Ollie just won't have it. You'd think the poor boy was a dog."

I swallow hard, choking a little. We let Ollie out of the carrier and I immediately spot the infection. "How long has his eye been bothering him?"

She runs a hand over Ollie's back. "A few days now. When I saw the gunk, I figured it was time to see a vet." She pauses. "I am just so thankful to have a vet back in the area."

She watches me put a few drops of dye in Ollie's eyes. She still has a ghost of a smile on her face. "I wondered how long it would take those motorcycle boys to find you."

I grab a small flashlight and shine it in Ollie's eyes, checking for scratches. "Took them exactly one day."

She hoots at that. "Oh, they had such a special friendship with Maria. She would defend those boys come hell or high water."

I give her a side glance. "Do they require defending?"

She shrugs, watching me work. "Some folks aren't big fans. Maybe Maria rubbed off on me, but I say Hill City is lucky to have them. Especially during the big motorcycle rally. God knows the police can't keep those rowdy crowds in hand."

I pass a hand over Ollie's back, instinct driving me to pass my hand over the same spot again. "Has Ollie had any bathroom troubles lately?"

Lorna looks up, surprised. "He's had an accident or two. In the bookshop, which is less than ideal. Why? Is something else wrong with him?"

I shrug, but instinct coalesces into a diagnosis. "We'll test to be sure." I glance at her. "Crying when he urinates?"

She looks aghast. "I thought he was just being talkative."

"I think he's got a little infection, nothing serious. He'd just need to be on antibiotics for a short while."

I glance up, watching Peter settle against the doorframe. He crosses his arms, watching me with open curiosity. I meet his gaze and I know what he's thinking. He doesn't have to say it. *Witch*.

41.

When Lorna and Ollie are safely loaded back into her car, Peter strolls back. He stops short of climbing the steps, reaching out to lean on a post instead. It puts him slightly below me, but it says something about his height and my general lack of it, that he's still almost eye level.

With his arm stretched out, his biceps flex in fascinating ways. He smiles at me, an expression that's all in the eyes. "Did you heal that hell cat with your witch powers?"

I bite back a grin, tilting my head. "You and Ollie aren't on the best of terms, are you? Not a cat person?"

He comes closer, hands slipping over my hips. "I don't mind cats. Problem is, they don't like me."

He wiggles his thumbs along my ribcage, tickling an unflattering squawk out of me. Amused by my reaction, he tugs me into his arms and slowly lets me slide down his body until my tiptoes hit the ground. "What about you— are you a cat or a dog person?"

There's a growl in his voice that sends a delicious shiver down my spine.

"I'm a vet. I love all animals."

His voice drops a little, low and honeyed. "How about wolves?"

Trying to hide my blush, I duck my head, pressing my cheek against his chest. I breathe him in as sneakily as I can. Soap. Fresh air. He smells amazing.

I catch sight of his sleek bike parked next to my SUV. "How'd your bike get here?"

He follows my gaze, arms wrapping around me. "Angela, of course."

"Why Angela, of course?" I'm still not a big fan of Angela. Not since she left Luna and Baby alone.

"She was never particularly impressed by me, but she loves that bike."

I tilt my head to look at him. "Did you want her to be impressed by you?"

He smirks at me. "Is that jealousy I hear?"

"Dream on."

He tugs me closer. "Still can hear your heartbeat."

"Still haven't answered the question."

I can feel a soft chuckle vibrating in his chest. "I'm a people pleaser. What can I say? I didn't want her to *like* me, but I wanted her to like me. If that makes sense."

"Not even a little."

"It's like with that damn cat." A wry smile curves his lips. "Nothing I do seems to win him over."

I can't keep the hint of a pout out of my voice. "You had no issue with me not liking you."

He pulls back to look at my face, a twinkle in his eye. "When did you not like me?"

"Immediately."

He laughs. "Liar. You took one look at me, and it was a done deal."

"Your hubris knows no bounds." I squeeze his sides. "What makes you so sure of this?"

His arms tighten around me. "Because that's how it was for me."

"Love at first sight?" I meant it tongue in cheek, but as soon as the words are off my tongue, I want to reel them back. Too much, too soon.

But he holds my gaze with his steady blue eyes. "Yeah, maybe." He looks away, glancing at his bike. "We're supposed to meet everyone at the club later tonight."

"Andy's house?"

He gives his head a little shake. "The club by Hill City."

Yeah. Not going to a biker bar. I disentangle myself from his arms. "Okay, have fun with that."

He catches my wrists. "You're coming with."

"An interesting theory, but incorrect, my friend."

He plants my hands on his hips. "You don't want to?"

"Not even a little." His torso is hard and warm under my hands.

"I'll have to drag you," He murmurs. "Is that what you're saying?"

"I'm saying you'll have to make a convincing case."

He drags my hips against his. "I can be very convincing."

I nuzzle my nose against his neck. "How are you with pipes?"

He pushes his hips against mine. "Very good."

"Because I think something's wrong with the hot water heater."

He laughs. "If I fix it, you'll come with me tonight?"

"That's assuming you can fix it."

He takes my hand and leads me up the stairs. "It's a deal."

Thirty minutes later, he's reattached some loose wiring on my heater and sealed my fate. Changing out of my scrubs, I throw on a pair of jeans and a tank top. I'm not excited about meeting everyone at the club, but I do love riding on that bike of his.

We head out early so he can stop by his house for a quick shower and a change of clothes.

The road leads right past Andy Haugen's massive cabin. We pass two more driveways nestled in the pine trees. He's going slow enough he can shout and be heard over the rumble of his bike. "Dante's place." He gestures to the south. "And Dusty's."

We take it slow on a road that weaves hairpin turns ever higher up the mountain. Just when it seems like maybe we'll sail right over the peak, he slows and turns down an impossibly steep driveway. It occurs to me that I may be required to take that driveway in the future, possibly in snowy conditions. A bubble of fear rises in my chest. I'm not sure if it's the idea of heights combined with ice, or if it's the fear of commitment. Regardless, my traitorous pulse gives me away yet again.

When Peter helps me off the bike, I can see it in his eyes. He must think I'm incredibly high strung. I make a mental note to work on breathing exercises to keep my heart steady, otherwise I'll have no secrets.

He leads me to his cabin, which perches on the very edge of the rocky cliff face. It requires an honest-to-God gangplank to reach the front door. The exterior is built from gray, weather-beaten plank. The view is breathtaking. Pine-covered mountains that spread below us in prickly spines. He opens the door, letting me in first, before tossing keys on an end table behind me.

My first thought is that it smells like Peter in here. Leather. Soap. Campfire.

My second thought is that's a rather wolfish observation to make. But even my human nose recognizes that this is Peter's home, and it's a scent that envelops me, makes me feel just a little at home, too.

He watches me carefully, uncharacteristically hesitant. "I'm just going to hop in the shower, quick."

I realize with a sudden rush that the steady rumble I was hearing is actually his heartbeat. I know this, because it picks up when he meets my gaze.

42.

The fact that he's nervous now too does nothing for my state of mind.

Maybe it's my fault he's on edge. "Okay."

I watch him go, wondering if I was supposed to join him. Left alone in his living room, I make a slow circuit. There's a retro fireplace in the corner. One of those freestanding conical ones, painted red. He has low slung couches and bookshelves loaded with books. I let my fingers run over their cracked spines, noting with a surge of pleasure that his most worn books are some of my favorites. There's a picture frame on one of the lower shelves, turned to the side. I peer at it. Three boys, all tall and handsome and clean cut. Peter is clearly the one in the middle, though his brothers look so much like him. He wears a polo, his arms and neck are free of ink. It's hard to compare that young man to the one I know. They seem like completely different animals.

I suppose, according to the laws of nature, they are different.

Easing the frame back into place, I step out onto a wide deck. A breeze rushes over my skin, clearing my lungs. I peer out over the mountain, black with dark pines, and spot a few rooftops. Dante's and Dusty's. And there, to the east, is Andy's sprawling cabin. After a few minutes, Peter joins me, the smell of soap rolling over me. He comes to stand beside me, and I sidle closer. He quickly puts his arm around my middle.

I turn more completely, liking the way my ass fits up against his hips. I allow my back to ease into his chest. "Do you all live on the same hill?"

"Not the entire pack." His voice rumbles against my back. "But a bunch of us, yeah."

I peer up at him. "How big is the pack?"

"Locally? There's twenty-four of us. A handful more live in the region."

I try not to blanch. "That's a lot of werewolves."

He studies my reaction, turning to look out over the hills.

I follow his gaze. It's hard to separate what happened with Rabbit from my feelings about the pack. Andy explained himself, and I get it, but that doesn't erase the fact that they would let a friend perish without trying to fight for him first. I'm not so blind as to think that I would get special treatment, especially being an outsider.

At least I have Peter on my side. He was willing to fight his own wolf brothers to keep me safe.

"I saw a picture of your family." My voice cracks the silence. "What do they think of the werewolf thing?"

He doesn't stiffen or freeze up, but when it takes him a few beats to respond, I realize just how nosy the question was.

He clears his throat. "They don't know."

I crane my head to look at him. "Seriously?"

He tilts his head. "Have you talked to your family about being a witch yet?"

"No."

He holds my gaze. "Why not?"

I sigh. "I'm not sure they could handle it. My grandma when she was alive, yes. My mom? No."

He nods. "Then, you understand."

"Do you still see them often?"

"No. Not at all." He gives a short laugh. "They think I've gone to the dark side. All the tattoos and everything."

"I'm sure you're still the same person."

"I'm definitely not." He pulls back, easing his hand down my wrist, where his fingers slide over my palm. "Not even close to that same kid. We grew up in a very traditional household. Country clubs and all that bullshit. All three of us became engineers, but I'm the only one who isn't… well, anyway. A lifestyle like I lead now? It doesn't even compute to them."

I don't like the sadness I see creeping into his gaze. I really don't like the fact that I'm responsible for that expression. Enough prying for one night. "You ready to meet up with your friends?"

"At Staggers?"

"Oh, God," I groan. "Is that what it's called?"

He laughs, weaving his fingers through mine. "Come on, you'll love it."

"Are you sure?"

"I have no idea." He grins, tugging me behind him. "But I won't leave your side. You can bet on that. I'm not letting any of those silly motherfuckers fall within two feet of you."

We go back outside, and I climb onto the back of his bike. It's already becoming second nature to swing my leg over that seat. I slip my hands under his t-shirt, bracing against his hard stomach. His skin still has that dewy, just-out-of-the-shower feel. The short hair at the nape of his neck is slightly damp and the scent of his soap fills my head.

I'm having serious regrets about not slipping into the shower with him. His bike kicks into gear. The rumble of the motor and the road vibrate below us. I lean in, pressing my body to his to make up for the missed opportunity.

When I'm with him on his bike like this, the pine forests don't seem so scary. It feels like part of our territory.

It's when I'm by myself that the shadows creep in.

Night slips over the western slopes, reflecting the orange and red colors of the setting sun. I could stay like this with him forever, flying through the warm summer evening, but all too soon, he pulls up to the bar.

It's a strange building right off the highway. Strange, because to the outside eye, it looks like a bar. But it's also clearly not public. There's something forbidding about the entry and the line of bikes parked outside.

Peter climbs off first, turning to face me. He pulls his helmet off first. I'm still staring at the bar, so he takes my helmet off for me. My hair falls in front of my eyes, and he gently pushes it back. His gaze is mirrored by the steady, reassuring beat of his heart.

43.

I look over his shoulder. Staggers is missing all the usual hallmarks of a bar. There are no neon lights in the windows. No sign by the highway. It's clearly not meant for the public.

His voice is soft. "I'm taking you out of your comfort zone, aren't I?"

"Yes and no." I swallow hard. "Back in St. Louis, we used to hang out at places like this a lot. One of the places was owned by your very own hallowed leader."

"Lennon Accetti?"

I nod.

"Was that one full of werewolves, too?"

I grimace, swinging my leg over so that I'm sitting sideways on the bike. "Worse. Boxers."

But now that I know what I know about Accetti, maybe that boxing club was full of werewolves.

He settles between my legs and pulls me into his chest. Kissing the top of my head, he breathes deeply. "We don't have to go in."

I pull back, peering up at him. "I can't keep avoiding them. It's just... after everything that happened with Rabbit... I'm not sure if I *want* to trust everyone just yet."

He nods, expression stony. "I know. A fucking mess. They were just following protocol, though."

"Were you following protocol when you tried to fight your way into that basement to get me?"

He hesitates, hands sliding down my back. "No."

"Maybe you're just more forgiving than I am."

He shrugs. "We don't really have a choice. The wolf pack... We're all we have." His eyes are bright blue even in the fading light. "I know our laws must look strange to an outsider, but it's how we survive."

"It's just a lot to take in." I pause, patting his chest. "Let go in before I lose my nerve."

"You sure?"

I nod and he helps me off the bike. Weaving his fingers through mine, he leads me across the dark parking lot. "I won't leave your side."

I squeeze his hand. "Better not."

If the outside of Staggers looks like a strange, forbidding building, the inside looks like a standard bar. The wood paneled walls are covered with Harley Davidson memorabilia and there are colorful Christmas lights above the bar. Gritty blues music rocks through the speakers overhead. As soon as they spot us, there's a general outburst, but it's not Peter's name they call.

"Doc!" At least twenty people shout the name in my direction, christening me with my very own biker nickname.

I was expecting a lot of things. Testosterone. Stale beer smell.

I was *not* expecting such an enthusiastic reception. More than that, I would never have guessed a nickname would fill my chest with gooey affection. Treacherous heart. So easily won.

I was an only child. I never understood the whole nickname thing. My experience with that kind of thing was relegated to junior high, and those nicknames were never meant to be nice.

But with the way they're all looking at me, I realize it's a term of high praise.

165

And I can see the source of that high praise. My miracle patient.

Joy blooms in my chest. "Rabbit!"

He comes forward, a grin stretching his features. Damn, he's a cute one. Closing the distance, he drags me into a tight, breath-stealing hug. "My angel."

Holding me at arm's length, he studies my face with something close to reverence in his eyes.

I'm not so sure I deserve it, but I am glad to see him doing so well. "They let you out of your cage."

He grins, moving on to hug Pretty Boy. "I think Andy just wanted me out of his house."

Peter slaps him on the back. "How you feeling, man?"

"Better than I should." Rabbit's gaze strays to me again, before he leads us back to the group. There's at least a dozen of them circled up around a few tables, pitchers of beer spread out in front of them.

Dante pours me a beer, then one for Peter. It seems like everyone wants to take a turn introducing themselves to me, or thanking me for helping Rabbit.

Only one person holds back.

Angela.

It's not that I don't like her. I don't know her well enough to have an opinion. My only personal experience with her wasn't exactly flawless. And then, there's the fact that Peter hinted that they might have had a past together.

I've been told I have a shitty poker face. I'm not sure what expression I make when I look at her, but she seems reluctant to meet my gaze.

But Rabbit seems rather attached to her. He motions for me to sit with him, which means I get to sit next to her. Peter tries to follow, but gets waylaid by Dante and Dusty. So much for not leaving me alone.

44.

I keep my eye on Peter, smiling distractedly when Rabbit sits on my other side.

Peter breaks away from Dusty and Dante, an apologetic look on his face as he makes his way over. I can guess what he's going to say before he says it.

"They need your help?" I ask.

He nods. "I'll just be in the back. Five minutes. Tops." He runs a hand over my shoulder. "You can come with me..."

Rabbit leans back, putting an arm around me. "I highly doubt Doc wants to watch you fix the freezer."

Peter gives Rabbit a dry look. "I highly doubt you want to put your arm on my girl like that."

Rabbit holds both hands up with a sly grin. "Point taken."

"Rabbit's the lady's man." Angela says. "He's hopeless."

"Hopeful." Rabbit laughs. "Always, always hopeful."

I look up at Peter. "I'll stay here."

He nods, squeezing my shoulder. "I'm just in the back if you need me."

"Yes, dad. We know." Rabbit drawls.

"Thin ice, my friend." Peter says, but the growl in his voice isn't very convincing.

Rabbit gives very strong little brother vibes. Chuckling to himself, he smiles at me. "He's fun to fuck with."

"That is true." Angela says.

"Have you two met?" Rabbit asks. "A lot happened while I was in lockdown."

"We've met." Angela says, wincing at me. "And I promptly fucked up."

Rabbit pulls a face. "I'm very familiar with fucking up. What'd you do?"

I put up a hand. "She didn't do anything."

Angela holds my gaze. "I definitely did. I let the good Doc down. I was supposed to look after her clinic, and I dropped the ball. It's just because I was just in a hurry to get back to see your sorry ass."

"Damn," Rabbit whistles. "Everyone's been pushing Doc's buttons. Thank God she's still here."

Angela tilts her head. "What? Who else fucked up?"

There's a rumble of bikes outside and Rabbit pauses, looking towards the doors. "That the country boys?"

Angela grins. "You know they'd come out to check to see how their favorite pup's doing."

Rabbit smiles at me. "I'm kind of a big deal around here."

Angela shakes her head. "You're something alright."

The doors bang open and half a dozen big, bearded men come in. I don't have the werewolf's sense of smell, but one look, and I know they're all werewolves. The leader of their group, a blonde man with a thick beard, scans the bar. His face lights up when he spots Rabbit.

I watch with mounting trepidation as they barrel towards us. It's like watching a wall of muscle close in on you.

Angela leans in, murmuring in my ear. "Rabbit's the only one who can keep up with these boys when they're partying."

The first guy swoops in on Rabbit, picking him up with a bear hug that lifts him from the chair.

He swings him back and forth, growling happily. "Rabbit, you slippery motherfucker. We thought we were going to lose you."

Anticipating the return arc, Angela leans across me, shielding me from Rabbit's helpless limbs. "Watch it, Cam. You're going to crush the rest of us."

Cam pauses, noticing me for the first time. He sets Rabbit down slowly, moving to stand in front of me. "Who's this beauty?"

I have to crane my head to see his face.

Angela swats him, urging him to back up. "*This* is Doc."

"You're the doc?" Cam asks, looking down at me like I'm some sort of new and wonderful species.

"Yes, she is." Angela says. "And she's with Pretty Boy, so go slobber over someone else."

As though summoned by his name, Peter appears like a thunderhead behind Cam. "You better back the fuck up."

Cam whirls around. I catch a glimpse of shock on his face before Peter is shouldering past him.

Acting like a shield, he eases me to my feet and pulls me back a few paces. Slipping his arm around my waist, he gives Cam a very cold, level stare.

Cam frowns, confused, then his gaze drops to Peter's forearm. "Ho-ly shit." He looks back at Peter. "Pretty Boy. Did she mark you?"

The question drops like a stone on a pond. It ripples outward, leaving silence in its wake.

Blues music still pipes through the speakers, but every other conversation dries up. We suddenly find ourselves the center of attention.

I shift uneasily from one foot to the other, not really sure what to make of the pack's reaction.

Cleo Mercer

Peter's fingers slide along my hip, anchoring over the mark he gave me. Tugging me closer, he holds his arm aloft.

There's a brief pause, and then pandemonium breaks out.

45.

I try to imagine what it would be like if I went to a family reunion and announced something like this out of the blue.

I'm sure my family would be shocked. Excited, even. But I doubt I know any group that would react quite like this. And that's including my ex's steroid-jacked gym friends.

The pack loses its ever-loving-mind and a rowdy gathering turns into an outright rager. Apparently, marking your mate is a thing worthy of celebration. And these guys know how to celebrate.

We're shuttled towards the bar where shots are being passed around. Peter gamely takes his first, but refuses the second. He wants to be able to take us home at the end of the night.

I bravely take it on his behalf. He eases onto a stool, pulling me against his lap. His lips brush my temple as he leans in to murmur in my ear. "I thought you didn't drink."

I grin. "Are you going to remember everything I say word for word?"

"Damn right I am."

He tugs me up against his hips, cradling my ass in his lap. His arms weave under mine, locking around my tummy.

Little by little, I'm coming around to this pack. They live by a separate set of rules and that part is going to be hard to adjust to. It still smarts that I found myself on the wrong end of that harsh justice. The pack must always come first, no exceptions. Not for loyal members like Peter and definitely not for an outsider like me.

Except, I'm not a complete outsider anymore. I'm a pack member's mate.

And a witch, as it turns out. I may be a different kind of beast, but we all live outside the constructs of polite society. I won't lie, that idea sends chills across my skin.

Peter notices. Of course he does. He notices everything. His arms fit over mine, bringing his warmth to my bare skin.

As I lean into Peter, I realize I'm grateful to have found them. I was bound to realize I was a witch sooner or later, but they were there to guide me through it. If I had been by myself, I don't know what would have happened to me.

The mate thing is actually harder to wrap my head around than werewolves and witches combined. I can't deny the literal beat of his heart, a deep and resonating answer to my own. I feel his presence deep in my body. When he's away from me, I feel that, too.

But there's an insistent voice in my head that whispers this isn't how things are done. I don't believe in love at first sight, that's why I was so glib when I asked Peter about it.

I did not expect him to take me seriously.

It feels a little lopsided; him being so sure while I'm hanging back. My head is a mess, but my body seems content. Sitting together, our breathing has synced. Even our hearts have settled into a rhythmic beat, two of my fluttery pulses for every one of his deeper beats. I can hear and feel that even over the ruckus in the bar. I turn partway in his arms, so that my side is against his hips and his chest, and peer up at those clear, blue eyes.

He's studying me with that observant gaze, not missing a thing. He sees the flush in my cheeks and when his thumb slips under the hem of my top, my eyes flutter. He notices that, too. Leaning in, his nose lightly brushes over my cheekbone. He presses a kiss to my temple before working his way down to my ear. He sucks my earlobe into his mouth, giving it a sharp little nip.

I jerk in surprise, ass shifting in his lap, and he groans quietly in response. "Want to head home?"

"You don't want to hang out with your friends?"

His fingers slip up to the small of my back. "I want to be *alone* with *you*."

"Well, I'm not going to argue about staying, that's for damn sure."

Chuckling, he eases me to my feet and follows close behind. He waves at Andy and is met by a chorus of catcalls and whistles. Pushing the door open, he lets me step out first.

It's like stepping between dimensions. Behind us, the glow of the bar lights, the loud music and laughter. Out here, it's quiet. The mountains rise up around us, nothing but wind in the trees and distant road noise. He leads me to the bike and hands me my helmet. My heart flutters happily as soon as my ass hits leather and Peter grins at me before shoving the helmet on his head. He settles on the seat in front of me and I lean into him, fingers slipping under his t-shirt to stretch across his hard stomach. He guns it, gliding onto the highway.

We're nothing but light and speed as we cut through the cooling summer night. The wind flows over my body like fleece and I snuggle closer, fitting my body to the broad curve of his back. His bike purrs between my legs, just enough to sensitize my skin. My hardened nipples press against him and I tighten my grip on his middle. It's not until he kicks the bike into high gear, speeding up, that I realize his heart is pounding. It's the steady, pulsing undercurrent to my own, pouring gasoline on fire.

46.

Peter pulls right up to the front door, barely parking before he's already climbing off the bike. Not bothering with the helmets, he puts his hands around my waist and lifts me from the seat. My feet touch the gravel and I look up at him. It's a little unnerving to see him with his helmet on, looming over me. He's got his hands on my hips and I take a hesitant step backward. He stays with me step for step.

My heart is racing. Somewhere deep in my bones, my body registers that he is a predator, and that understanding fills my veins with adrenaline. But at the same time, my logical side is feeding me snapshots of the time he was between my legs. As a result, I'm a giddy, half-terrified mess as he backs me up the stairs and to the front door.

I turn and struggle with the key, acutely aware of the exact places where his hips press into my ass. As soon as the door opens, I make a break for it. He catches me by the kitchen, tossing me giggling over his shoulder. His hands brace over my upper thighs and I'm treated to a nice view of his backside as he carries me up the stairs.

Setting me down on the edge of the bed, he finally lifts the helmet away. My hair fans down over my shoulders and my cheeks feel like they're on fire. He takes off his helmet and even though I've seen him countless times, my lips still part in surprise. The werewolf is present in the raw hunger in his eyes, the tense set of his jaw. But those features are statuesque. He's not pretty, he's beautiful. And I'd feel way out of my league if not for the desire scrawled across his features.

He pulls his shirt off with his signature one-handed move. I reach for the hem of my shirt, but he gets there faster, easing it over my head.

Funny, with my shirt in a pile on the floor, I feel hotter than I was before. His fingers trail lightly over the lace edges of my bra. "Were you trying to get that pretty little pussy off on the back of my bike?"

The growl in his voice has me transfixed. "You noticed that?"

"You were squirming up against me, so yes." His gaze drops from mine to my breasts. His fingers unbutton my jeans. "Does my bike turn you on, baby?"

I lift my hips, letting him pull my jeans off. Guiding his hand to curve over my damp panties, I nod. "Yes."

He closes his eyes briefly, breathing deeply through his nose. I reach up, dragging his zipper down. His tattoos form fascinating whirls over hard, curved muscle. My fingertips find the vee in his hips, hooking his jeans and boxers as I go. He's got a dark line of hair disappearing underneath the line of his boxers. He unhooks my bra as I push his jeans off his hips. Tossing my bra, he kicks his boxers off and lifts me around the middle before I have a chance to appreciate his erection. I can feel it pressing against my thighs as he drags me to the middle of the bed.

Settling to my side, he braces himself over me, fingertips dimpling my tummy as he slowly, slowly reaches beneath my panties. His fingertips tease at my entrance, gathering wetness, before nudging inside.

"Been thinking about this all day." He pushes in to his knuckles. "Jerked off in the shower and still didn't take the edge off."

I suck in a breath when he pushes a second finger inside. My voice is shaky. "Maybe I should have joined you in there."

He meets my gaze, leaning in to nip my jaw. "Why didn't you?"

"Gotta keep you on your toes."

"Stringing me along, you mean." He shifts over me, easing his hips between my legs. Reaching over to my nightstand, he locates a condom in the drawer.

I push up on my elbows. "Where'd those come from?"

"What'd you think I was doing while you took care of the devil cat?"

"Not that."

He rolls the condom on and positions himself at my center. Strong hands hook my thigh over his hip and I expect him to thrust deep. But instead, he nudges inside and presses in with excruciating slowness. He watches me carefully, my lips parting, my back arching, as pushes deep.

Kissing my jaw, he draws back and does the same thing again, ensuring that I feel every last inch. My fingers stretch across his back and I try to pull him into me, to encourage him to go faster. But he seems determined to draw this out. Even when I roll my hips against his shaft, he presses them into the mattress with his strong hands.

I whimper in frustration, arching against him when his mouth moves down to my nipples. Tangling my fingers in his hair, I hook my ankles around his hips. "You're driving me crazy. Fuck me, Pretty Boy."

He nips my breast at the use of his nickname, moving up to kiss my jaw. I catch a glimpse of pleasure in his eyes before he scoops me close in his arms and drives his cock home in one quick, hard thrust.

I cry out, tears leaking from the corner of my eyes. "Yes. Like that."

He picks up the pace, hips driving mine into the soft bed. Pressing my thighs up by my hips, he tilts my hips and pistons down, deeper. I can feel pleasure building between my legs, in the center of my hips. It pulses with his heartbeat, with mine, winding tighter and tighter until, like a coil, it springs loose. Pleasure cascades outward, a sweet euphoria that sails out through my fingers and toes. In the haze of my bliss, I feel him go entirely still and then, with a sharp inhale, he's tensing, coming hard with a broken groan.

47.

Peter cleans up and comes back with a satisfied calm on his face. He crawls into bed beside me. Laying on his back, he waits until I curl up against his side, before closing his arm around me. "You called me Pretty Boy."

"Does that make you happy?"

"I never would have thought so, but yes." His fingers trail up and down my arm. "You're part of the pack now."

My lips curve upward. "I use the secret code names and everything."

"I knew you'd come around."

"What's it like?"

He curves his fingers over my arm. "What?"

"Becoming a werewolf... what's it like?"

He's quiet for so long I begin to fear I've taken a misstep in asking. He takes a deep breath. "It's not fun."

"Would you ever think about turning me?"

"What? No." He's vehement. Almost angry. "Absolutely not."

So much for being part of the pack. I can't quite keep the hurt out of my voice. "Why not?"

"The lycanthropy virus... not everyone survives it. We're not going to risk that."

"But you said the werewolf virus slows aging, right?"

He's slow to respond. "Yes."

"So I'm just supposed to get old and gray and you'll stay the same age? How do you think that's going to work, Peter?"

"Back to first names now, are we?"

"I'm dead ass serious, *Peter*."

He sighs. "I know." He pulls my body closer, ignoring the angry, hard angles of my limbs. "I can't risk it, though. I barely survived it. If anything happened to you…"

I can hear the dread in his voice. "You barely survived it?"

"Yeah. It wasn't good." He pauses. "You really want to hear this story?"

"Do you want to tell it?"

He shrugs. "I guess I'll have to sooner or later." He weaves his fingers into my hair. "I'm originally from Iowa, did I ever tell you that?"

"No. That explains the obscene height. One of those corn-fed Midwestern boys, huh?"

He chuckles. "Correct. My brothers and I were all tall. Big into sports in high school and college. I did alright at track. Even after college, I loved running. My buddies and I did this Iron Man thing in Utah every year. It was our way of staying in touch after college. That was the last thing I ever did with them."

"Is that where you were attacked?"

He nods. "Yeah. I was on a trail and this wolf came out of nowhere. It got me by the ankle. Thank god there were other runners right behind me. They managed to fend it off. I came away with a few stitches and a rabies shot and thought that was the end of it. I got as far as Rapid City before I started to feel sick."

"Oh, no."

"I thought I caught the flu or something. I'm just grateful I made it off the range before the virus took over.

Everything west of here is pretty rough. Andy's territory marks the start of a more civilized region of wolves."

"The Black Hills wolves are the civilized version?"

He grins at the skepticism in my voice. "If you wanted civilized, you should have stayed in St. Louis. Anyway, to make a long story short, Dusty happened to be in Rapid City and he caught my scent and drug my ass back to Hill City."

"Did they put you in one of those rooms?"

"Yes. And I'm glad they did. My transition wasn't pretty."

I'm quiet for a few beats, mulling that over. "Rabbit said the same thing about himself. Why do they have to lock you up, though?"

He's quiet for a few beats. "So, we don't go on a rampage."

Fear coils in my belly. "Nobody does that, do they?"

"Unfortunately, yes. That's why it's key that each region manages its own population. If the mainstream world were to catch wind of us, Lord knows what would happen. Our freedom would be at its end. We know that much."

I wait for him to continue and when he doesn't, I peer up to gauge his expression. I'm surprised to find a grin tugging at his lips, dimple and all. "What are you smiling about?"

He nudges my ribcage. "You want to grow old with me."

"Who said that?"

He chuckles. "You did."

"God, I've really got to watch what I say around you."

"I'm always paying attention. Especially when it's you."

I rest my cheek on his chest, distracted by the sound of his heart. The pulse drums in my ears, thumps alongside mine in a strange harmony. It's nothing short of magical.

48.

Sunlight tracks across the bed, a bright square of light crawling over the quilt. But it's not the intrusive sunshine that wakes me, it's the sound of Peter's phone. It vibrates and buzzes in a crazy dance across my nightstand. I want to snatch it before he can, toss it out the window. I was having such a nice dream, waking up cocooned in his arms is pretty damn good, too. He lies on his side, body conforming to mine, his arm snugged up under my breasts. Keeping his arm firmly in place, he reaches out with this other hand.

Pressing the phone to his ear, he sighs heavily. "What?"

I don't have a wolf's hearing, but I can hear Andy's distinctive baritone on the other end. "We got it."

Peter's upright in an instant, leaving me chilled to the bone, dread coiling in my tummy. He gives me a careful look before sliding to the edge of the bed. Keeping his back to me, he rests his elbow on his knee. "Where?"

"Deadwood."

I scoot across the bed, kneeling behind him. "Tell them to bring it here."

"No." Andy's response is immediate—he must have heard me. "Bring Doc with you."

"Alright." Peter hangs up, tossing his phone to the side. He turns partway to look at me.

I hook an arm around his chest and lean up against his back.

181

He sighs. "You heard that?"

"I'm coming with you?"

He nods, but his back feels tense under my chest. "What's wrong?"

"These vargulfs... it won't be like it was with Rabbit. This could be dangerous. Rabbit was hanging by a thread when we brought him to you. He was weak. This wolf won't be."

"We don't know what condition it's in."

"That's true." He pauses. "You're determined to come along?"

I rest my chin on his shoulder and nod. "Yes."

"Okay. Just promise me you'll be careful. No unnecessary risks, okay?"

I nod again, turning to kiss his neck. "I promise."

But just going out there is an unnecessary risk. I was willing to risk my life for Rabbit and if there's a chance we can save this person, I'll do whatever it takes.

I can't tell Peter that, though. He'd never let me out the door.

We take my SUV and by the time we pull up to Andy's cabin, there's already half a dozen bikes lined up in the long drive. Peter pulls my crate of supplies from the back of the SUV and walks with me, step for step. I can tell from the tense lines of his body, and the revealing pounding of his heart, that he's worried. For once, I'm the one picking up on his mood, not the other way around, and it's filling me with a growing sense of dread.

Dusty meets us at the door. Peter slips past him. "How bad is it?"

Dusty's expression says it all. He shakes his head, glancing at me like I'm a complicated math problem. I peer into the living room. Kali's curled up next to Rabbit. He's pale and my first thought is that the virus is back, but if that was the case, he wouldn't be up here with the pack leader's woman.

This is the same wolf who attacked Rabbit. It's probably hard for him to be in the same house as his attacker. They all have the same look on their faces. They want to believe I can save the wolf, I can see it in their eyes. If I can recreate my cure, it's a game changer. But it's pretty obvious—they're skeptical.

I don't blame them. I'm skeptical, too. This goes way beyond my veterinarian training, tangling my schooling up with half-cocked memories from my childhood. Instinct and magic. A thin defense against a deadly virus.

The pack might be willing to take risks based on instinct, but it's harder for me. Dusty nods towards the basement and we follow behind him.

Even before we reach the bottom of the stairs, I can hear it. The snarling sounds of a cornered, injured animal. It kicks something into gear for me. My medical training takes over. Stepping around Peter, I stride down the hallway. Andy and Angela stand outside one of the holding cells, their conversation pausing as I arrive.

Andy steps back so I can peer in through the window. "This one might be too far gone, Doc."

It's in wolf form. I recognize it instantly from my first morning in Hill City. Its gray fur is in worse shape than before and its hips protrude at painful angles. It backs up until its rear hits the far corner, then lunges at the window, snapping at the glass. It falls back, leaving streaks of blood and foam.

I glance up at Andy. "Any chance we can tranquilize it?"

He looks over his shoulder and nods. Dusty turns without a word to find a tranq gun in one of the lockers in the exam area. No one is saying much. There is a heavy feeling of foreboding as they quietly pass the tranq gun to Andy. I'm glad Kali isn't down here to see what I'm exposing her man to.

Cleo Mercer

I push past Dusty and Angela, putting my arm on Andy's forearm. "Let me do it."

"No." Peter growls from behind, reaching between Angela and Dusty to drag me backward.

A faint smile tugs at Andy's lips. He locks gazes with Peter and shakes his head. Turning to look at Angela, then Dusty, he gives them a sharp nod. A pit opens in the center of my stomach when I see that they've both pulled out firearms.

Peter drags me back even farther. "Go upstairs and wait."

"No."

Andy glances at Peter, waiting to see what he plans to do with me.

I growl at them. "I'm staying."

Peter lets out a shaky breath, but shrugs.

With a final nod, Andy swings the holding cell door open and levels his tranq gun.

49.

Andy times it carefully. He waits until the wolf is backed into the corner, facing away, before throwing the door open. There's two quick shots, pneumatic puffs of air, followed by a ragged yelp.

I expected that to be it. My mind was already back in the exam area, thinking about how I would lay my treatment out. But there's a shocked intake of air that forces me to look up.

Andy backs up, shoulders hitting the wall, gun leveled. He fires two more shots, but the tranquilizer can't work fast enough to slow the wolf down. Claws scrabbling on the cement floor, it tears through the door frame. Ignoring Andy altogether, it turns its bloodshot eyes on the two people blocking its escape. Coiling back on its haunches, it leaps at Angela and they go down in a tangle of fur and limbs. She's changing into her own wolf form, firearm long forgotten. The handgun spins across the floor, spiraling to a stop at my feet. Not as though we could use it. The rabid wolf has locked onto Angela. She's in wolf form, a black wolf with silver points, and the two rip viciously at each other.

There's a lot of confused shouting, but not much of it registers. It's like I'm hearing everything from underwater. There's Peter, lowering to his knees, leveling his gun. In my shock, all I can wonder at is where he got the gun. Andy and Dusty have moved to the side and, with a single shot, a loud pop that clears my fog, Peter shoots the rabid wolf in the flank.

It staggers to the side, knocked to the floor by Angela. The fight is still pounding through her, but she's staggering, too. I'm staring at her, shocked at the sight of dark blood soaking the silver tips of her fur, blood on starlight, and a tranq dart thumps into her flank. She yelps, turning those blue eyes on me, beseeching me, before stumbling to the floor.

I rush forward, but find myself suspended midair. Peter has me around the middle. "No, Zoey."

Andy and Dusty are rising to their feet, chests heaving. They exchange shocked looks that quickly settle into stony acceptance.

Andy's fingers curl into fists at his side. "They're both down?"

Dusty's closer, he carefully squats beside the vargulf. "Yes."

Coming closer, Andy takes the firearm from Dusty's limp fingers and points it at the vargulf's skull.

"No!" I shout.

Andy pauses, giving me a tortured look, before turning back to Peter. "Take her out of here."

"It will be all for nothing." I shout, struggling in Peter's iron grip. "That vargulf is still alive. We can test my treatment on it."

Andy pauses, clearly conflicted. In the space of three heartbeats, the Black Hills pack started reverting back to their old ways. Execution as the solution.

"Please." I peer up at Andy. "Let me try."

He sighs. "Fuck." Looking at Dusty, he tucks the gun into his waistband. "Peter, grab the gloves. Let's get them up."

Working with militant efficiency, Dusty, Peter and Andy gingerly pick both injured wolves up. Angela is carefully laid on the exam table, the vargulf is put on a counter. They tie them down, seeming to only worry about containing the wolf. Even if one of them reverted back to human form, they wouldn't be contagious. It's the wolf that can infect.

I pause between both wolves, conflicted. Angela is more valuable to the pack. They're close to her. They love her. She's in bad shape, bleeding heavily from rips in her flank and underbelly.

But the vargulf is hemorrhaging badly. If I don't stop that bleeding, he won't last ten minutes. "Peter, put pressure on her wounds."

He complies with a practiced hand that reminds me he used to be the man they'd call on in emergencies like this. I feel like an imposter and I come with a medical degree. I can't imagine what kind of pressure that must have put on him.

Andy stands back, arms crossed, his expression like thunder. I hear Kali's choked cry, followed by Rabbit's ragged moan. "Angela. No."

Dusty goes to them, holding Rabbit back before he can throw himself on his friend's prone body. I'm focused on the vargulf's gun wound, but I can feel Rabbit's gaze boring into my shoulder. "Help her. She's bleeding out."

I can't formulate a response, but my heart twists with guilt. I'm fully aware that all of this could have been avoided if the pack had put the vargulf down immediately. They kept it alive for me. Because of the promises I made. And now their pack sister is hanging by a thread. If the blood loss doesn't kill her, the virus might.

That's if I can't save her.

My shoulders bunch up, but I keep my focus on the wolf in front of me. If I can solve this, if I can beat the virus, I'll save more lives than just these two.

Dusty manages to take Rabbit back a few steps, but he refuses to leave. I wish they'd all leave, to be honest. Peter

Cleo Mercer

is the only one who's helping. Having an audience, feeling their cold gazes on my back, is making my hands shake.

50.

Despite the pressure, I get the vargulf sewed up before turning back to work on Angela. There's a set of couches in the far corner, and Peter manages to talk everyone into taking a seat. A little space is what I needed.

Lining the treatments up on the counter, I resist the urge to rest my head on Peter's shoulder when he stands beside me. "What do you need?"

I glance at him. "Do they have any syringes?"

He goes to the cupboard and pulls out an assortment of syringes, plastic and glass, big and small. It's a reminder that Andy's cabin isn't just his personal residence. It's part headquarters, part medical clinic. And Peter was their stand-in vet. I take the plastic syringe and fill it with my elixir, hoping against hope that it will be enough. There's a sick feeling in the pit of my stomach. Everything in my medical training rebels against relying on a questionable tea I brewed in my kitchen, but short of taking them to the hospital and becoming a national headline, this is our best shot.

I should fill the syringes and walk away—let them administer the treatment so that I'm not an accessory to this tableau. But some voice deep inside me tells me that this might work, that it's worth it. I understand why none of them wants to seek medical help. If it was legitimate help, that would be one thing. But if they blew their cover,

189

their well-being as individuals would be forfeit. They would become specimens not patients.

Peter told me they fear becoming government property, being locked up in a facility somewhere. They have no choice but to operate outside the bounds of the law. A week ago, I might have sided with the US government on this one. But now that I realize I could potentially end up in one of those facilities myself, my perspective has shifted.

We start with Angela this time. Peter carefully pries her muzzle open, and I insert the syringe's long catheter into her mouth. We're both careful to avoid her teeth. When I'm sure all of it has gone down, I glance up at Peter.

He gives me a reassuring nod. We both know what's at stake—that this is a hail Mary. But I glance over at the couches, meeting Rabbit's strained gaze. He's living proof that the medication works. There's still a chance.

We move onto the vargulf. Peter dutifully opens its mouth, but its breathing is ragged at best. I've worked with enough patients to recognize a death rattle. We still need to try. Making sure that the wolf takes the entire treatment, I back up.

Andy's on his feet, moving forward, exhaustion heavy on his shoulders. "Now what?"

I glance at the two wolves. "I... I'm not sure, but I think they're going to need another treatment as soon as they can take it." I pull the gloves off. "We probably shouldn't move them yet."

Andy nods, before turning to look at Dusty. He jerks his head and Dusty's on his feet. "You stand guard." He makes eye contact with Kali. "Take Rabbit upstairs."

Rabbit resists Kali's attempt to help him to his feet. "I'm staying with her."

There's a break in his voice. I don't know the pack well, but even I can recognize the love Rabbit has for Angela. I can't say I would call it romantic love, but they were clearly close. Andy turns his attention to me. "What do you need from us, Doc?"

I look at the small collection of jars on the counter. "I don't think there's enough here for both of them. I need to make more. Stronger this time, I think."

Andy nods. "Get what you need and hurry back."

I'm loathe to leave my patients in the hands of these people. But the fastest way to get what we need is for me to get it myself.

Peter and I hop back in my SUV and ransack the last of Maria's herbal stores. Sunlight filters in bars over the exam room counters. In the hall, Maria's grandfather clock stands sentinel. Its steady ticking seems all too ordinary considering the circumstances.

I pause, looking around. "We're going to need more of everything before long."

Peter nods. "Make a list and I'll send someone after it."

I jot down a list as he drives us back to the cabin.

We bring Baby with us this time. He senses the mood, dark eyes ping-ponging between the two of us. When we get back to the cabin, Baby trots ahead of us. He knows the way, and he's got a good instinct for who needs a visit from a big, fuzzy baby. Hopping up onto the couch, he lays his head on Dusty's lap.

Dusty runs his fingers over Baby's head. "Dante's downstairs. Rabbit, too."

Peter nods, setting my crate of supplies on the counter. He turns to look at me, blue eyes scanning my body. "You okay for the time being?"

I nod, recognizing the fact that Peter needs to check in with his pack leader. Familiar with the kitchen now, I get started on making a concentrated treatment.

The next hours pass in a fog. I administer the elixir the same way my grandma would have forced her teas on us when we were sick. Every three hours. By the third treatment, the vargulf is barely hanging on. His breathing is labored, the pause between each breath grows longer and longer. I'm standing by its side when it takes its last ragged breath. I put my hand on its brow, smoothing its fur back. Despite its wretched appearance, it was just as human as the rest of us once. Someone's child. Friend.

I take a deep breath, like I'm breathing for the both of us, and look up at Peter. His gaze is steady but heavy.

It didn't work.

I knew it was a long shot—the virus had progressed too far by the time we got to this wolf. Even so, I nursed the hope that my elixir would be the miracle cure everyone has been searching for.

We both look at Angela at the same time. There's still hope for her. We've been administering treatments before symptoms can even surface. If this was rabies, she'd have a good shot at a full recovery.

But there's the matter of her injured body. She's got to recover from a vicious attack on her outside even as the virus attacks her from the inside.

51.

Day bleeds into night. They take the vargulf away, I'm not sure what they do with it. Tension hangs over the cabin like a dark miasma. Thank God for Baby. Those soulful eyes seem to convey the empathy we all need.

He has a future as a therapy dog if we can ever get past the never-ending late nights.

Sensing Dusty is struggling, Baby sets up shop next to him by the fireplace. Before long, the two of them are conked out on the rug together.

People doze where they sit, catching scraps of rest between guard duty and the next bit of news.

Maybe this is just how life is on the fringe of things— one foot in the shadow, one in the light. Never quite living in either world.

I begin to understand why Peter threw his whole lot in with the pack. There's no way he could have kept up a day job with unpredictable nights like these.

I'm barely keeping up with it and my clinic is only partway open. If I had a kennel full of cats and dogs, I couldn't be here. I'm not sure what kind of vet I'll be if I have to get through many more late nights like these. As it is, I'm dead on my feet.

Peter notices, because, of course, he does. He finally coaxes me to the guest room. Pulling me into the small bathroom, he helps me shed my scrubs. I watch, arms wrapped around my middle, as he pulls his shirt over his head. His muscles glide up and down, ink stretching this way and that. He kicks off his jeans and boxers and leads me into the shower.

If it was humanly possible, I would sleep standing upright, the calming spray of warm water massaging my back, resting my forehead on his slick chest. He turns me so that my ass brushes against his cock. His body responds to mine, shaft growing heavy, but he holds back. I would willingly give him whatever he needs, but the fact that he's holding back speaks volumes. His fingers massage my scalp, lathering up shampoo, before turning me so that he can rinse it out. I weave my arms around his middle and lean into him. His aura hovers just out of sight. I can't see it with my eyes, but I can sense his strength. I get the feeling I could syphon some of that off him if I really wanted to, but he's barely hanging on, too. Turning off the shower, he snags some towels and we dry off in silence. With his towel hanging low on his waist, he slips into the bedroom and comes back with a pair of sweatpants and a t-shirt courtesy of Kali. I struggle into them, watching him slip on a loaner pair of sweats from the supply the pack keeps on hand. Taking my hand, he leads me to the bed and pulls me in beside him.

I let him drag me closer, pulling my thigh so it rests on his hips. My mind spins dizzily with dark thoughts. I could pepper him with questions. Does he think Angela will pull through? What happens if she doesn't? Would they consider it a mercy kill to put her down if the virus continues to progress?

But this is one of those things where only time will tell. With Angela in the forefront of my thoughts, and Peter's heart beating a steady rhythm in the background, I fall into a fitful sleep.

My consciousness stays right at the surface, it's hard to differentiate between when I'm awake and when I'm asleep. Music pulls me closer to the surface. It reminds me of electronica, a woman's distorted voice wavering like a bow across strings. The sound coalesces into one word—*help*. And then, just as quickly, it's gone. I lay in bed, heart racing, straining my ears. There's Peter's heartbeat, steady and deep. Outside, wind passes through pine branches, but nothing else interrupts the night's silence. I peer at Peter. I've been using his arm as a pillow, he's got his other arm slung over his chest. In the cold moonlight, his tattoos look like spilled ink. I study his face, following the little worried crease between brows, the tense set of his jaw.

There's another sudden pulse in my awareness. One that is soundless, but I can only describe as a plea for help. I have no question in my mind about where it's coming from. Easing out of Peter's arms, I pause, waiting to see if I woke him. When he doesn't stir, I slide to the edge of the bed and climb to my feet. I could wake him, drag him along. But he needs rest as much as I do. At least one of us should recharge. Slipping down the hallway, I wince when my bare feet come across a creaky floorboard, but when no one comes looking for me, I continue. I haven't been freaked out by this wolf pack. Blame it on the shock, but even when I was fighting to protect Rabbit, the strongest feeling I had was anger. But now, as I pass through their shadowed headquarters, my every nerve is on high alert. I half expect a wolf to slink out of every shadowed corner.

Tiptoeing down the stairs, I find Dante standing watch over Angela. Rabbit is dozing on a couch in the corner. Dante follows my gaze. "I finally got him to stop pacing."

Rabbit looks gaunt. He's barely recovered himself. My chest tightens. "He needs rest."

Dante grunts, nodding. We both turn to look at Angela. Her black fur has lost its glossiness. I pull on a pair of gloves and start checking her vitals. "How's Dolores?"

Dante's tired expression immediately lights up. "Fabulous. As always." He shoves his hands in his back pockets. "My mom is dog-sitting. When you're ready to take her back, you just say the word."

"Dante." I wait until he's looking at me. "Do you want to keep her?"

He gnaws at his lower lip. "I don't want to take her away from you."

I laugh, trying to keep my expression placid as I take note of Angela's weakened pulse. "She was mine for all of five minutes. You found her. If you want her, she's yours."

He grins. "I have gotten pretty attached."

I smile. "I've noticed."

His gaze drops to Angela's prone form. "How's she doing?"

I smooth my hand along her back. "Not great."

52.

Turning my back to Dante, I get to work preparing Angela's next treatment.

Dante walks closer to her. "Is this what it was like with Rabbit?"

I glance over my shoulder, first to look at him, then to look at her. "No."

He meets my gaze. "Worse?"

I nod, turning back to my work. "Her injuries are more severe than his were. She's up against a lot more than he was."

"Doc."

The strain in his voice has me jerking around. I watch, dread coiling in my stomach as her fur starts falling away. I'm no expert in werewolf shifts, but the ones I have seen have been graceful. Fur melts into skin and back again. Angela's fur is falling off like we're watching a time lapse of decay. Her bones snap, puncture, and crack their way back into place.

It's grotesque.

I'm sure I'll be haunted by the images later, when and if things settle down, but all I can do in the moment is worry for my patient. Rushing forward, elixir forgotten, I start blotting at her skin making sure that her flesh has sealed itself back up.

Cleo Mercer

As blood drips off the table, I start worrying about how much blood she can afford to lose.

Does it replenish itself after each shift or is she draining her already strained reserves?

"What can I do?" Dante's voice is low.

"Help me clean her off."

He gives me a sharp nod, before pulling more towels from a cupboard. Angela's head rolls from side to side, her coppery hair is wet with blood. "Help me." Her voice is little more than a hoarse whisper.

But I recognize it the plea. I know without a doubt, that this was the sound that pulled me from my fitful sleep.

"I've got you, girl." I say in my most soothing voice. "How are you feeling?"

"My chest." She grimaces. "It aches."

That surprises me. "Your head? Your throat?"

She shakes her head. "My heart."

Rushing for my stethoscope, my gaze strays to the tea I brewed. When I was preparing it, I was thinking about the traditional rabies symptoms. Headache. Sore throat. Respiratory issues. She's saying vascular and that shifts part of my thinking. I could adjust my treatment. Herbs flutter through my thoughts like snowflakes. Coneflower. Lachesis.

Possibly even arsenic. I'd have to source arsenic first. I'm not sure where I'd get it, but I get the feeling someone in the pack would know. Briar would know.

"Doc." Dante grunts as he tries to hold her down.

She's seizing.

Rabbit's on his feet, rushing forward. "What's happening to her?"

"Don't fight her." I hurry back to the table, watching her limbs jerk against the loosened restraints. Now that her form has shifted, the restraints do little to hold her back. "Just be ready to catch her if she falls."

I can feel Rabbit's gaze burning into me before he turns his attention back to Angela. He circles around to her head, brushing her hair back even as her head turns side to side.

It's all happening so fast, too fast for my sleep-addled brain to keep up with. I should know what to do for her. But I'm a vet, I don't have training in dealing with human patients.

This is why I didn't want this responsibility. They are counting on me to take care of her, trusting her to me, and I'm frozen.

Her limbs flail so violently, at first we don't notice the change in length. The way they bend. She's on her way back to wolf form.

Dante notices first. "Get back."

My gaze flicks up to his face just as Angela shifts in a nightmarish twist of flesh and fur. She's dying, but her body and soul fight it. Faster than we can react, she twists in the restraints, knocking into all three of us. Head, muzzle, and limbs battering my body. Her clawed paws knock into my stomach with surprising strength and I stumble and fall. I'm just pulling to my feet when I hear a loud, percussive pop that makes my ears ring.

Sudden stillness fills the room, except for the high-pitched whine in my ears, it's silent.

Dante stands over Angela, his face pale and drawn.

And there's Rabbit, a firearm hanging from his limp fingertips. I don't need to look at Angela's body to know what I'll see. She's no longer struggling.

Rabbit ended it for her.

Angela's fight is over.

A pair of arms reach around me, lifting me to my feet. I look up, surprised to see Peter's face staring down at me in concern. His lips are moving, but I can't make out what he's saying. Slowly, like listening to someone speak underwater, his voice reaches my ears. The words rearrange themselves into sounds with meaning.

Andy's voice is the first to reach my ears. "Is anyone hurt?"

Rabbit huffs a broken laugh. He's slumped up against the counter, the gun discarded. His expression reminds me of a renaissance painting. One of the ones depicting hell. Tortured souls. I've never seen an expression of despair like that. It feels like someone has scooped my chest out.

Peter takes my face in his hands. "Are you injured?"

53.

I shake my head, not trusting myself to speak.

It's my fault. They put their faith in me, in my blind reaching, and we failed.

We move away from Angela's limp body. Peter takes me to one of the couches and sits with me cradled in his arms. I feel like I don't deserve this kind of tenderness. That's not justice. I failed Angela. She's gone and he's taking care of me?

Dante stays with Rabbit, crouching beside him, talking to him in a low, soothing voice.

Andy follows us to the couch, sitting on the edge of the seat. "She's okay?"

Peter's hands curl around my upper arm, my thigh. He peers down at me and I nod weakly.

He sucks in a deep breath, tightening his grip on me. I want to stay in the shelter of his arms, but it feels wrong.

Slipping out of Peter's arms, I forced myself to stand on wobbly legs.

Peter's fingers curl around my waist. "Zoey."

I gently twist my wrist out of his hand. "I need to take care of her body."

"No." He starts to stand. "Leave that to someone else."

"Who? Someone who knew and loved her? No. I'll clean her up and then the pack can take over."

He frowns. "That blood is probably contagious."

"I know." I glance back at the table, the floor. It's a disaster. "But it poses a risk to any of us. Someone needs to take care of it."

"Why you?"

Because this is my fault.

If I had known about the heart complications... If I had tweaked the treatment just a little...

But I got it wrong. Cleaning up my mess is the least I can do. "Why not me?"

Peter starts to argue, but his gaze falls on Andy. He takes a deep breath. "Be careful."

"I will."

Walking towards the exam area feels like walking towards an execution. The fact that we're in a basement starts to weigh down on me. It's like we're already buried underground. It's hard to breathe and every fiber in my being is screaming to run upstairs. Get fresh air. Feel the sun on my face.

But I force my feet to go towards Angela's body. Towards Rabbit who is now weeping and Dante who is trying and failing to comfort him. I find heavy lab coats in the cupboard, along with more gloves. Moving to the sink, I fill it with water so hot it steams. I dump bleach in and breathe in the vapors, hoping it can cleanse my body too. I feel absolutely wrecked, I can't imagine how the rest of the pack is going to take this loss.

Over the sound of the faucet and the water pouring from the tap, I can hear Rabbit's restrained moans. I can hear Andy's voice, too. "That was too close."

The sound of his baritone voice slips down my spine.

"We'll need to restrain them better next time." Peter says.

"There won't be a next time."

It takes an incredible amount of discipline to hold still, to not stare at Andy.

Peter's voice is familiar, something that I can hold onto. "What do you mean?"

Andy pauses. "I mean, next time, we go back to the old way."

"But Rabbit..."

"Rabbit was a fluke," Andy replies. "It's not unheard of for people to recover."

"It's happened, but it's rare." Peter's voice is pulled taut. "And you know that."

Andy grunts in response. "Next time, we don't hesitate. I'm not risking any more pack members."

There's a finality in his voice—an alpha tone that even I recognize. Peter drops the issue because he has no other choice. He has to recognize pack order. It's the way things work.

My chest feels like it's collapsing. I struggle to process Andy's words. I didn't know it was possible to recover from the virus—I assumed it was a death sentence the same way progressed rabies is a death sentence. If there was even a sliver of a hope that a pack mate could survive Vargulfism, why wouldn't they let it play out every time? My mind is supplying possible answers, but nothing sticks. Anger and dread swirl together in my stomach, but I force myself to focus on cleaning up.

The water in the sink turns pink before I drain it and start over. I've been feeling unsure of myself from the moment they asked for my help. But I know, I just *know*, that Rabbit wouldn't have recovered without that elixir. Something, some deep ancestral root, guided my hands. I'm starting to believe that miracles are possible. Magic is possible.

That's what makes it doubly frustrating that it didn't work for Angela.

I glance at her limp form, forcing myself to scan the injuries to her body. They're severe. Rabbit was in bad shape when they brought him in, but Angela was already hanging by a thread. We'll never know if it was the virus or the wounds that defeated her body. But there's still a chance my treatment works.

Andy's doubt only fuels me. I'm certain I can fix this, but I need their faith if I'm ever going to try again. If it's even remotely possible that I hold the key to defeating this virus once and for all, I have to try.

I'm just not sure if they'll let me.

Peter joins me, exhaustion evident in the strained lines of his shoulders. His expression. "You've done enough, Zoey. Let them take over."

I glance over, noticing Dante and Dusty standing nearby.

I step back, watching them carefully bundle Angela's wolf form into a heavy blanket.

"What will they do with her?"

Peter keeps his voice low. "She'll be cremated. And returned to her family."

"Her family?"

He nods, watching Dante and Dusty carry Angela upstairs, Rabbit on their heels. "She was from Wyoming."

"Did her family know about her?"

"Yes." He pauses, reading my expression. "Some families can handle our secret. Hers was one of the good ones."

He nods his head towards the stairs, and I follow behind him. "Rabbit and I are going to return the ashes to Wyoming. Will you come with?"

I want to cling to him. I don't want to be left behind without his protection.

But I know I can't.

I have no choice but to stay.

54.

Angela's family lives four hours away. By early afternoon, Peter and Rabbit are climbing onto their bikes. Rabbit carefully tucks a black box into his saddle bag—her ashes. I don't ask how they managed to have her cremated so quickly, and on a Saturday to boot. In the grand scheme of things, it doesn't seem that important. At least a dozen pack members have turned out to escort her ashes back home. Peter comes to stand in front of me, putting his hands on my hips. "Sure you don't want to come along?"

I shake my head, keeping my voice gentle. "This is pack business."

His eyes scan my face, trying to read between the lines. Leaning forward, he presses a kiss to the top of my head and pulls me into a tight hug. "The funeral is tomorrow. We'll be back by late Monday."

I nod, whistling to call Baby over.

Baby leans against my leg and I rest my hand on his head. We watch as the solemn progression rumbles up the steep drive way. We stand there for a long time, Baby and I, listening to the bikes for as long as I can. When the last rumble dies away, I glance at the pine woods and I swear they're watching me back. The rogue wolf is gone. As far as we know, the woods are safe again. But with the pack completely gone, it feels like the hills have lost their guardians.

Cleo Mercer

Every last pack member will be at Angela's funeral, leaving their mountain unguarded. No one seems concerned with that when there's a fallen comrade to honor. There's no enemies out there. No dark forces. But now that the door to the paranormal world has been cracked, I can't help but wonder what else might be out there. Feeling like my skin is itching, I pat Baby's head. "Let's go home."

A crate sits abandoned on the porch. Partially consumed bottles of potion fill it like a failed science experiment. I heft it and carry it to my SUV. Shoving it in the back, I help Baby inside and sit behind the wheel. It's so quiet.

Too quiet.

I hit the road, cranking up the radio louder than I usually like, but even that can't seem to drown out the strange silence that presses down on me with almost physical pressure. I turn the wheel, easing around a bend and am reminded of the times I've taken that same turn on the back of Peter's bike.

That's it. That's the silence I'm noticing.

There is usually a constant beat of a drum, his strong heart, thrumming in the back of my mind. I didn't realize how familiar I had gotten with it. Now that it's gone, it feels like a loss. The feeling gets worse and worse with each passing minute. It occurs to me that the feeling might be getting worse because we're getting farther away from each other.

Which means this homesickness I'm feeling is only going to get worse. Just add it to the list.

My skin itches again, this time almost throbbing. I pull up to Strawberry Moon, finally taking the opportunity to tug the sleeve back on my scrubs.

Two angry welts no longer than my thumb slash across my upper arm. They're scratches, really, even if they were made with canines.

She only just managed to break my skin. But where Angela's fangs pierced my skin, the swelling is spreading. Streaking in red curling lines.

I couldn't tell them. Not after hearing that they're back to their old policies.

I'm going to beat this virus once and for all.

My heartrate flutters as fear crawls its way up my throat. I wish Peter were here.

I'm glad he's not.

If he was, he'd hear my heartbeat and then he'd know something was wrong.

He's already demonstrated that he would battle his own pack to protect me. If he knew what I was planning to face, it would turn into a one-man war. I couldn't let him do that.

Sucking a deep breath, I straighten my spine and let myself out of the SUV. Pulling my cell out, I make two calls.

One to Hitch.

The second, to Briar. I'm forced to leave a message.

I'm in the kitchen, peering over Maria's notes when I hear wheels on gravel. Baby perks up, leading the way.

I called Hitch to ask him to dogsit for Baby. I had a bullshit excuse ready and everything. But as I stand in the doorway, something very obvious suddenly occurs to me.

Angela bit me. In wolf form.

I thought I was just battling the vargulf virus. That alone was scary enough.

But if I've been bitten by a werewolf, that means I might be battling the wolf as well.

Hitch smiles as he crosses the driveway, but his grin slips as he gets close. "What's wrong?"

I try to smile. "Nothing, my mind's just wandering."

He comes close, filling my nose with the scent of his soap, and puts a steadying hand on my shoulder. "You need to sit."

Cleo Mercer

I try to bat his hand away, but realize I'm feeling lightheaded. Heaving a sigh, I ease down onto the porch. I could take him inside, but then he might stay. The longer he stays, the closer he could get to my secret.

55.

Hitch sits down next to me, pulling back far enough to peer down at me. "Don't take this the wrong way, but you don't look good."

A headache is starting to grip the base of my head. "I'm not feeling too good, if I'm honest. Thanks for taking Baby for me."

He shrugs. "Of course."

We sit in silence for a few moments. I'm cataloging the ingredients I need to pack up. The plans have shifted. I thought I could lock myself in the house, work in my own kitchen. But I wasn't thinking far ahead enough. I wasn't thinking about the fact that I could turn violent. Strawberry Moon isn't going to cut it. I need the pack's headquarters. I need their padded holding cells.

A shiver works its way down my spine and Hitch notices. "I think you need to go to the hospital."

I shake my head. "It's just allergies."

He huffs a skeptical laugh at that. "I've never seen allergies that looked like that. You're pale. Sweating and shivering. Seems like a bad combination."

"I just need some rest."

He stands up, offering me his hand. "And you will. You'll get plenty of rest in the hospital."

"Hitch... that's very sweet, but I'm not going anywhere."

He frowns. "I'm not trying to be sweet."

It's the second time he's said something like that to me. We stare at each other for a few heartbeats. His eyebrows twitch, then crease together in a frown. "This has to do with the pack."

My shoulders hitch until I remember that the pack publicly refers to itself as a pack. I force a smile onto my face. "I got allergies from my mother's side."

He doesn't return my grin. "Tell me."

"There's nothing to tell."

He runs a hand over the scruff on his jaw. "If you're in trouble, Zoey, you need to let me know. Let me help you."

My head is really starting to pound. "I have troubles, but not the kind you're thinking of."

"You have no idea what I'm thinking of."

There's a tone in his voice that catches my attention. I peer up at his strange, amber eyes. "Okay, Officer Florean. Surprise me. What are you thinking of?"

He pauses, holding my gaze. "Wolves."

The blood leaves my head all at once and I'm feeling lightheaded again. Thank God I'm already sitting down.

He comes down on one knee. "That's it, isn't it? The pack... don't tell me... were you bitten?"

I try to focus on his eyes. "You know?"

He tips his head slightly. "This is my county. Nothing goes on that I don't know about."

"But you know about them?"

His gaze turns towards the dark forest. "That they're werewolves?"

The word seems to plunk down between us, too dark and thorny for such a bright afternoon.

He puts a hand on my knee. "Were you bitten?"

"Are you a wolf?"

He shakes his head. "As human as they come."

"Are you going to turn them in to the authorities?"

He huffs a laugh at that. "Baby, I am the authority."

"And you're not going to call the marines or something?"

He shakes his head. "I don't like them. I've made that clear, but they've got a right to be here as much as anyone does."

"You weren't shocked to learn about them?"

He shakes his head. "I'm the third generation of Floreans to serve these hills. My grandfather told me about those wolves long before I ever pinned a star to my chest. And he told me my job was to protect them just like I would any living being. But Zoey... were you bitten?"

I swallow hard. With a feeling like I'm giving in to something, I pull my sleeve back and show him.

A tendon ticks in his jaw as he stares at the festering cuts. His gaze pulls up to mine and I find myself staring at those warm brown eyes, wondering just how far I can trust him.

He holds my gaze. "Does the pack know?"

I shake my head. "They can't."

"They need to know, Zoey. They'll help you through this. You shouldn't be alone right now."

"I can't tell them." I cover the bite mark up. "It wasn't just any wolf, it was a rabid wolf."

He shakes his head, not understanding. "Okay?"

"If you're bitten by a rabid wolf... it's a death sentence."

"A death sentence?"

I can't stand to look at him anymore. I study the mossy shingles on the barn's roof. After a while, I swallow hard. "They'd execute me."

He moves to sit at my side again. "Okay. We won't tell them, then."

"We?"

He shoots me a sidelong glance. "If you think I'm going to let a new wolf roam my hills on her own, you're dead wrong. I'm sticking with you until I know you're not a threat."

A tired smirk tugs at the right side of my lips. "How sweet."

He barks a short, dry laugh. "I guess you've got me figured out."

"I've got a few days to figure this out. The pack is in Wyoming for Angela's funeral."

I tell him the story, only stumbling once or twice over my words. When the tale finally dries up, we sit in silence, watching the pines at the edge of my property.

He glances at me. "So, what's the plan?"

"I'm going to work on a cure." I swallow down a bubble of panic. "And it will work or it won't."

56.

Hitch agrees to support my plan with one exception. He doesn't like the idea of locking myself in the wolf's den. We search Strawberry Moon, looking for alternatives. The basement could potentially work, but Hitch thinks it's too damp and dark. We look in the barn next, realizing that one of the stalls was reinforced for horses. Big ones, apparently, because the last stall is reinforced with steel beams.

Maria was full of secrets and I can only guess what the backstory was for this stall.

Hitch helps me set up a makeshift kitchen in the barn, using an old camp stove and the exam table as my work surface. With every passing moment, my health dips. If this was another day, I would assume I really did have allergies. It reminds me of hay fever.

But the itchy skin, the clogged throat, only add to my sense of urgency. The clock is ticking. I ransack Maria's hidden chest again. I find a small vial of arsenic, mercy of mercies, but it won't be enough for a full regimen of treatments.

Hitch watches me line a paltry collection of herbs up on the counter in the clinic's exam room. He tilts his head. "Do you have what you need?"

I suck in a shaky breath. "It will have to do."

He comes closer. "What are you missing?"

213

I glance up at him. "You don't happen to have a big jar of arsenic on hand, do you?"

He starts to smile, frowning when he realizes I'm serious. "Not that I know of."

I start piling the half-empty jars into a basket. "I need coneflower and Lachesis, too." I pause. "Is there a health foods store in Hill City?"

He leans a hip against the counter. "The closest thing we have is a gas station with a sad supply of potato chips and skittles." He pauses, thinking. "There's one in Rapid City."

That's forty-five minutes away. A ninety-minute round trip.

He pushes upright. "Do you need those things?"

I nod.

"Okay. We'll get you set up and secure and then I'll head out."

I'm sure the pack would be furious to know that I'm collaborating with a human on werewolf business. Peter will be irate. But if I don't survive, none of it matters.

Besides, if I had told them, they would have killed me. Andy said so himself.

They didn't really leave me with much of a choice.

Swallowing hard, I march back outside and Hitch locks me into the reinforced stall. We've swept all the straw out, revealing a concrete floor beneath.

He carries my camping stove into the stall and peers up at the barn's arched ceiling. "Normally, I would caution against using a portable stove indoors. We've got a good amount of airflow, though."

With both doors to the barn open and every window, there's a constant breeze toying with my hair.

He pauses by the stall door. "Are you sure you're going to be okay?"

I look at him, considering my response.

The short answer is *no*. I'm not going to be okay. Even if I do survive the vargulf virus, I might not be human anymore.

He seems to register that response in my eyes. With a sharp nod, he swings the door shut and locks it. "I'll be back in two hours."

Whistling for Baby to follow, he walks away.

I watch him retreat, listening to the sound of his boots on gravel, then the sound of his patrol car starting up. When that sound fades, too, I find myself alone again.

Fear squeezes the back of my neck, making my aching head throb. I sit down, spreading Maria's notes out on the floor. My own notes are mixed in with hers now, adding my own observations and theories to hers. It's almost like I can feel her spirit looking over my shoulder. It gives me the boost of strength I need. With a deep breath, I find my mortar and pestle.

I'm grinding herbs when my phone rings.

For a split second, I imagine its Peter. But he's only been gone a few hours.

Snatching my phone, a pulse of nerves blasts through me when I see her name. She's using the video call feature. My finger hovers over the button for a second before I take the call. Her image fills the screen. Black hair dyed red at the tips. Her cherry red lips match. She's beautiful and elegant in ways I could never aspire to.

"Briar."

"Hi, honey. I got your message." Her tone is calm but stretched at the edges. I didn't tell her much in my message, but she knows something is up.

"Thanks for calling me back. I just have a few quick questions."

"I'm glad you reached out. What's up?"

I hesitate, wondering how much to tell her. "Do you have any healers in your community?"

215

Cleo Mercer

"My coven?"

That's the word. Coven. I nod.

Her expression becomes guarded. "I don't really interact with my coven anymore, but I do have a few contacts."

"I need help."

57.

Briar tilts her head, nibbling her lower lip as she watches me from her side of the screen. "What do you need help with?"

"I'm working on a cure for Vargulfism."

Her eyebrows fly up. "You are?" There's a guarded skepticism in her tone that she doesn't quite cover. It's the same tone as the response I got from the Black Hills pack. It's like they want to hope, but recognize that the foe is too big to take on.

I hesitate, unsure of how much I should share. I don't know what Andy has relayed to their pack.

"Baby, if it's pack knowledge, it's Barone's knowledge. He's their pack alpha." She pauses, seeming to choose her words carefully. "We heard about Angela. Barone flew out for the funeral."

That surprises me. "He did?"

"Of course. He cares about each and every wolf in the region. Angela was a special person. I didn't know her very well, but everyone around here is pretty wrecked when we got the news."

"So, you knew about Rabbit, too?"

"Rabbit?" She tenses. "Is he okay?"

"He's fine." I fiddle with the pile of herbs in front of me. "He was the vargulf's first victim."

Briar frowns, tilting her head. "But he's okay?"

"Yes. Because… It might have been a fluke, but I found the old vet's notes and I combined that with the wisdom my grandma passed along, and I think I might have found a cure." I take a breath, realizing the words are tumbling out faster than my thoughts can keep up with.

"You found a cure?"

I pause. "Yes. I think so. But it didn't work for Angela."

"Oh." There's a creeping understanding pinching her words. Like she knows where this is going.

"But I think it didn't work because her wounds were too severe. I'd need to test it again, but I don't have the ingredients I need. And I wanted to bounce my ideas off another healer, see if they agree."

"Zoey? Are you okay?"

A hysterical laugh slips past my lips before I can tamp them down. "I'm fine."

"Then why are you in a jail cell? Where's Andy? And Peter?"

"It's not a jail cell." I angle the camera so she can see the barn. "It's a horse stall. And they're at the funeral."

"That doesn't explain why you're camped out in a horse stall." She pauses, eyebrows flying up. "You were bitten."

I don't reply.

"Oh my God. Oh, Zoey. Do they know? Of course not. They would never leave you. You shouldn't be alone, honey. I never made the change, I was one of those cradle wolves, but it's not pretty, honey. You wouldn't want to do it alone."

"They can't know." I cut across her.

She pulls up short. "They need to know."

"Then tell them after the fact. Either I'll survive it, or I won't." I should never have called her. The moment she ends our call, she'll call Andy and then it's game over.

"Why can't they know, Zoey?"

"Because I was infected by a vargulf."

She's quiet, as the weight of the information settles in—as she hears of my death sentence.

"Please don't tell them, Briar. I just need time. A day... two tops. By the time they return, I'll either be recovered or dead. But if they come back now, I'll just be dead. You know that."

She nods. "I know. You're right."

"And I'm not alone. There's a local here who knows about the pack. He's the one who locked me up."

She doesn't seem as surprised to learn that a local knows about the pack as I would expect.

"Can you trust him?" she asks.

I nod. "With my life. Yes."

"Okay." She takes a deep breath. "I won't tell them. Not yet."

"Thank you. Thank you, Briar."

"You've got one day."

"Okay. That's fair. If things aren't turning around by then..."

"What do you need from me?"

I almost sob in relief. "I'm short a few ingredients. Hitch went to track down the Lachesis and coneflower. I have a theory about arsenic, but I don't have enough in my supply to test it out."

Briar listens to my hypothesis, and Angela's final symptoms, taking notes while I talk.

"I've got a friend I can bounce this idea off of," She says, setting the note pad aside. "And I might be able to track down some of those ingredients. I know some Chicago coven expats living in Rapid City."

"Hitch is in Rapid City right now."

She nods. "Okay. I'll start there, see if we can arrange a meeting."

Tears are threatening to spring from my eyes, but I can't start feeling sorry for myself. Not yet. "Thanks, Briar."

Cleo Mercer

She gives me a smile. "Of course. Us witches have to stick together."

58.

The first hour passes with me chanting the mantra: I'm fine. I'm holding steady.

But it's a wish not a reality.

The reality is, I'm getting sicker and sicker. My joints begin to ache, and my headache makes it almost impossible to focus. The fever has to be the worst part of all. It feels like I'm burning up. My clothes itch and burn against my skin. It's all I can do to hold it together. I read my notes and carefully prepare the elixir's ingredients with shaking fingers.

When my phone rings again, it almost feels like a cosmic joke. I'm possibly dying and if that's the case, there's half a dozen people I should be talking to. And the person who's calling wouldn't make that list.

It's my ex, Dax, of all people. I can't begin to guess what he wants. He's a proud man, one more inclined to cut someone off than apologize. When he's 'done' with someone, be it friend or family, he's just done. That's it. No second chances. Our breakup came as a surprise to him, but despite two years together, he didn't put up much of a fight. He never called. Certainly not to grovel or ask me to come back. I don't know if he's even aware I left St. Louis. But there he is, trying to talk to me on the phone. I can't begin to imagine what he would want, but I don't have the time or the bandwidth to deal with an ex.

Cleo Mercer

When I hear car tires on gravel, I freeze, listening. Baby's bark rings out across the lot and I sob in relief. I need water. And a fan.

Baby appears first, nails clicking on the floor. He stops outside the stall, whining as he peers at me. Hitch is right behind him, a Natural Grocer's sack in one arm, a purple bag in the other with the words "*Vape Witch*" emblazoned on it. "You have some strange friends."

I sigh in relief. "Briar came through."

He nods, opening the door. I climb to my feet, and he hands me the purple bag. "I asked what was in it and they said it would be best if I didn't ask questions."

I smile at that, trying to picture straight-laced Hitch accepting a bag from a stranger. My laughter fades. "You couldn't get in trouble for this, could you?"

He leans against the stall's doorway, watching me with a neutral expression. "I was careful."

"I can fend for myself. I don't want to drag you into anything."

"If it's happening in my county, I'm already involved. Nobody is making me do anything I don't want to do." He pauses. "How are you feeling?"

I shake my head, avoiding eye contact as I lay the coneflower and Lachesis out.

"Zoey?"

I force myself to look at him. "I'll be better once I can start taking these treatments."

He nods. Leaving the stall door open, he sits down just outside, leaning up against an opposite stall. Baby takes up a post beside him, eventually laying his head on Hitch's thigh. They watch me in silence as I force my heavy fingers to mix herbs, to simmer and stir. I barely have the capacity to do this much. Small talk isn't something I can pull off and thankfully, Hitch is content to sit and observe in silence. They watch me carefully meter the tincture out into six jars.

I take the first dose immediately. It tastes like a strong herbal tea. Bitter and grassy.

I line the jars up and pass them to Hitch. "As long as I'm in this body, you can give me these. Force my mouth open if you have to. But if I change into a...wolf... just lock me in and don't come anywhere near me."

He studies the row of jars for a few moments, before looking at me. "Are you hungry?"

I huff a surprised laugh. "No."

"Could you force something down? Soup?"

I tip my head. "Soup, maybe."

"If you can eat, you should. You need to keep up your strength."

He's right about that. My strength is waning, slipping away like sand in an hour glass. With the solution brewed, I finally allow myself to rest. Backing up to a wall, I let my legs splay out in front of me. I stare at my worn tennis shoes. My blue scrubs. They seem so ordinary. I can't believe I ever took something like the ordinary for granted. The ability to go for a walk. To live and work and play. But now, if things don't go my way, I might only have hours on my side.

It's hard to keep my eyes open, to fend off the virus taking hold in my body. I stare at my toes, wondering which virus is winning, the vargulf virus, or lycanthropy—the werewolf virus. Maybe they're banding together, because with each passing moment, it's getting harder to keep my head above the surface.

All I want to do is lay down. I need the rest, but with the way I'm feeling, I'm not sure I would wake up again.

Not as myself, anyway.

When Hitch comes back with the soup, I force myself to eat half of it. It fills my stomach, but does nothing to recharge my fading lifeforce. There's a way to cheat, to buy myself time, but I hate to ask for yet another favor.

Cleo Mercer

Pain lances out through my chest like forking lightning. This is what Angela described near the end. "Hitch." I clear my throat. "Can I borrow some of your energy?"

He makes eye contact, one side of his lips quirking up.

I lick dry lips. "I mean that literally. Can I siphon off some of your energy?"

"How?"

"By touching your arm or hand."

He tilts his head. "Werewolves can do that?"

I bite my lip. "Werewolves can't, but witches can."

•

59.

Hitch laughs at that, scrubbing a hand over his jaw before rising to his feet. He crosses into my stall, squatting down beside me. After a beat, he holds out his hand.

I look up at him, keeping my hands pressed beneath my thighs. "Are you sure? You're not going to ask if it will age you? Turn your hair gray or give you wrinkles?"

"Will it?" He's got a glimmer of a smile in his eyes. It's the expression of a man who's had one too many surprises for one day.

"No."

"Then, go ahead."

Taking a breath, I tentatively reach out and brush my fingers over his palm. It's warm and callused. I look up at his face right before I start borrowing from him, which is a mistake, because something passes through his eyes that looks suspiciously like affection. Like more than affection.

Feeling guilty and confused, but mostly, tired, I close my eyes and focus on finding his energy. I'm careful to only sip, but even that small amount is renewing. Hitch's energy is all courage and determination. It's exactly what I need. Letting my eyelids flutter open, I look up at him. He's looking back at me with hooded eyes.

"Okay?" I ask, leaning back.

"Did it work?"

Cleo Mercer

I sigh. "Yes. I don't feel like I'm drowning anymore. How about you? Do you feel okay?"

He returns to his spot on the opposite side, easing to a seated position. "I feel oddly relaxed. Whatever it is you do, you should charge admission."

I smile, exhausted. "I'll consider that."

"You should rest."

I let my eyes fall shut. "I think I can now."

Funny, that a boost in energy would make me feel like I should take a nap. But before, I felt so close to the edge, that if I closed my eyes, I wouldn't open them again.

Now, I feel like rest might help. Between that and the elixir working its way through my system, I might just have a fighting chance.

"Close your eyes, Zoey. I'll keep watch."

I obediently close my eyes, letting my head rest on the wall behind me. "Hitch?"

"Yeah, Zoey?"

"Thanks."

He's quiet for a while. "Whatever you need, Zoey. You only have to ask."

With his words echoing around in my head, I fall head first into a deep sleep.

When I hear voices, I claw my way back to the surface. It takes me a second to acclimate, to remember where I am. The stall in the barn. I crane my head towards the open doorways. It's dark. A few hours must have passed.

There's two men arguing outside—the voices that woke me.

And there's something else.

The deep, familiar racing of a heart. It's pounding so fast, I'm afraid it might break.

And it means only one thing, Peter is back.

He shouldn't be here. He should be in Wyoming for the funeral.

I listen carefully for the sound of more bikes, other voices. But it's just Hitch and Peter.

They're arguing.

"What's wrong with her?" Peter's voice cuts through the night air.

Hitch's voice is like the crack of a whip. "That's far enough, Mackavoy."

Peter repeats his initial question, this time his voice has dropped an octave. "What's wrong with her?"

"You would know if you hadn't left her alone."

There's a few tense seconds. "Get the fuck out of my way, Florean. You're not in uniform and I won't hesitate to take you down if you keep standing between me and my woman."

A few more beats of silence. I push upright, head swimming. When the dizziness abates, I crawl up to my knees, then shakily get to my feet. I'm straining my ears, desperate to know what's going on, hating this cage. Hating the necessity of this cage.

Peter laughs. "You wouldn't dare."

The unmistakable sound of the safety on a gun being drawn. Hitch's voice is hard. "I know what your kind will do with her. A mercy kill, right? If you want her, you'll have to come through me."

"A mercy kill? Get out of my fucking way."

Standing by the stall's locked doors, I wrap my fingers around the bars. I'm struggling to find my voice. "No!" I cry out, to what, I'm not sure. But my voice comes out as a croak.

Hitch's voice is percussive, cutting through time and space. "Stop right there!"

Boots on gravel and then a sharp pop. The sound of yet another gun being fired.

I hate guns. Have always hated guns.

First Angela. And now… Peter? Hitch?

227

"No!" I shout again, this time my voice obeys me. "Hitch! What's happening?"

There's a long silence and gasping breaths.

I rattle the bars on the stall. "Hitch! Peter!"

"Shit." Hitch mutters. "You stubborn bastard."

Sobbing, I cast about for Peter's heartbeat and find it, racing at an unnaturally fast pace.

"You shot me." Peter's tone is accusatory.

Hitch huffs a dry laugh. "I did warn you."

"You fucking shot me."

"You'll live."

"You won't, not for long."

There's the sound of boots scraping on gravel and then they come into sight. Hitch has Peter's arm thrown over his shoulder. "I ought to kill you for that."

Hitch grunts under Peter's weight. "Strong words from a man who can't lift his arm."

"The other arm works just fine." Peter's words dry up when he spots me standing at the locked stall gate. "Zoey!"

He has blood blossoming out over his shoulder, soaking his gray t-shirt, but he's looking at me with a stricken expression on his face.

I crane my neck to try to see his wound better. "You're bleeding."

"You're locked up." He glares at Hitch. "Why is she locked up?"

"I asked him to do it." My knuckles are white from gripping the bars so tightly.

"Why?" But I can tell from his tortured expression that he knows the answer to that question.

"She's been infected." Hitch helps him up towards the door.

Peter winces, shaking Hitch off. "Let me in."

I pull my gaze away from him, looking squarely at Hitch. "No."

Peter pushes Hitch's hands away. "You can't infect me, Zoey. I've already got the virus."

I swallow and it feels like swallowing broken glass. "Not this one, you haven't."

Peter stares at me, stumbling closer, he wraps his fingers around mine and we look at each other through the bars. "Let me in, anyway."

"No." I whisper.

60.

Peter tries to peer at me through the bars, his eyes are roving my body searching for injuries. "Are you badly hurt? When did this happen?" He studies my expression. Understanding dawns in his eyes. "It happened when everyone was still here."

I nod.

His face falls. "Was it the rogue wolf?"

I consider lying, but the hesitation is long enough to hint at the truth.

His voice is haggard. "Angela."

When I don't correct him, he knows it was her. He squeezes his eyes shut, heartrate dipping before he looks at me again. "You didn't tell me?"

"I didn't want to make you choose."

"You didn't have a right to make that decision for me."

Hitch crosses his arms over his chest. "Maybe she didn't want to face the executioners."

Peter rounds on him, wincing at the pain in his bleeding shoulder. "What the fuck do you know about it?"

"More than you can guess."

Peter's gaze flicks back to mine. "You told him?"

I shake my head. "He knew already."

Hitch studies Peter's shoulder. "You better take care of that wound, Pretty Boy. Before you bleed out." Hitch turns to look at me. "I'm not much with a needle and thread. Think you can sew him back together?"

I nod. "Yes. You can open the gate, Hitch. I'm not an immediate threat. Not yet."

Hitch opens the gate, stepping back. "You got everything you might need in your clinic?"

I rattle off a list of supplies and we both watch his retreating back. Peter turns back to me and the space between us feels like it stretches for miles. "Why didn't you trust me?"

My heart twists in my chest. "I do trust you."

"Just not enough to tell me you'd been bit." He frowns. "Do you have any idea how dangerous that was?"

"I'm quite aware."

"Why didn't you tell me?"

I wish I was in his arms, his fingers threading through my hair. Maybe he could ease the pounding of my headache. Instead, I ball my fingers into a fist. "I heard what Andy said. About the next vargulf. I won't go docilely to my end, Peter. I'm going to fight. I want to fight, and Andy wouldn't have let me. And you know it."

"I don't know anything." Peter hisses. "You need to give Andy more credit. He was upset. We'd just lost a good friend. She was like a sister to us."

"Exactly. How would it have looked if you stayed behind instead of going to her funeral?" I pause. "Why are you back, anyway?"

"I felt it in your heartbeat. I knew something was wrong."

"You could feel me from that far away? I lost touch with you after a few minutes."

"You're not a wolf."

"Not yet, anyway."

He doesn't smile at that joke and Hitch returns with an armful of supplies. Peter finally steps closer, brushing past me as he comes to sit in the middle of the stall. I want to curl up in his lap, but I hold back. He scans my temporary

231

lodging, making note of the camp stove and the empty pot. "Were you able to make more medicine?"

I nod, taking the supplies from Hitch before joining him on the floor. "I adjusted it, too. Angela had chest pains. I didn't think about the vascular aspect when I made the first treatments."

"You improved it?"

I shrug, peeling his shirt back. "Time will tell."

We awkwardly struggle to take his shirt off, first his left arm. We pass the shirt over his head and I carefully slide it down his right arm. He's got blood streaking down his tattooed chest, his arm. The actual site itself is a ragged hole, but the bleeding has slowed down. It looks like the bullet passed clean through his body. He watches me in silence as I cleanse his wound and sew him back up. Hitch paces outside the stall for a few minutes before offering to take Baby up to the house for more food and water.

Peter watches him go. "You didn't trust me, but you trusted Hitch."

I bandage him up, studying his profile. "I didn't trust him with anything, he guessed on his own. He said he's known about the pack for a long time. Said his father and grandfather knew, too."

That catches Peter's attention. He frowns, thinking that over. "I guess I always wondered why the county sheriff's department never hassled us more. God knows we give them plenty of reasons to."

With Peter's wound bandaged, I ease back. My headache and lightheadedness have only grown over the last few hours. I scoot back, leaning against the barn's wall.

Peter comes closer, sitting next to me. He takes my hand and wraps it with both of his. "Borrow my energy."

"You just got shot."

"You're fending off vargulfism."

I give him a weak smile. "And lycanthropy."

He mirrors my smile. "And lycanthropy."

"I can't borrow from you. I need to know if my treatment works. We can't intervene with magic."

"Fuck that. We need to keep you alive, no matter what."

I sigh, tipping my head back. I could tell him that I already borrowed from Hitch. But he's already a little jealous about Hitch, I don't want to add fuel to the fire.

He knows what it feels like when I borrow energy from him. I can't fake it and he seems determined to give me what he can. Closing my eyes, I let his familiar energy roll over me, taking the smallest amount, but just enough to satisfy him.

He sighs like he was holding his breath and finally, *finally*, takes me into his arms.

61.

Hitch and Peter work out shifts to watch over me.

Peter takes the first shift, mostly because he refuses to leave my side. Hitch reluctantly shuts us both inside the stall before going off in search of the saddle blankets I told him about. He drags them back setting up a makeshift bed in the stall opposite mine.

Peter coaxes me into laying my head on his lap. His fingers lace through my hair, rubbing soothing circles across my pounding temples. I take his free hand in mine, weaving our fingers together. His heartbeat is steady and familiar. It lulls me to sleep.

The next time I wake up, my head is resting on a pile of blankets. I squint at the windows. Pale, pink light filters through them. Sunrise, then.

My head is pounding even worse than before. I pause, listening, but it's hard to hear much over the blood pulsing in my ears.

They're there, just within range. Peter and Hitch having a low, tense conversation.

Peter's voice is haggard with exhaustion. "We're not forcing anything down her throat."

Hitch's response is exasperated, like they've been arguing the same point for a while. "She said to force her to take the treatment no matter what."

"I'm up." I call out, wincing as the effort sends another stabbing pain through my temples. I force myself upright, but the sudden movement gives me a wave of vertigo. It takes everything I have not to throw up.

When I force my eyes open, Hitch and Peter are squatting next to me. Peter has a cup with the tincture in it. "Can you swallow?"

I swallow my own spit and it feels like swallowing razor blades. I nod. "Yes. I can still swallow."

He eases down next to me, putting one arm around my back. Holding the glass for me, he lets me guide it to my mouth and watches me closely while I swallow the tincture sip by sip.

It seems like every focus is trained on this one, silly task, but then we hear tires on gravel.

Baby barking from the yard.

Peter and Hitch look at each other. Hitch shakes his head to say he doesn't know who we've got coming.

Peter turns to look at me and I shake my head, too.

Hitch climbs to his feet. "I'll go check."

Peter stays by my side, I can feel his body vibrating with the need to investigate. Hitch returns quickly, looking directly at Peter. "I think you better come out here."

There's no need, though, because Briar followed him right into the barn. "Where is she?"

She strides right past my stall before backing up. She looks me over with disapproval in her eyes. "Oh, honey. They've got you in the barn?"

I try to sit taller in the protective circle of Peter's arms, but I'm too exhausted. "My choice." I nod towards the steel beams stretching overhead. "It's reinforced."

Peter's head pivots towards the barn door. Moments later, two more men stride into view. The first is a tall Thor-look alike. Shaggy blonde hair, kind blue eyes. Massive, massive shoulders.

The second man I recognize. Lennon Accetti. St. Louis business tycoon, and apparently, also one of the top dogs in a werewolf crime syndicate. He grins at me. "How you doin', kid?"

Thank God at least one person realizes pity isn't going to make me feel better. I give him a weak smile. "Not great."

"Where is she?" That's yet another familiar voice I could go a decade without hearing and not miss it. I'm hoping it's just the virus causing me to hallucinate, but when Dax comes into view, I swallow wrong and start coughing. "You're all seeing him, too, right?"

Dax can hold his own next to the werewolves, he's easily as tall and athletic. If someone had to look at all three St. Louis guys, they would probably take one look at his crooked nose and neck tattoos and figure he was the werewolf.

Briar rolls her eyes. "My mistake for mentioning your name while Dax was with Lennon."

Lennon shrugs. "You have a very determined friend."

"What's wrong with her?" Dax asks, staring down at me and Peter with a frown. He's vibrating with anger. "What's wrong with you people? She should be at the hospital. Babe, come with me. I'm going to get you help."

Dax starts to move forward, but Lennon puts a hand on his shoulder to stop him. He shrugs Lennon's hand off with a growl. "She needs to go to the hospital."

The first man, the blonde giant eases Dax back. "If she's going anywhere, it's to a more secure facility."

Dax whirls on him. "You're going to lock her up? Look at her, she can barely keep her head up."

Peter's arm tightens around my waist. "She's staying here, Tate."

The blonde man, Tate, turns to look at him. "We just want what's best for Zoey."

Peter's voice rumbles against my back. "What's best for Zoey is to stay right here. With me."

"Is she safest here?" Tate tilts his head. "We're fully aware of the Black Hills pack's policy towards vargulfs."

Peter tenses at my side. "And I'm fully aware of your little lab and coterie of human guinea pigs. You're not turning her into a lab rat."

Lennon leans on the side of the stall gate. Dax has been watching Tate and Peter argue like he's at a tennis match. His gaze lands on Peter. "I agree with the tattooed guy. She's staying here."

Lennon laughs at that. "You have no say in this one, brother."

I see what's coming only because I've been to dozens of Dax's boxing matches. I know his secret tells, even if some of the best boxers can't spot them. Apparently, that includes werewolves because Lennon doesn't notice the tick in Dax's jaw. His hand balls into a fist and cuts through the air like an arc of light.

His fist connects with Lennon's jaw and all hell breaks loose.

62.

Lennon wasn't braced for the hit, so it knocks him back a step. When he finds his footing, his easy-going grin is long gone and he has murder in his eyes. He barrels into Dax, taking him back several steps, crashing into Tate. All three men stumble to the side, nearly knocking into Briar. Hitch is there to shield her from flailing limbs and lowered shoulders.

Dax might have one of the meanest, fastest right hooks in the boxing world, but he can't hold a candle to a werewolf. Any edge he gained with the element of surprise is quickly turned upside down and he finds himself literally facedown on the barn floor. Lennon has his knee pressed between Dax's shoulder blades. His expression is one of barely contained fury. He lowers his head so that his lips are by Dax's ear. "Don't. Move."

Dax growls, turning his head so that he can look directly at me. "Don't worry, babe. I won't let them take you anywhere."

Briar laughs at that, gingerly stepping around him. She glides into the stall, lowering to her haunches beside me. This girl is beautiful. There's something dangerous and mysterious about her. Yes, she has tattoos up her arms and across her chest, but the power resonating from her comes from within. I've never met a witch before, not one that I was aware of, but I recognize a sameness in us.

She tilts her head. "Your aura, Zoey." She winces, turning to look at the guys. "Even if she wanted to come with us, we can't move her. Not in this condition."

Tate walks forward, stopping in the doorway. He looks at Peter, then at me. "May I?"

I nod and he comes forward to examine me. His hands are cool despite the warming temperatures outside. He presses his fingers to my wrist, keeping time with his watch.

I peer up at him. "Are you a doctor?"

"You bet." He releases my hand. "I usually focus on research, but I have walked countless wolves through the transition process. We're going to make this as painless as possible, Zoey."

I swallow, wincing at the pain in my throat. "What about the Vargulfism?"

Tate has a well-trained doctor's face. He doesn't give away much, even though we all know how dire my condition is. "First things first, Dax, would you go get my suitcase from the car?"

Lennon reluctantly lifts his knee from Dax's back. Dax dusts himself off, hesitating. "You're not going to drag her away?"

Tate turns his head to shoot Dax a look. I can't see what his face looks like, but Dax's face blanches in response and he scampers off without another word. By the time Tate turns back to me, his expression is placid once again. "Has Andy been made aware of your condition?"

I look up at Peter who shakes his head. "Not yet."

Tate nods at that. "Well... how do you want to play it? I can't say everything will go your way, we still have to conform to pack law, but I think we can buy some time." He pauses. "Our pack hasn't had to deal with the vargulf virus for at least a decade. Long before any of us guys were in the hot seat to make decisions about it. How does the Black Hills pack deal with it… the same way?"

"Yes." Peter's response is rigid. "We're still handling it the same way."

Tate's gaze lands on me. "If she was part of the St. Louis pack, she would be subject to our laws, not yours. We could shield her from those desperate measures."

"If Zoey makes the shift, she'll be in the Black Hills pack." Peter's arms tighten around me. "She and I are a package deal."

Tate's gaze lands on my bite marks, two crescent moons tattooed across Peter's forearm. He nods. "Ah. I see."

Dax returns with the suitcase. He hesitates in the stall doorway. It's clear he wants to pepper me with questions. I have one or two for him as well. It's strange to be so close to someone I used to share my every thought with and feel like there's a wall between us. He hesitates, like he's waiting for a signal from me. Some sort of cue that I want him to rescue me.

But I don't need rescuing. Not from him. The only person who can save me is *me*.

A beat passes and Dax seems to realize I won't be begging him for help. He reluctantly backs out of the stall, finding a spot on the opposite wall. He leans against it and crosses his arms. It's a casual pose, but I know him well enough to know the difference between relaxed Dax and a man who's poised and ready for battle.

I struggle to sit up taller, accepting help from Peter. "I've been working on a cure."

Tate's gaze swings back to me, I see a spark of curiosity there. "Briar mentioned that. It's why I insisted on tagging along, to be honest. If you've found a cure for Vargulfism, that could be revolutionary."

"I think I have." I pause. "It worked for Rabbit. Maybe it was a fluke, but I don't think so. I thought I'd figured it out, but then we tried it on the rogue wolf and Angela, too, and it failed."

Tate shakes his head. "The road to discovery is never straight. Do you have any theories on what could have gone wrong?"

"Yes." I nod at my notes, stacked up in a neat pile. "I've been working on a new formula."

"Do you think it will work?" Tate asks, picking up my notes.

"I believe in it enough that I took it myself."

Tate's gaze meets mine and I see respect in his blue eyes. He looks over his shoulder. "Lennon, update Barone. Dax, you stand guard outside. If any visitors come, we need to know. Officer Florean, would you mind standing guard as well?"

Hitch nods, following Dax outside. Tate motions Briar closer and the three of us bend our heads over my notes.

For the first time in almost twenty-four hours, things are starting to look up.

Only issue is, my health is failing fast. I might not last long enough to see this thing through.

63.

Time bends in funny ways. As the virus threads its way through my nervous system, past and present weave together in ways that leave me dizzy. Time loses meaning.

I am five years old, watching how my breath carries dandelion seeds into the summer sunlight.

I am twenty-three, meeting Dax for the first time. His face was bruised and bleeding from a cage fight and yet, his crooked grin melted my heart.

The barn, and the stall that's become my hospital room, rises and falls in my consciousness. I stare at the aluminum lights overhead until my vision goes blurry.

People come and go, and I can see their auras clearly drifting ahead of them like iridescent bubbles. It's beautiful and mysterious to see their intentions and their thoughts manifested into something the eye can see.

A witch's eye, anyway.

And through it all, there is always Peter. His heartbeat is the steady drumbeat of this affair, a war drum, anxious and determined.

I'm laying in the stall, my head resting in Hitch's lap. He's fallen asleep with his hand threaded through my hair. The muscles in my neck are stiff and protest as I turn to see Dax. He's leaning up against the opposite wall, arms crossed over his wide chest. We make eye contact. Without a word, a look can say so much.

Here we are.

It's a fucked up world, isn't it?

You're still a part of me.

I feel safe with these two. Hitch and Dax.

I'm not surprised I feel that way about Hitch. From the start, he's only had my best interest in mind. None of this pack bullshit. None of his own prerogatives.

But I'm surprised to find I still have space in my heart for Dax. All of our past fights, the pettiness, seems incredibly silly. What matters, is that he showed up. He's here now and I can tell from his posture alone that he's ready to fight for me.

Fight whom, though?

I don't know if I can trust the Black Hills pack—especially not after hearing Andy say they were going back to the old ways. If that's the case, I'm a dead woman.

But is the St. Louis pack any better? From what I can tell, they're just a more powerful, more polished version of Peter's pack.

Peter's aura snakes through the bars of my stall, splitting and reconverging like water. His voice is low, but what I can't hear with my ears, I can see in his aura, and I can feel in his heartbeat.

"She's at Maria's place." Pretty Boy's boots scuff through the dust and straw just outside.

Even in my fevered state, that statement irks me. It's not Maria's place. It's mine.

Strawberry Moon is mine.

"Tate and Lennon." Pretty Boy continues. "And Briar."

There's a pause, while he comes closer. I close my eyes and focus on calming my heart rate.

I can feel him standing in the doorway, his gaze drags over me. There's a silence where I imagine him studying Dax and Hitch, too. The uptick in his heartrate tells me that he's not thrilled with their proximity to me.

"I didn't alert you because I didn't know they were coming. I'm telling you now, Andy." Pretty Boy's voice carries an edge. "I didn't call St. Louis." There's a pause. "Zoey must have."

Betrayal slices through my chest.

So much for holding my heart rate steady.

Pretty Boy pauses. "I better let you go, she's waking up."

The sound of his boots brings him closer and still, I keep my eyes closed. I can't look at him right now. For the first time in days, I'm not sure I can trust him. That feeling of doubt scoops through my chest leaving me feeling hollow.

"Zoey?" Pretty Boy's fingers touch my arm. "How are you feeling, baby?"

Betrayed? Scared as hell?

I frown, squeezing my eyes shut. "Sick."

"I know, baby." He kneels beside Hitch and worms his arms between us. Lifting me from Hitch's lap, he carries me a few feet and sits down. He glares at Dax. "Aren't you supposed to be standing watch?"

Dax glowers right back. "That's exactly what I'm doing."

Pretty Boy stiffens behind me. "Go stand watch somewhere else."

Dax huffs a laugh. "Go fuck yourself."

I feel the tension in the air, the fight that is brewing between them. I'm not sure where my loyalties lay, but we can't have friendly fire right now. There's too much at stake. "It's okay, Dax."

Dax holds my gaze for a few moments before shrugging. "I won't go far, Zoey. Call out if you need help."

Peter tenses around me. "I've got her."

Dax shakes his head. "I see that."

Once Dax is gone, Peter begins to stroke my hair. "How bad is it?"

I look up at him. "I should ask you the same thing."

He turns his gaze towards the deeper reaches of the barn, towards the place where Briar and Lennon are holding quiet conversation. "I'm not sure, babe. This is all new territory."

"Because normally we'd put a vargulf down?"

His gaze jerks back down to mine. His tone holds a note of admonishment. "Zoey."

"Pretty Boy." I echo his tone. Swallowing, my throat constricts painfully. "Just give it to me straight. They're going to kill me, aren't they?"

"Who?"

I heave a ragged breath. "You know who I mean."

He pulls me closer, fingers gripping my arms like he can pull me back together through sheer will. "I won't let anything bad happen to you."

"Are they coming?" I look up at him, beseeching him. "Pretty Boy. Please."

He holds me closer. "I won't let anything happen to you."

I wish I could believe him. Exhaustion weighs heavily on me, filling my stiff joints with cement. I let Pretty Boy run his hands up and down my muscles. Perhaps he's acting from his own memory of when he made the change.

I force my eyes open. "If I survive the vargulf virus..."

He lifts my knuckles to his lips and presses a kiss against my fevered skin. "You're going to pull through."

"Right." I reply. "*When* I survive the virus, what's the lycanthropy going to do to me?"

He's silent, rubbing gentle circles over the pad below my thumb joint.

I curl my fingers around him, beseeching him with my gaze.

He licks his lips. "It's different for everyone." His gaze grows distant, lost in memory. "Some people fight it. I sure as hell did. Rabbit damn near lost his mind."

245

"Does anyone lose their mind altogether?"

He tips his head, expression carefully neutral.

I frown. "Pretty Boy."

"Not everyone survives it, Zoey. But you're strong. You're determined. And when you come out of this, you're going to be a wolf to reckon with. Of *that* I'm sure."

64.

The next time I open my eyes, the sky beyond my barred window is thick with stars. The overhead light in my stall has been turned off, but the oxidized light from the lamps outside filters through in cold stripes of light.

Pretty Boy's heart is hammering in my consciousness—this is the beat that broke my fitful sleep. He holds me in his arms, my head rests in his lap, but his body has gone rigid as he listens.

I listen too and after a few moments, my human hearing registers a low rumble.

Motorcycles.

Lots of them.

Pretty Boy eases out from underneath me. "I'll be right back."

At the sound of his voice, there's a scuffle in the dark corners of my stall. Dax climbs to his feet and steps into a box of moonlight cast through the window. They exchange silent glares and then Pretty Boy pushes past him.

Dax's gaze falls on me. He comes closer, lowering down to one knee. Pressing callused fingers against my forehead, he hisses. "You're burning up." He looks back over his shoulder, listening to the roar of engines. "You can't keep suffering out here, Zoey. This is inhumane. You need a doctor."

I give him a weak smile. "I am the doctor."

He turns his hand, gently brushing his knuckles against my cheek. "I know you are, babe. You sure you've got this?"

I am sure? Hell, no. The idea that I might die has been my constant companion, a shadow that keeps me company. I nod, putting my hand over his. "I've got it."

He smiles. "Well, alright, then. I know better than to doubt you, babe." He pauses as the motorcycle engines cut off. "How many do you figure are out there?"

I peer through the window, seeing nothing but stars and the black outline of pine trees. "At least a dozen, I'd wager."

"The whole pack?"

I shake my head. "Not even close. Where's Hitch?"

Dax sits next to me, one hand automatically coming to rest on my hip. "Who's Hitch? The sheriff?"

"Yeah."

He tips his head towards the window.

"Out there somewhere. Your boyfriend made him stand watch." He pauses. "Is it serious between you two?"

I think of the bite mark permanently etched into my skin and close my eyes. "Yes and no. I don't know, Dax. I don't know anything, anymore."

"Join the club." Dax huffs, keeping his voice low. "Zoey… back in the day, the way I treated you…"

"It's fine, Dax."

"No." He squeezes my hip. "It's anything but fine. I was going through the shit back then when we were together, but that's no excuse. If I had it all to do again, I would treat you like the queen you are."

"I'm no queen."

His hand gently cups my cheek. "On that topic, you're completely wrong. I'd follow you anywhere."

We hear the scuff of boots on gravel. I can't see them, but it isn't hard to picture. At least a dozen trespassers out there in my own damn yard, arguing about life and death.

Tate's voice, even and confident, cuts across the silence. "Andy. Didn't expect you so soon."

"Didn't expect to see me in my territory?" Andy doesn't bother dampening the anger in his voice. "Need I remind you it's common courtesy to let an alpha know when you're planning to invade his land?"

"Invade?" Lennon's voice is light. Amused. "That's a bit strong, Andy. We're just here on a social call."

Andy barks a hard laugh. "We're not taking callers tonight, brother. I think it's best you all head on home."

More footsteps and then Tate can be heard again. "We'll leave, but we're taking the vet with us."

"Like hell you are." Peter's voice cracks through the air. "She's not going anywhere."

"Peter." Lennon's voice is gentle. "We know what your pack does with vargulves. She's dead if she stays here. Let us take her to safety."

"A cage in your lab is hardly safe." Andy replies. "Go play the self-righteous card in your own backyard. Your opinion doesn't stand here."

Tate's voice is hardening. "According to pack by laws, it does."

"We know all about your labs, Tate." Andy continues. "What you do to vargulves. How you treat them like rats. You're not trying to save her any more than we are. At least we won't make her suffer first."

"At least she'll have a chance with us," Tate replies.

"It's not your call," Andy says.

Dax and I hold perfectly still, listening. His hand is cupped over my body, like a steel shield.

"We don't want any trouble." Lennon says. "But we can't let you kill that woman."

"What we do with her is our own business." Andy replies.

"Nobody's killing Zoey." Peter says.

"You sure about that?" Lennon asks.

"I've never been more sure of something in my life." Peter replies.

"Fact of the matter is, you're violating pack law." Andy says. "She is ours to decide what to do with."

"She's part of your pack?" Tate asks.

There's a pause. I know, as well as they do, that I'm not an official pack member yet. I'd have to be a wolf for that to be the case, and no one is sure I'll survive the change.

"She's my mate." Peter says. "That's all you need to know. If you want her, you'll have to come through me."

"We're wasting time with this." Lennon mutters.

Dax shifts out from underneath me, silently moving to the far corner of the stall. He returns with my boots and begins slipping them on my feet. "Can you move if you need to?"

I test my weak limbs, finding them impossibly heavy. "I'm not sure."

Dax shrugs. "Doesn't matter, I'll carry you."

"Where?" I whisper back.

Dax presses a finger to his lips, reminding me that wolves have incredible hearing. He circles his finger towards my make-shift workbench. I swipe my hand through the air, indicating that I need all the herbs. He nods and begins stuffing bottles and wax-wrapped plants into his backpack.

The tension outside grows and grows until it explodes in a flurry of shouts and scuffed gravel.

The first wolf's snarl rolls down my spine like an icy finger. Some, or all of them, have transformed into their wolf form. Yelps and growls fill the air.

Dax freezes, listening to the war storming outside.

He shoulders the pack and crouches over to me. "Let's get the fuck out of here."

I let him wrap my arms around his neck. "Where's Hitch?"

"Right here." Hitch appears in the doorway. He watches Dax lift me with a grim nod. "They're all out front. We'll have to go out the back way."

Hitch turns suddenly staring into the dark reaches of the barn, hand going to the gun holstered on his hip. "We're taking her to safety, Peter. Don't try to stop us."

Peter appears on the other side of Hitch. He looks almost frantic and that scares me more than anything. His gaze bobs from Dax to Hitch, then back to me. "Zoey, come with me, baby."

Dax tightens his grip on me. "You can't keep her safe, Peter. We can."

Peter glares at him, a tight smile curving his lips. "You? A pair of weak-ass human beings against a pack of wolves?"

Hitch pulls the gun from his holster and levels it, the barrel pointing at Peter's heart.

"No." I cry. "Please, Hitch. You'll kill him."

Hitch rolls his shoulders, holding the gun level. "Only if he tries to stop us."

65.

Peter's gaze is icy. "If you think I'm going to let you take my woman away, you're out of your damn mind."

Hitch pulls the safety back. The solid click can be heard over the battle din. "She's coming with us. Be smart about this, Peter."

"I can't stay here." I hold Peter's gaze. Confusing emotions roil through my chest. "It's not safe anymore."

Peter winces. It's a gentle rebuke considering the situation. He's the one that brought the Black Hills pack down on us. Judging by the pounding in his heart, he's not certain his brothers will keep me alive.

If he wasn't sure—why would he call them here?

The answer is simple. His true loyalties lay with the pack—they beat stronger than the rhythm of his mate's heart. That understanding passes between us. He had no choice.

But I do.

I tighten my grip on Dax's neck. "Let's go."

Peter steps closer. "I'm not going to let you disappear from me, baby."

Hitch holds his gun steady. "Not another step, Peter. I'm warning you."

Dax side-steps Hitch; Peter's gaze tracks our movement like a predator. When Dax begins to carry me towards the rear entrance, Peter growls in frustration. I peer over Dax's shoulder just in time to see Peter lunge around Hitch.

But Hitch is faster.

There's the percussive *pop* of gunfire. Hitch stands frozen, watching as Peter brings a hand to his chest. He holds his fingers up in the moonlight. Black blood drips from his fingers, blooms across his shirt.

His heart rate drowns out all other sounds. It's pounding too fast, hastening blood towards an unholy exit.

His heart stutters and he stumbles. My mouth is open and my throat hurts. I must be screaming, but Dax carries me farther away. The last thing I see of Peter is him falling to one knee as Hitch turns and sprints after us.

We plunge into the darkness. Here, at the rear of the barn, the cold white lights don't quite reach. It's three long strides and then we're out of the gravel and into the tall, overgrown grasses.

Hitch's fingers close around Dax's arm, yanking him to a stop.

Dax turns, chest heaving. "We can't stop."

Hitch shakes his head, peering back towards the barn. "We can't outrun a pack of werewolves, either."

Dax looks like he wants to argue, but the truth is evident. He growls in frustration. "I rode here with those sons of bitches."

Hitch nods. "My cruiser is in the lot, but we've got two packs of warring wolves between us and it."

Briar's voice materializes from the shadow. "They're distracted. Now's your only chance."

Dax and Hitch startle, surprised to find Briar stepping into the thin moonlight. She places a cool hand on my forearm. "You're going to be fine, honey. You're a strong one."

Dax studies her. "You're not going to call your boys down on us?"

She scoffs at that, turning to gaze towards the din of the battle—wolfish roars and snaps and whines. "There's no talking sense to them right now." Her gaze swings between Hitch and Dax. "You've got somewhere you can go?"

Hitch nods. "Yeah, we'll go west. I've got a cabin up in the…"

Briar holds up a hand, cutting him off. "Best if I don't know the details." She squeezes her other hand around mine, then unhooks a necklace from her neck. "I want this back."

I study the sad smile on her face and look at the pendant she's holding out. "What is it?"

"A witch's amulet." She reaches up and Dax lowers so that she can hook the necklace around my neck. "It was my mother's—she's a powerful witch. This should give you extra protection."

With the green jewel resting on my breastbone, I can almost feel a soft power humming through it. "Thanks, Briar."

She grins at me, winking. "Us witches got to stick together, you know?" She turns her gaze towards Hitch. "If you're headed west, Big Paul Carter might be someone to ask for help. He's a piece of shit, I'm not gonna lie. But he hates the Midwest pack, and I'd bet good money he'll jump at an opportunity to fuck them over. Just don't trust him too far."

Dax holds me closer. "Where do we find him?"

She huffs a dry laugh. "The Rockies are his region. He'll find you." She places her hand on Dax's arm, studying both men with a serious gaze. "It's going to be rough going for her. She knows this. I don't have time to candy coat it. She's either going to live or die. There's nothing you two can do to help her. It's up to Zoey now. What you can do is stay out of the way of her fangs. And keep her locked up. Nobody needs a new werewolf rampaging around."

I feel my strength fading and turn my gaze back towards the dark barn. "I can't feel him."

Briar looks up at me. "Who, honey?"

"Peter." I swallow hard. "I can't feel his heart."

Briar follows my gaze. "He's in the barn?" When I nod, she squeezes my arm. "I'll look after him. You just get to safety. Good luck, Zoey. May the goddess be with you."

She turns without another word, leaving the three of us in her wake.

Dax and Hitch exchange weary glances. Dax shrugs. "It's now or never."

Hitch nods. "Let's move quickly. Don't stop for anything."

Hitch takes point, sticking to the shadows near the encroaching trees. We avoid the halo of light cast by the barn lamps, but it's impossible to avoid looking at the carnage.

The wolves are still in full battle mode. I count at least four limp bodies, laying lifeless amongst the bloodied gravel. Are any of those wolves people I know? Friends I've shared drinks with over the last few days? I squint into the battle, trying to see if I can identify Rabbit or Dante or Cherry.

But no, I don't recognize them in wolf form and even if I did, they all just look like bloodied blurs to me—lunging and tearing at one another.

Hitch pauses at the edge of the light. We hide in the last bit of shadow while he points at his cruiser. "It's over there. We'll have to run now."

Dax hefts me closer to his body and nods, expression grim.

Hitch holds up his fingers and silently counts down from three.

And then Dax is running, trailing right behind Hitch. I glance over his shoulder and grip him tighter when I see a huge white wolf closing the distance between us.

Its snowy fur is splotched in blood and gore. I can't tell how much of the blood belongs to the wolf or its victims.

Hitch gets to the cruiser first, fumbling with the door handle before throwing it open. It's like time slows down. Dax barrels into the back of the cruiser, taking me with him.

Hitch slams the door shut on us and turns to open the driver's side. At the last moment, the wolf loses footing on the gravel, giving Hitch the slight edge he needed to slip behind the wheel. The wolf crashes into the car door, forcing it shut. Its maw gnashes up against the glass, streaking blood.

Then Hitch is revving the engine, spitting gravel as he whips a U-turn.

Dax peers out the back window, crowing in relief. "That's right, motherfuckers. You done fucked up."

Pushing past the pain in my joints, I lift myself up to peer out the back window. Wolves are hastily shifting back to their human form, rushing to their bikes.

But it's too little too late. Dax turns back, thumping the bars that separate the front of the cruiser from the back with pure joy. "Hell yeah, brother. Let's burn some rubber."

I turn, too, allowing Dax to settle me into the crook of his body.

He's far from perfect. Rough around the edges. But I know what I'm getting with Dax. Strength. Bravery.

And most importantly, loyalty. I know Dax will side with me no matter what comes. If either of these men wanted to save their skins, their best bet would have been to turn me over.

But they chose to save me, instead. I won't forget that.

If I survive this thing—if I become a wolf, I'm going to need a pack I can count on.

And it sure as shit isn't going to be the Blackhills pack.

Strawberry Moon

They gave us the window we needed to escape.
And we aren't looking back.

66.

We make it as far as the Wyoming border before I begin the transformation.

At first, I think I'm going to throw up. But there's an internal heaving, a pulling sensation, that goes deeper than my gut. I feel it in my bones. It's like they're stretching, shrinking.

Rearranging.

My tongue tracks the sudden growth of fangs, the elongating of my palette. "Get up front, Dax."

"Zoey?"

"Now, Dax!" My voice comes out garbled in a strange harmony. My human voice mixed with something that sounds demonic. "I don't want to hurt you."

"Pull over, Hitch." Dax holds me, despite my weakened attempts to wiggle out of his grasp.

Hitch pulls over so quickly, both Dax and I are thrown up against the front seats.

My vision goes wavy, like a fun-house mirror, as my eyes transform. I see Hitch pass a pair of cuffs through the bars. I reach out for his hand, unsure if I'm looking for comfort or to stop him. My hands have begun melting and I'm not able to caress or stop Hitch as he passes the cuffs off.

Dax grabs my leg and I'm startled to see that I look more like a wolf than a human. He snaps one end of the cuff around my haunch and the other around the headrest.

I'm strung up, mostly upside down, twisting wildly. Another voice joins my own thoughts, one that speaks in images and feelings and actions—but not words.

Trapped.

Escape.

Fight.

The arms that bound me are the ones to blame for my entrapment. I snap furiously at a long forearm, but he backs away. I try to lunge again, but the car door is slammed in my face. I scrabble at the handle. Foggy human memories blend with panicked wolf thoughts. I know the handle is the key to escape, but I no longer have fingers. My claws click and scrape uselessly at the handle. I turn my gaze up in time to see two males staring at me through the window. They are simultaneously familiar and a threat to me. I lunge at the window, in part to reach out for rescue, in part to simply escape.

My head thumps painfully against the glass, but I do it again and again.

Until darkness takes over.

A nightmare follows.

Streaking light and darkness. Highway flying by. The low, unintelligible mutter of two men in the front seat. My mind seems to recognize their speech and yet, I can't make sense of it. Like a drowning swimmer, I struggle to stay at the surface, certain I'll never survive this.

But I wake up again and again and eventually, fresh air settles over my body like a soothing caress. I'm being carried. Dawn breaks through the trees, shedding reddish-orange light over Dax's solemn features. He glances down, smiling wearily. "Good morning, sunshine."

"Where are we?" I croak.

"Colorado. Hitch's family has a cabin up here."

Dax carries me up a set of steps and then Hitch is in my field of vision. His hand gently brushes over the back of my head. "How are you feeling?"

"Terrible."

He huffs an exhausted laugh before swinging the front door open.

"Are we safe here?" I ask, watching Hitch toss a set of keys down on the counter.

Dax and Hitch exchange sober glances, not bothering to reply.

Hitch nods towards a hallway. "This way."

Dax follows behind, his shoulders stiff. "Just rest now, Zoey. You're going to be alright."

Odds are, he's lying.

But what else can I do but rest? With heavy eyelids, I close my eyes and slip into the darkness once again.

The next time I wake, I'm laying on a garage floor, my head cradled in Hitch's lap. I pause, listening to my surroundings. I hear wind traveling through pines and granite. A few birds sing crisp songs in the distance.

And there is an echoing, percussive beat that I feel, rather than hear.

I lay with my eyes closed and study the qualities of the rhythms. There are two separate rhythms, but they beat in tandem.

Quick-slow. Quick-slow.

One rhythm weaves alongside a faster rate, *thrum-thrum-thrum*.

Two hearts, but neither of them matches the man who stole my heart.

Pretty Boy.

Peter.

My heart reaches out, searching for him. But either he is too far away, or something worse has happened.

I squeeze my eyes shut at the thought, turning towards Hitch.

He wakes at my sudden movement, hand automatically coming to rest heavy and reassuring on my head. "You doing okay?"

"Yeah." I mutter. "How about you?"

He laughs. "I've had better days."

"How long have I been out?"

He sighs. "We've been out three, maybe four... days."

"Days?" I push upright, surprised to find my limbs obey me once again. His words process through my sluggish thoughts. "What do you mean *we*?"

The door that separates the house from the garage swings open. Dax steps into the doorframe. "She's awake?"

He looks terrible. His dark hair sticks up at odd angles and his five o'clock shadow has morphed into a straggly scruff.

My gaze sweeps between the two of them, associating their heartbeats with their bodies. "Why can I feel your pulse?" My hand grips Hitch's thigh. "What's happened?"

Dax steps into the garage. "What's happened is we've formed our very own pack, Zoey baby."

My hand shakily rises to cover my lips. "No."

Hitch squeezes my shoulder. "Afraid so."

Horror and guilt threaten to overcome me. "I bit you?"

Hitch shrugs. "We got in your way. It's not your fault."

"Of course, it's my fault." Tears threaten to spill over. "I'm so sorry."

Hitch catches a tear on his thumb. "We both knew what the risks were when we chose to side with you."

The weight of their choice is too much to bear. Their futures are forever shattered thanks to me—thanks to this virus. I shake my head, willing the nightmare to go away. "It makes no sense. Why would you do that?"

Hitch cups my cheek, tracing my lower lip with his thumb. "Why? I should think that would be obvious by now."

I stare at him for several heartbeats before looking to Dax. My appeal to his better sense is lost when I see his expression. He gives me a shy smile. "I never stopped loving you, baby."

I sniff back tears. "But to throw away your lives for me..."

"I'd do it again in a heartbeat." Hitch says.

"Same." Dax comes forward to help me to my feet.

Hitch climbs upright more slowly. I can tell, through sensations I can't explain, that he's struggled more with the transformation than Dax and I did. But his pulse is strong, and his body still works. He'll just need more time to rest.

Dax places my arm around his waist and after a moment, he takes Hitch's arm and throws it over his shoulder. "Think we're fit for public, yet?"

Hitch huffs a dry laugh. "That's a matter of perspective. But I don't think we're at risk of going feral anymore."

I glance back at the garage, noticing for the first time the state it's in. Shelves pulled down. Streaks of blood. Food wrappers and bottles. It's clear we spent a very chaotic three days together.

Dax leads the way, silently taking us through the cabin. The walls and ceiling are paneled in pine. The furniture is also from pine and woven material. We pass by a wood stove and I breathe in the comforting scent of wood smoke. Dax opens a set of French doors and we step onto a long, sprawling deck. It hangs over a sharp drop off, giving me the feeling of floating in the clouds. The sun is just rising over the distant mountain tops. They look harsh and unforgiving, but that soothes me. We've chosen a good place to hide. Mother nature's very own fortress.

Dax takes us to the railing and we lean on it, watching the sun crest over the mountain ridge. It paints the snowcaps orange, then gold.

"We're a pack now, huh?" I murmur, finally breaking the quiet.

Dax grins, bumping into me. "A three-pack."

"Three musketeers." Hitch adds.

I nod, silently thankful to have these two men at my back.

As long as I've got them, I won't have to face my future alone. At one point, I thought Peter was my future. The connection still holds, like a painful, bluesy note in my heart. It's faint, but it gives me hope that he lives. I can't say Peter and I will have a life together, though. Not after he sold me out to his pack.

I look at Dax, then Hitch. "So... who's in charge?"

Hitch laughs. "You are."

"Me?" I squeak. "Who decided that?"

"You did." Hitch says. "Your genes, anyway. You're a natural alpha. We didn't have any say in the matter."

"Although we would have voted for you." Dax adds. "What'd I tell you, Zoey? You're the queen."

Queen of what?

Queen of nothing.

Queen of disaster.

Queen of not giving up.

There's still a lot to do. And more importantly, I survived my transformation, and so did my boys.

The evidence is clear—I must have healed the vargulf virus before I bit them. That means, between the three of us, we hold the power to save lives.

Even more reason to avoid capture. There's too much to do to become a pawn in another pack's politics.

I sidle between the two of them, slipping my arms around their waists. "Alright, boys. Let's take on the world."

☾

Thank you for reading <u>The Wolf Vet: Strawberry Moon</u>. Consider leaving a review or rating. Check out what the rest of the pack is up to in the Blueblood Series and be sure to find me on social media. I'd love to hear from you.

Xoxo

Cleo

Cleo Mercer

The adventure doesn't stop here. Read the first few episodes of Season Two of <u>The Wolf Vet: Buck Moon</u>.

Episode 1: Zoey

The coneflower springs from a crevice in the stone. Roots cling to the mountain's granite, sponge up morning dew as it trickles past lichen and moss. My boots scrabble against the giant slabs of granite, showering the plant with bits of gravel as I try to climb down into the small space. Hovering over it, I'm almost ashamed to clip the little warrior, its purple bloom is bright against the harsh mountain. A Lupine Blue butterfly floats past me, landing lightly on the flower's petals. It doesn't belong this far up in the mountains, but then again, neither do I.

I retreat a few feet to allow the little critter room to drink. For a few moments, I watch nature carry on the way it does, outside of human concerns. I envy it, trying to remember a time before werewolf viruses and warring wolf packs. There's comfort in the knowledge that the world will carry on no matter how bad things get for me.

A small shadow flits overhead and quick as a wink, a pinyon jay swoops down and snatches the butterfly in its beak. I gasp, hands covering my mouth, and startle the bird. It readjusts its prize, crushing delicate wings, and flies away.

We are hunted, all of us.

From the smallest creature to the biggest—this is the circle of life. Clinging to my perch, I turn and look at the mountain pass behind me. Hitch says the Rockies are mean mountains—that they will chew you up and spit you out. And that's before you add in the fact that we are hunted by not just one, but two werewolf packs.

Pulling my pack from my shoulders, I hunker down by the coneflower and quickly snip the bloom. Snagging a page from an old newspaper, I fold the bloom between crosswords and want ads, and tuck the bundle back into my bag.

It's a short hike back to Hitch's cabin. I never stray far, none of us do. I know the safety of our hiding spot is thin, but I still heave a sigh of relief when the old fishing cabin comes into view. It's tucked back behind a little offshoot of the river, hidden behind a stand of pines. I hurry across a little foot bridge and pause on the front porch. If I settle my racing thoughts and the worries that never stop dogging me, I can feel them out there. Hitch and Dax. My own little wolf pack.

Hitch tugs at my consciousness, he's farther away— probably down by the highway, standing guard against hunting parties.

Dax is closer, somewhere to the north. Slipping inside our tiny cabin, I set my pack down on the kitchen counter. I pour a mug of coffee, warming my fingers against the cup. A fox stares back at me from his wire crate, golden eyes baleful as he watches me check his water. It's still lethargic, but it's no longer foaming at the mouth or snapping at imaginary foes.

The screen door squeals on its hinges and snaps shut against the frame. I don't need to turn to see Dax standing by the door, kicking his boots off. Dark haired, tall, and rugged. He was never much of a pretty boy. With a boxer's broken nose and tattoos from his neck to his fingertips, he is the very definition of the bad boy. Sometimes I question why I put up with his bad behavior for as long as I did, but I've never questioned why I was attracted to him. The man smolders.

He's holding a cat pet carrier under his arm, a limp racoon captured within. "Brought you another patient."

I come closer, smelling fresh air and wood smoke on him as I peer past the wire bars. "This racoon is dead, Dax."

"You never specified."

I stand upright. "That we need living patients?"

He gives me a crooked grin. "You're the witch, can't you do something about it?"

"I'm a witch, not a necromancer." It still feels strange to say these words aloud, knowing that they're true. A wolf and a witch. The double threat—one the other packs can't abide by. It's only part of why they want me dead. The other part has to do with wolf rabies—vargulfism. Through a combination of vet science and old wives' tales, I beat the virus and now its just a matter of replicating the cure.

I think I have the recipe, what I don't have is time.

He tilts his head. "Are there really necromancers?"

"I have no idea."

He huffs a laugh at that, setting the carrier on the coffee table. "This little fella probably had rabies, though." He pulls his shirt off. "Look at its little mouth."

I examine the foam drying on a rictus snarl. Easier to look at the face of death, than to face the way Dax's half-naked body makes me feel.

Desire.

Desire like flames eating up all rational thought in my brain. Desire that seeks to burn up feelings of betrayal and guilt. Because while I'm going into heat at the sight of my ex, my *mate* Peter, is out there alive... but barely.

I can feel him, but the connection is faint. I'm not sure if it's distance or his health that makes the beat of his heart so faint. I cling to it, wondering if I'm imagining the steady thrum. The last time I saw Peter, he was bleeding out. Shot by Hitch's own hand.

"I'm going to take a shower." Dax balls up his shirt. "You had breakfast yet?"

"No." I murmur, feeling overcome by feelings of loss and guilt and fear. This happens to me, now. Most of the time, I can stuff the feelings down so deep they can't reach me. But occasionally, something will remind me of Peter and the reality of our situation comes back so hard it leaves me breathless.

"Hey," Dax whispers, coming closer. "Where'd you go, baby?"

I shrug, trying to keep a neutral tone. "I'm fine."

"Liar." He puts callused hands on my arms and studies my expression. "I can feel your heart, you know."

He's right and that makes me feel naked with nowhere to hide. Our connection isn't as poignant as it was with Peter, but we can still feel each other. We have a sense of proximity and we can feel each other's moods.

"It's just a lot." I mutter, standing stiffly in his grip.

"That's an understatement." He gazes at me for a moment, before pulling me into a fierce hug. "But you're not alone."

This feels comfortable. Familiar.

Was it so long ago that we would have found comfort in each other's arms, coming together without a second thought? For a moment, I push the feelings of guilt aside and lean into Dax's embrace. His bare chest is warm against my cheek. Emotions overwhelm me, unspent tears burn the corners of my eyes.

"I got you, babe." Dax's low voice rumbles in his chest. "And don't forget about Hitchy."

A smile tugs at the corner of my lips. "Yeah."

Dax rubs small circles on my back. "Although I still think we should invest in a shock collar."

Cleo Mercer

I sniff back tears and laugh. "That's inhumane."

We were all turned by the virus at the same time, but Hitch struggles to reign in his wolf more than Dax and me. It's like watching a naughty puppy every time we practice running as a pack.

Hitch is usually pretty buttoned up and straight-laced. His wolfy side? Not so much.

This contrast is the source of endless amusement for Dax.

The screen door protests as it opens, slapping shut. We yank apart, but there's a neutral look in Hitch's face that tells us he knows exactly what was going on.

Both tall and dark-haired, Hitch and Dax could almost be cousins. Hitch's features are finer than Dax's and he's generally tidier in his appearance than Dax. But time in the mountains is chipping away at Hitch's hard exterior. He gave up fighting the scruff on his strong jaw, and now sports a short beard.

He takes off his gun holster, carefully setting it on the table. "Did I hear my name being used in vain?"

Dax laughs, sauntering over to pour himself coffee. He slaps Hitch on the shoulder as he passes by. "Only good things, brother."

Hitch pretends to frown, but there's a glimmer of amusement in his eye. "I bet."

I use those spare moments to pull myself together. "How were the roads?"

I'm not asking about weather or road conditions. We all know this.

The amusement evaporates from Hitch's face as he meets my gaze. "Busy." He shakes his head. "It's only a matter of time, Zoey."

A matter of time before Andy Haugen figures out where we're hiding.

A matter of time before his pack rips us limb from limb.

Episode 2: Zoey

Dax was right about the raccoon. It died from rabies, but I have no way of knowing how similar traditional rabies and werewolf rabies are. The wolves don't even refer to the virus as rabies—they call is Vargulfism.

That's what I am to them. A contagious *vargulf* that needs to be put down.

It just goes to show, they don't know me very well.

I never go down easily.

Without a lab setting, there's nothing I can do with Dax's deceased raccoon. Burying it outside, I wash my hands at the sink, listening to laughter waft in from the deck.

Hitch and Dax make an amazing odd couple—their friendship has surprised the heck out of me. Up until a week ago, Hitch was Hill City's most strait-laced sheriff. And Dax was a St. Louis boxer with morals so bruised up they were black and blue. Despite their differences, they seem to appreciate each other. Turns out, going through your first werewolf transformation together is a bonding experience.

Crossing the small living room, I pause in the doorway, listening to Hitch recount hunting trips he used to take with his dad. They're grilling the rabbits he and Dax caught earlier.

"She's lurking again." Dax stage-whispers to Hitch.

Hitch turns, a wry grin on his lips. "Come on out, Zoey. We won't bite."

Dax laughs. "We won't—but she will."

Gallows humor. We arm ourselves with it.

Facing doom with a joke our lips.

Hitch shakes his head, but there's a twinkle in his eye as he looks at me. "Hungry, darlin'?"

"Always," I admit, stepping onto the deck. It's late June, but the breeze that skips across the patio is almost chilly. Noticing the shiver that wracks my body, Dax drags me into his arms. I offer a mild protest, but Dax's warm body is a welcome balm for my aching muscles.

Hitch watches the exchange without comment.

Convincing myself that platonic friends can hold each other, I stop struggling and lean against Dax. We watch Hitch rotate pieces of meat.

"Who caught the rabbits?" I ask.

Dax's laugh rumbles against my back. "Hitch—the beast master."

A faint, shy smile tugs at Hitch's features as he turns away, focusing on the grill.

Dax squeezes me closer. "He may pee on the carpet, but damn if that boy isn't fast."

Hitch huffs an annoyed laugh. "I don't pee on the carpet."

"*You* don't, but your wolf does." Dax says.

"One time." Hitch sighs. "And you're labeled for life." He points his grilling tongs at Dax. "At least I didn't hump the pillows."

Dax shrugs. "What can I say? My wolf was hard to tame at first."

"Zoey had no issues." Hitch says.

Dax rubs small circles along my forearm. "Yes, but Zoey is the ultimate wolf."

"Am not." I disentangle myself from Dax's arms.

Hitch catches my gaze. "You are, Zoey."

Dax sneaks a morsel of meat from the grill, juggling the steaming bite from hand to hand before popping it in his mouth. "I don't know why you deny it, babe. I'd be thrilled to be an alpha."

I open my mouth to argue with him, but there's no point. As much as I'd like to pass the duties along, I am undeniably an alpha wolf. It's not something I chose, but rather, something that chose me.

My wolf senses are more in tune. I have a better sense of the boys' locations, a natural radar. They listen to me in wolf form and out. Even Hitch, in his feral wolf form, will sit down and beg if I tell him to. To me, being an alpha seems like an inconsequential genetic variation. We've evolved past allowing our DNA dictate our actions. But the boys don't see it that way.

They see me as the woman in charge.

I wish they wouldn't.

Time passes in strange ways up in these mountains. We waver between moments of desperation and periods of stillness so quiet it's like everything stands still.

We eat our dinner, the boys arguing over football stats, while I watch clouds gather behind mountain peaks. In times like these, I can almost pretend like life is back to the way it was. Back when Dax and I were together, when we were innocent to the world of darkness that lay just beyond the veil.

Their conversation morphs from football to wolf transformation techniques.

"You gotta pull from here." Dax is motioning at his flat stomach. "From the belly—like you've got a bungee cord tied around your spine."

Hitch cocks his head. "From the core?"

"Yeah." Dax stands up. "Here, I'll show you."

Without a care in the world, he pulls his shirt off one-handed, shrugging out of his pants just as quickly.

Cleo Mercer

I avert my gaze, but I don't miss the way he winks at me. Dax has always been athletic. He's got the grace of a boxer, so channeling that agility towards the wolf transformation was natural for him. My gaze is drawn back as he contracts his spine. I've seen him transform dozens of times, but I never get tired of seeing it. His change is awe-inspiring. He spins on the ball of his foot, seeming to twist into ribbons of downy fur and flesh. One moment he is there, the man I once loved, and the next he is a gigantic gray and white wolf. He sits on his haunches, tongue lolling.

"Show off." Hitch murmurs, but he's grinning.

With a playful bark, Dax leaps onto Hitch's lap, nearly turning the chair over. Hitch just barely manages to settle all four chair legs back on the ground. "I hate you so much." Hitch mutters, but his fingers scratch behind Dax's ears.

My cell rings, sounding foreign and unexpected after days of silence. All three of us startle.

Trying to shake off a feeling of foreboding, I slip inside and dig my cell out of my purse. "Hello?"

"Zoey." It's Briar LeFay. Mate to the St. Louis alpha who wants me captured.

I feel short of breath. "Briar? How'd you get this number? Is everything okay? Do you know what happened to Peter?"

Her voice is rich and melodic. "Slow down, baby. One thing at a time."

I can almost picture her on the other end. Long black hair, limbs covered in tattoos. Lips as red as blood. She's the only witch I've ever met and the only other wolf I think is on our side.

I take in a shaky breath, looking at the boys. Dax has hopped off Hitch's lap and is standing near the door, ears perked. Hitch slowly climbs to his feet as well. They're both alert. Wary.

I swallow hard. "Do you know what happened to Peter? Is he okay?"

"He's here with us."

It's like a stack of bricks have been lifted from my shoulders, but immediately, I want more. I want to hear his voice. I want to be in his arms. "In St. Louis?"

"Yes. He's here with me, in the other room."

I turn away from the boys, gripping the phone. "Let me talk to him."

"In a second, Zoey."

"Why's he there? Why isn't he in South Dakota with his own pack?" A faint hope lights in my gut. Between the two packs, it's comforting to know Peter sided with St. Louis. The Black Hill pack wants me dead. The St. Louis pack just wants to study me for science. Of the two options, I'd rather be a lab rat. But I'm still in charge of my own destiny—so the choice I make is to be free.

"The aftermath of that battle." Briar's voice fades before she steadies herself. "It was pure chaos, Zoey. A blood bath. Peter needed medical help, so we took him with us."

Doubt creeps in around my feet. "He didn't want to go with you?"

"Not particularly." Briar's voice is wry. "We don't have a lot of time though. I need you to listen to me."

"Okay," I say.

"This phone I called you on? Destroy it, baby. Anybody could use it to track you."

My shoulders tighten. "How will I find you if I can't call?"

"I'll find you." She pauses. "Listen... I really shouldn't say this, but wherever you're hiding, just stay there for now. Nobody's agreeing on what to do about you."

"What do you mean?"

Briar clicks her tongue. "You're an unknown female with unknown powers. Trust me, babe. The wolves do not take kindly to unfamiliar threats."

"Do they want me dead?"

"The Black Hills pack definitely does." Briar says. "But St. Louis? I'm not sure what they're going to do."

I swallow down a lump. "Let me talk to Peter, please."

Briar sighs. "Okay. Stay safe. I'll be in touch."

There's a pause and then Peter's voice is there. "Zoey."

The sound of my name on his lips washes over me, filling the cracks in my heart. "Peter. Are you okay?"

"I'm fine. Where are you, baby? Are you okay?"

"I'm..." I hesitate, unsure if I should tell him where I am. "I'm fine, Peter. I'm not hurt."

"Are you trapped?"

I look out at the boys and the mountains beyond. "Yes and no."

Peter breathes out at that. "Are you safe?"

"Are you?"

He sighs. "I'm fine. I'd be better if you were next to me so I can keep you safe."

"Come find me then, Peter. We can hide out until this blows over."

"I'm not hiding," Peter replies. "I won't hide from anyone. You won't have to, either."

"I don't think I have a choice."

"You belong with me." Peter says.

"Agreed. Come out here so we can be together."

"You know I can't."

I tense. "Why not?"

"The pack..." He trails off. "There are rules, Zoey. I have to follow the chain of command."

I'm quiet.

"Zoey." He murmurs. "Talk to me."

"Your pack wants me dead."

He sucks in a breath. "You know I won't let that happen."

"If the chain of command demanded it?"

He pauses. "They wouldn't."

I shake my head. "They would. They have. Those people want me dead, Peter. How can you side with them?"

"I'm not siding with anyone."

Tears start to gather in the corners of my eyes. "That's clear."

He sighs.

I turn away and catch sight of Dax in his wolf form. He's no longer sitting on his haunches, but upright and alert. Every line in his wolfish body is tense—his tufted ears are perked forward.

A few heartbeats later, I hear it, too.

Motorcycles. And they're closing in.

It's suddenly hard to breathe. "I've got to go."

"Zoey... what's wrong?"

Feeling like I'm being split in two, I grip the phone. "Stay safe, baby. No matter what happens, just know I love you."

Episode 3: Briar

Peter grips the phone like a man holding onto his last lifeline.

Truth be told, he is.

That's his mate on the other side of the call. The longer they're apart, the worse his health is going to get.

And that wolf is already in bad shape.

He goes quiet, turning to me with a pale face. "She hung up."

My heart aches for him. "Sit down, Pretty Boy."

His thoughts are a thousand miles away, deep in the mountains with his mate, as he absent-mindedly hands me the phone. I wrap my small hand around his bicep and usher the giant of a man back to the bed. He sits on the edge, refusing to lay down.

The moment my pack returned to St. Louis, they put me in charge of guarding this biker with an attitude. My first thought was that there wasn't a chance in hell I could stop this beast of a man from doing anything. But he's injured. Worse, he's separated from his pack and his fated mate.

Day after day, I've had to witness the energy literally leaking away from his aura. I've learned a few tricks, though. One of which being to call him by the nickname his pack gave him.

Pretty Boy.

A name not given for his looks, though he is handsome in an all-American sort of way. Strong jaw, blue eyes.

Peter told me they called him that because he insisted on shaving when the rest of the pack members let their scruffy beards grow. He's a well-groomed wolf to say the least, though he's got almost as much ink on his skin as I do.

I step back, studying his tense shoulders. "Why'd you lie to her?"

He looks up at me, gaze slowly focusing. "What?"

"You told her you were fine. You're definitely not."

He shrugs, irritated. "I *am* fine. I just need rest."

"Well, that I won't argue with." I fluff the pillow. "Rest."

He huffs out a breath, reluctantly laying back.

I resume my station—curled up on the armchair reading steamy romance on my phone. It's the only distraction that keeps my thoughts from spiraling.

Pretty Boy turns onto his side, watching me with hooded eyes. "I didn't want her to worry."

I set my phone down and look at him. "She would want to know how you're doing, Peter."

He turns onto his back. "I should be protecting her. Not the other way around."

"Men," I mutter.

His head turns, those bright blue eyes shine on me. "Women."

"I'd just like to point out that not a single woman has anything to do with the situation we all find ourselves in. It's been all men, huffing and puffing." I sit upright, crossing my legs. "This is why witches prefer female led covens."

"You don't have alphas?"

I smile at that. "No, we don't have alphas. We have a council. Wisdom and common sense are our guiding principles."

"How'd you end up with the wolves, then?"

I study his face, realizing he genuinely doesn't know. Admitting the truth brings patches of color to both cheeks. "They excommunicated me."

His eyes widen. "Why?"

"For being a wolf."

He props himself up on an elbow. "Seriously?"

I heave a deep breath. "Seriously."

"Damn."

He doesn't know the half of it. We don't have alphas, but if we did, my mother would be the witch in charge. Selene LeFay. Her power is unmatched, but her daughter was a cradle-born wolf. When the secret became too big to hide, she sent me away. "So now you understand why I relate to your girlfriend as much as I do. My people turned on me, too."

"We didn't turn on her."

I study him with a patient gaze.

He huffs a sigh. "They'll come around." His gaze pops up to mine. "And she's not just my girlfriend."

"Mate, then."

"She's my everything."

I watch him carefully. "Why not go to her then?"

He studies me with shrewd eyes. "Did your old man tell you to say that?"

I feel myself bristling. "Harris doesn't tell me what to do."

Peter tilts his head. "Not even as your alpha?"

I shrug. "He's not the alpha yet. Not as long as Rudolfo is still in charge."

Peter clicks his tongue. "We all know Rudolfo isn't the wolf he once was."

"That's the chain of command." I say, repeating Peter's own words.

"Okay, fair enough." He threads his fingers together, resting them on his chest. "It's a mind fuck, I'll be honest."

"What is?"

"The chain of command," he says. "Who do I submit to? Andy Haugen—my alpha? Or Rudolfo—my alpha's alpha?"

I'm quiet for a moment. "I think you know the answer to that."

He shakes his head. "I don't know *what* I know anymore. It's all fucked. I would never in a million years have predicted that Andy would go against the St. Louis pack."

The St. Louis pack didn't predict that, either. The Black Hills pack was always our last bastion of civilization, the guard against the more brutal western wolf packs. If Andy's turned sides, what's to stop the Rocky Mountain pack, and their alpha Big Paul Carter, from setting their sights on the east?

I bite the inside of my cheek. "Think Andy will come around?"

"Seek out a peace agreement?" Peter turns to look at me. "I'm not sure. I've never seen him so pissed off."

"Harris always talked about Andy like he was this big, lovable teddy bear."

Peter smiles at that. "He usually is. Until someone tries to mess with his pack." Peter glances at me. "I shouldn't be talking to you, though."

"Probably not." I smile.

"You're the enemy."

"Am I?"

Peter studies me. "Harris Barone's mate? Yeah. Doesn't get any higher up the chain than that."

Except it does—the king on top of the hill is my lover. I demurred when Peter said Harris was the alpha, but the truth is, he's right. Rudolfo's best days are long past. Harris has been running a shadow command for at least a year now. He's the one with the power, but what good is being an alpha's mate when all I'm allowed to do is babysit?

If they would listen to me, I would tell them to work with Zoey, not against. As both a wolf and a witch, there's so much she could accomplish.

That little witch has more power in her pinky finger than even my mother, the great Selene LeFay.

Zoey just hasn't recognized it yet, but I knew it from the moment I first heard her voice. We first met over the phone and even then, I could sense the awesome power emanating from her aura. I've seen her once in person, for just a few heartbeats, but she stole my breath away.

Maybe some primal part of the wolf pack recognizes this power in her.

Maybe they want her controlled, or eliminated, because they don't want a woman like that running around under her own power.

I shouldn't think like this because I genuinely do love my mate. He has a good heart—and he just wants what's best for the pack. He's holding the entire region on his shoulders and that kind of responsibility doesn't allow for much empathy. There are rules for a reason, I understand that.

But I also understand that a power like Zoey's could do so much good for the werewolf population.

If only they would take the time to listen.

The Wolf Vet: Buck Moon

More books by Cleo Mercer

Fallen Warriors – SciFi Alien Romance

Tooth and Tusk
Flying on Clipped Wings
Bull by the Horn
Hunter's Eve

Dark Haven – Fae/Fantasy Romance

Girls Just Wanna Have Faun

St. Louis Blue Bloods - Werewolf Mafia

Syd King: Werewolf Attorney
Make Him Grovel
Mine to Punish
Bound to Protect
Easier to Submit
Got You, Babe
Cute Little Freak Show
Strawberry Moon: The Werewolf Vet
Buck Moon: The Werewolf Vet

Cleo Mercer

Cleo Mercer is a paranormal romance author and unapologetic monster lover living in the Midwest. She writes steamy, haunting love stories where wolves, witches, and otherworldly lovers find their happily-ever-afters. Born and raised in a small town, Cleo lives in the city now but is forever chasing a bit of magic. She believes everyone deserves a little romance—even the beastly ones. *Especially* the beastly ones.

Don't miss out!

Sign up for my newsletter! You'll get updates on all my books, plus tons of freebies.

www.cleomercer.com